# The Sentinels' Mother

## Tay T.

**www.authortayt.com**

**Join Tay's mailing list for information about new releases, teasers, sales, and giveaways. No spam, guaranteed.**

**http://eepurl.com/gWglqf**

# TO THE READER

If you haven't already, please take a look at my new werewolf romance series, The Cardinal Alpha series, which talks about the Cardinal Alphas and their mates, who are featured in this book.

I hope you enjoy The Sentinels' Mother, and I will see you again in the next book.

# CONTENT

# OTHER BOOKS BY TAY T.

**The Cardinal Alpha Series**

Book 1: Blood Bound
Book 2: Heart Bound

**The Breeder Series**

Book 1: The Alpha's Breeder
Book 2: Eros(A Short Character's Point Of View)
Book 3: The Sentinels' Mother

TAY T.

# CHAPTER 1

"Eros, do these pants make me look fat?" I asked nonchalantly, glancing at the curvaceous figure reflected in the mirror stationed on the wall close to our bathroom.

Ever since I'd lost the ability to see my own two feet, Eros had made it his job to make me more comfortable, by any means possible, including remodeling our room for my own convenience. Since I was constantly frustrated that I couldn't see my toes or the bottom half of my body, Eros had attached this fancy, full-length mirror to the wall a couple of weeks ago.

I didn't know why I even had this strange need to see if my toes were still there, but it had managed to make me cry several times now. Maybe it was just a psychological matter for me, since I didn't even clip my own toenails anymore.

Eros was the one who clipped them. In fact, he'd become my dietitian, personal nail technician—my everything—in the span of four months. And I felt kind of bad for how lazy I'd become, but I couldn't do anything about it because of how tired I got nowadays. If I wasn't eating then I was sleeping all day.

Literally.

Speaking of that, something mortifying happened a couple of days ago. And by mortifying, I meant downright horrifying and unforgivable.

Just last week, I fell asleep while Eros was going down on me.

*Shocking? I know.*

It was not because he was bad or the lovemaking was boring or anything. But my brain shut down on me, and the next thing I knew, I was dead asleep. I didn't even wake up until four in the afternoon… the next day. I still felt terrible thinking about it.

Could you imagine how Eros must have felt?

I grimaced.

"It's fine, Emira. You were tired," he said, dropping some papers on the nightstand before he made way over to me. His dark hair was still wet from his shower and was hanging over the top of his brow by over half an inch.

From where I sat, I saw the droplets trickle down from his hair, trail along the side of his handsome face towards his prominent jawline, and disappear beneath his grey shirt.

"I'm so sorry, Eros. If I ever do it again, you have my permission to slap me awake," I apologized with all the sincerity I could muster, feeling rather guilty about what had happened, although it was not within my control.

"You're tired easily because of the pregnancy. It's normal, Emira," he replied, pulling my un-resisting body up against his hard chest.

My shoulders immediately dropped, and I felt at ease again as I lay my head against him and let him wrap his strong arms around my body.

"You can always make it up to me later," he murmured mischievously against my ear, running his lips along the rim of the sensitive appendage. Goosebumps traveled up the expanse of my arms, and my body immediately heated up like a stainless-steel pot on the hot stove.

"You didn't answer my previous question, Eros." I cleared my throat and immediately changed the subject in case I made a dumb decision and fell into Eros' honey-filled trap that could lead to long hours of "grueling labor."

Eros sighed regretfully and answered, "Those pants make you look fat, but it's a sexy kind of fat."

*Sexy kind of fat?*

I breathed out a sigh of relief, not because Eros had confirmed that I looked fat in the pants, but because he was honest.

*Do you know how many men lie about this?*

I'd seen my grandfather lie one too many times to appease my grandmother in the past. Although it was nice of my grandfather, I was glad Eros wasn't like that. I would rather he be truthful than tell me lies just to make me happy.

Because who knew what else he could be lying about?

The mistress he kept in another house?

Or the child he secretly had with that mistress?

*Those are all purely examples. Don't take any of it seriously. Because I don't.*

"Thank you for being so honest," I said, turning to look at Eros before appreciatively pressing a wet kiss on his jawline. Then, I turned my attention back to my reflection.

From the mirror, I could see that my butt was bulging out as much as my stomach. And I didn't even have a butt before I met Eros! But now, I had way too much of a butt. It'd become almost obnoxious with how much it stuck out.

"Your butt is beautiful the way it is," Eros interjected. His fingers smoothed my hair behind my back, and he took the hairbrush from my hands to untangle the knot I had been working on for almost ten minutes now.

It was always the section in the back of my neck that became a giant wad when I got out of bed every morning.

"Butts aren't all that beautiful, Eros," I grumbled in reply, turning my head away from my reflection in distaste.

"Yours is," he stated firmly, leaving no room for me to argue with that certainty buried deep in the tone of his voice.

At his words, I suddenly felt flattered to the point that I didn't even care if I looked fat or not. Eros had, once again, managed to calm any feelings of unease and depression in me. Every time I'd start to build up with ugly emotions, he'd extinguish them right in the nick of time in a way that was rather tactful and flattering.

Though I'd heard people say the worst came out in their partner after moving in together, none of that was true for Eros. In fact, I didn't think there was a single thing I could think of that was even worth complaining about.

*Eros is a perfect lover and a perfect mate, in all ways.*

He knew how to pick me up when I was down. He put up with my stupidity and didn't make fun of me for it. He never put me down or complained about anything I did. And he was so mature and dependable that it made me childish and problematic at times.

Ugh.

*I'm supposed to be mature already.*

"Do you think I'm going to pop soon?" I asked, placing one hand on top of my overly large belly. Because of my current size, I had all sorts of back pain throughout the day, along with swollen feet that never went away.

As far as I could tell, my belly had to be at least twice the size of a regular pregnant woman's belly.

If I grew any bigger, I was going to scream. Because, by then, I wouldn't be able to walk, waddle, or do anything. I was either going to roll like a donut down the flight of stairs or Eros would have to push me around in a cart or wheelchair of some sort. There was no way I could carry any more weight without toppling over. No way Jose.

"I believe that we have close to a month left," he said, ignoring my overly active imagination like he always did.

"A month?" I squeaked out, gasping in horror. "Isn't that too fast? I've only been pregnant for four months."

"Four months and twenty-three days to be exact," Eros corrected.

Even though I knew my pregnancy might be faster than the regular human, I didn't think it would be *this* fast.

Originally, I thought that since I was a Breeder, my pregnancy might be a little longer than the four- or five-months Granny Ada said was common for she-wolves. Like seven or eight months long.

Wait.

No.

*I don't want to be pregnant for that long!*

"Well, I want a C-section," I choked out, curling myself against his warm chest and inhaling his comforting scent in an attempt to calm my rapidly beating heart.

How was I not scared about getting my abdomen cut open again to even suggest a C-section? Did I not learn my lesson the first time?

I shook my head.

"Your skin is stretched too taut and the pups are too close to the surface. The doctor can cut our pups too easily during such a procedure," Eros explained. "The pack Healer said your body was meant for this. She didn't want to mess with the natural order of things unless absolutely necessary. Your pregnancy is not like a normal one."

Eros rubbed my back slowly in a way to calm my rising emotions, but my dreams were seemingly dashed by his words. And I felt like crying all of a sudden.

"I have to birth all of them vaginally? Don't joke with me, Eros! I will have a heart attack!" I cried, nervously chewing on my bottom lip as my imagination started to carry me away again.

Eros' apologetic expression coupled with the grim look in his eyes told me otherwise.

I was going to birth all of my babies vaginally.

*Great. After everything is done, my vagina is going to become loose like the mouth of a—wait a minute.*

I forgot about the fact that my womb was rather magical. It could regenerate my lady bits too, right?

What I meant was that my womb and my skin had healed rather miraculously since the last traumatic experience, so I was assuming that everything else would too.

"I can't even imagine how terrible it is going to be trying to birth more than two babies through natural means," I muttered, wilting against his body like a flower in one-hundred-degree heat. "How am I going to birth a whole litter of pups?"

"We'll get through it together, Emira. Everything is going to be fine," Eros reassured, kissing my temple as I tried to shut off all the thoughts currently bombarding my mind.

I didn't say anything after that and let Eros finish untangling all of my hair.

Once he was done, we both walked over to the pack Healer's office for my usual checkup with Khanh. Khanh Dupont was a very kind and compassionate person with great skills in care and healing. She was very attentive and informative and had always made me feel very comfortable and welcome. At the moment, she wasn't just my doctor, she was also my gynecologist. From the last four times I'd visited her, I learned that she was half African American and half Vietnamese. Her mate was Sebastian, one of Eros' Gammas, and she had two pups who were already mated. Khanh had been a member of this pack way back when Eros' parents were still leading.

As soon as we entered the room, our pack Healer, Khanh, greeted us with a wide smile on her pretty face, "Emi, I was waiting for you."

Khanh's shoulder length black hair had been straightened this morning, her skin was still glowing beautifully as ever, and there was a bit of shimmery nude eyeshadow on her eyelids that made her brown eyes pop out even more.

"Hi," I greeted back as she led us into a different examination room.

Eros helped my waddling self into the room and onto the examination bed before he took a seat on one of the waiting chairs, trying not to block Khanh's way or overcrowd her.

"How are you doing today? Any heartburn or indigestion?" she asked routinely.

"I'm doing quite well. No heartburn or indigestion yet, but I've been sleeping a lot," I replied.

I'd heard of other pregnant woman getting really bad heartburn, but I was pretty lucky since I didn't have any of that. The only problem I had was always being sleepy nowadays. Especially during times that I was not supposed to be.

*If you know what I mean.*

"That's very normal. Sleeping is a very good thing during pregnancy!" Khanh said.

*Not all the time*, I thought to myself, giving Eros a glance from the corner of my eye.

"Do you want to do the ultrasound today?" Khanh asked as she checked my vitals and carefully documented it on her computer.

This was probably the second or third time that she'd asked me this question.

After I was told that Eros would be able to scent if anything was wrong during the pregnancy, I'd chosen to wave off on this procedure. Not getting an ultrasound made me less anxious and scared, because the thought of four to eight babies coming out of me was enough to make me emotionally distressed. If I were to know the exact number, I might explode into a million pieces.

But now that I sat in this room and really thought about it, I realized I was being selfish and kind of unfair to Eros. He probably wanted to see what the pups looked like, all stuffed inside of me like stuffing in a turkey, so I said, "Yes, but I don't want to see it. Can you show it to Eros only?"

Eros coughed, and I had to send him a look because I knew that he heard the comment I made about the stuffing.

"That is completely fine. I don't want you any more stressed than you already are," she reassured, smiling as she started to prepare her equipment. "I'll have you lie back for me."

"Okay," I replied.

Eros supported my back with one hand and helped me lie down on the examination table. Almost immediately, I felt the weight of my belly pushing down on my spinal column and rearranging my internal organs to accommodate my womb. The air almost left my lungs when the pressure fully settled.

*And I tell you, it is not a comfortable feeling.*

Nowadays, I really hated lying down because it was so damn hard to get back up. If I didn't have Eros to help me get out of bed every morning, I bet I would be like the bugs that get on their backs and couldn't flip themselves back over. Now that I put myself in their position, I felt kind of bad for them.

"I hope you're not annoyed that I keep asking you about the ultrasound. I just wanted to be on the safe side," Khanh explained. She lifted my shirt and tucked it under my breasts, revealing my swollen belly.

*The world definitely gets smaller whenever I lie back because my belly covers a big portion of my view now.*

"I totally understand. I know you only want what's best for me," I replied, a small smile forming on my lips.

Khanh smiled back and started to spread this clear gel on my belly. The gel wasn't cold since she'd kept it in a warmer of some sort next to the ultrasound machine. After that, she picked up the handheld device hooked to the machine and pressed it against my belly, with enough pressure that it didn't hurt. It was a rather strange feeling, if you asked me.

"Alpha Eros, you can come closer if you'd like," Khanh called.

Eros stepped a bit closer to take a look at the replicated image on the screen. I almost turned my head to look at him but had to keep it in place and look at the white ceiling in case I caught a glimpse of the image. I was still not ready to know the numbers. And I bet I was going to regret not looking later on in the future, but I was content with how things were at the moment.

*Sometimes, it's a blessing not to know everything.*

As the minutes progressed, the room was encompassed in total silence.

I took a deep breath and lay there anxiously while listening to my heavy breathing caused by the weight of my belly crushing everything vital inside my body.

Eros must have felt my nervousness through our bond because he held my sweaty hand in his warm one and tangled our fingers together in a comforting hold. The simple touch was enough to make my breathing even out again.

"Everything okay?" I asked nervously.

Khanh and Eros had become rather quiet ever since they started watching the ultrasound. It made me rather nervous because silence always meant that something was up, especially in a situation like this. But what could possibly make them both go quiet like that?

"Everything looks really healthy! All the pups are developing as they should. I think we might have over a month left, so we are on track for that due date," she replied slowly, moving the instrument along my belly, probably to capture better pictures of the babies.

"That sounds good," I said, glancing up at Eros, who was no longer staring at the screen.

Instead, he was staring down at me with this expression on his handsome face that made my heart melt with warmth and happiness.

Eros wasn't one to smile goofily in front of others, but his lips were curled upwards into a rather wide smile I hadn't seen before. And his beautiful blue eyes were filled with utter love and adoration, shining with what I thought could have been tears of happiness.

A wide smile immediately split across my face.

Seeing Eros so happy made me extremely happy too. And I really couldn't ask for more.

"Some of the test results came back from the other day, and it seems that we might have to stick with natural means of delivery," Khanh said.

Her words made me deflate faster than a balloon animal given to an energetic child. But this time, I wasn't as depressed because I'd already known this.

"Since your last injury, your skin is still trying to heal. Although the surface is seemingly smooth, the tissue underneath is a bit damaged. With how much you're growing from the pregnancy, the skin over your abdomen has become rather thin and overly stretched, in addition to the previous trauma," Khanh explained. "If we try for a C-section, I'm not very certain the results would be satisfactory. I don't want to take any risks with cutting you open again."

Hearing the "cutting you open again" made me kind of queasy.

"I understand. Eros explained it to me earlier," I replied, unable to stop the disappointment from filling my voice.

I was not disappointed about the fact that I couldn't get a C-section; I was disappointed that I was going to have to birth all of the babies vaginally.

Vaginally!

"Don't worry, Emi. Your body is rather resilient and miraculous in the aspects of birth. Natural birthing will be quite easy for you." Khanh grabbed a couple of napkins from the dispenser and handed them to me before turning around to finish documenting the pictures she'd taken from the ultrasound.

I glanced at the napkins and then looked up at Eros helplessly. The corner of his lips curved up and he was quick to take the napkins from my hand since he knew that I could barely reach anything with my short arms and fat midsection. He wiped off the mess on my belly, helped me pull down my shirt, and lifted me into an upright position.

After that, we finished setting up another appointment before we bid our goodbyes to Khanh. As soon as we left the room, I felt the sudden and urgent need to go to the bathroom hit me like a ten-ton truck.

"Eros, I have to go to the bathroom again." I tugged on Eros' arm and peered up at him through my lashes.

When I'd reached the third month of pregnancy, the constant urge to pee had become a chronic condition for me. Although I knew this was a normal byproduct of being pregnant, I was rather annoyed by the fact that I had to constantly go.

Before I was pregnant, I could hold my pee in until I got the chance to go to the bathroom, which could be hours due to a long shift at work. But now that I was pregnant, once the urge hit me, I had to go immediately or I would soil my pants.

*No doubt about it.*

It was strange how everything I'd come to know about my body had changed completely in the span of four months.

*I guess nothing stays the same once a woman gets pregnant.*

"We're coming closer to the due date, Emira. It'll be okay," Eros said. Before I could say another word, he tucked his hands under my thighs and lifted me off my feet.

I immediately wrapped my arms around Eros' neck to stable myself as he picked up his speed to travel back to our bathroom, before my bladder could leak and soil both of our outfits.

That would be rather embarrassing, because the whole pack would be able to smell it on Eros and me.

The scent of urine seemed to travel the extra mile around these parts, especially for those who had a rather acute sense of smell. So, basically, everyone in the house would be able to know that I peed on Eros.

# CHAPTER 2

While I was rambling to myself like usual, Eros had already opened the door to our room, walked us into the bathroom, and helped me sit on the toilet seat in less than a minute.

I didn't even realize that my pants were down by my knees along with my light blue underwear. When my brain caught up with reality, I'd tried to hold in the pee but failed miserably. My bladder let go full force, and the sound of me peeing resounded rather loudly in the bathroom.

Eros didn't say anything, but the drip-drop sounds made my face start to heat up along with my ears. The embarrassment was real at this point.

"Eros, don't look," I whined, trying to cover the sudden embarrassment with my words.

I'd never peed in front of Eros before, and it was really embarrassing to have anyone hear or see me pee, Eros included.

*Gosh, this is so embarrassing!*

"There's nothing to be embarrassed about. You're my mate, Emira. I don't mind any of this." Eros bent down to my level and brushed a strand of hair from my face.

17

"I know, but it's just so weird peeing in front of you," I replied, as if my excuse were any good. But, if Eros wasn't bothered by it, then why was I?

"Urinating is a very normal bodily function," he replied, chuckling.

"But I've never seen you pee before," I grumbled, not really knowing what I was saying at this point.

Eros glanced down at me with this rather incredulous expression on his face. His left brow was raised in question and lips were pinched together, probably wondering what was up with my strange thought process and why he'd gotten stuck with me as his mate. Then, he proceeded to undo his pants.

Eros' long, tapered fingers curled around the belt buckle on his waist and unbuckled it before he unbuttoned his pants and pulled down the zipper to where I could see his black boxer briefs. Suddenly, I realized that my mouth always got me into trouble.

"Eros, I'm still on the toilet!" I exclaimed, before he could do any damage.

We only had one toilet in the bathroom, so that meant Eros and I couldn't use it at the same time. It was not possible. I couldn't even imagine what that would look like.

Eros stopped in his tracks and softly acquiesced, "If you are uncomfortable with it, I will not do it again."

"I didn't mean that literally. I just—I'm not used to this," I admitted, quickly grabbing some toilet paper to wipe myself off before Eros could think to do it for me.

A shiver ran up my back at the thought.

Pee was not—in any way—sexy.

"And I think it's really weird to have a conversation while I'm on the toilet," I drawled out.

Eros helped me to my feet and washed his hands as I hurriedly pulled up my own pants—well, with the speed of a turtle, but at least I did it myself.

"I'll go get our lunch while you finish," he chuckled. Then, he proceeded to leave me to my own devices.

"Thank you," I called after him in mild relief.

Maybe someday I would get used to doing the number one... or the number two in front of Eros.

But that day was not today.

Once I'd washed my hands with soap and dried them properly, I left the bathroom to see Eros already seated at the table waiting for me.

In front of him were several plates of raw meat, semi-cooked meat, salads, and different kinds of cooked veggies. I quickly sat myself down and picked up a knife and fork. As my eyes swept over the heaping plates of red, my mouth immediately watered and I had to swallow repeatedly to keep from drooling all over myself.

Ever since Eros had fed me raw meat back when we were in his den, I'd become rather addicted to the metallic and bloody taste accompanied by consuming the chunks of red.

Before all of this, I wasn't even a fan of eating raw sushi because it was too fishy for my tastes. But now, I was all for it. Sushi. Red meats. Anything raw was fine by me.

Although I tried to eat cooked food like I'd used to, I didn't enjoy it as much as I did before. I could eat as much of it as I wanted but this feeling of emptiness—of missing something—never fully went away.

As the days passed, I gradually leaned towards eating food off of Eros' plate. Though I still ate veggies here and there, almost seventy to eighty percent of the food I ate was raw meat. And because of my change in appetite, Granny Ada had replaced most of my meals with raw meat while keeping in mind the other foods I had to eat to keep my-human-self healthy.

All this raw meat was probably not very good for me, being that I was pregnant and all, but I couldn't control my strange cravings enough to deprive myself of it. I'd read that pregnant women were prohibited from eating raw food due to the risk of bacterial infections, but Eros told me my case was different since the babies weren't human, after all.

It was still super strange how I went from being totally disgusted to totally addicted to eating raw meat. Maybe it was the pups in my belly that craved it.

*Who knows?*

"There will be a gathering with all of the other Cardinal Alphas this coming Friday to discuss the production of Ziron-e," Eros casually informed, wiping the corner of his lips with a napkin in a rather cultured way.

My lips pursed at the sight.

Every time I saw Eros eat, I was captivated by how well-mannered and perfectly refined his table manners were. He could eat bloody meat in such an impeccably precise way that I was always left feeling like a mongrel next to him.

Though most of my meal went into my mouth, there were times when the blood had managed to find itself splattered on my cheeks and chin or all over the table. I looked pretty scary after every meal. If I didn't go to the bathroom and wash my face or change into a new shirt, I would probably look like a serial murder on the loose or a crazed cannibal in a documentary on TV.

"I'm not very good at entertaining guests," I admitted regretfully, shoving a chunk of bloody steak into my mouth and getting lost in the delectable taste of good seasoning and raw beef.

"Don't worry. I'll take care of it," Eros replied. "You'll have to mingle and talk to the other Alpha Females. Nothing too stressful."

*Nothing too stressful?!*

"But Eros, I'm not good at mingling, either! I'm one of those people who gets nervous and chokes on their own spit and either keels over in a dead faint or pukes all over themselves," I exclaimed rather exaggeratedly.

Eros chuckled and said, "You did great with the pack members at the induction ceremony. I'm sure you'll do well this time, too."

My shoulders sagged.

"I'll try," I muttered, chucking a potato wedge into my mouth without much consideration.

In the end, I decided not to think too hard about it since Eros always kept his word. If he said he would take care of it, never fail, he would.

After a long pause to finish the meal, Eros asked, "Have you thought of names yet?"

"Names?" My brows raised in question.

"For our pups," he continued, reaching over to wipe the droplet of blood that had dripped down my chin.

My eyes widened dramatically, and I couldn't help but be surprised by his words.

Since this whole pregnancy, names had never really crossed my mind. I was too busy overthinking about other unnecessary things, like usual.

"I haven't really thought about it. You know how I like to procrastinate till the last minute," I said truthfully. "And I don't even know how many names we would need or what to name them. I'm terrible at names, Eros."

"We can come up with a few extra names together," he suggested, refilling my cup of water before I picked up the cup.

"I was thinking to name all of them starting with an E, since both of our names start with an E. But I don't think that's a very good idea, because I can't even come up with anything unique," I stated rather dejectedly. "It'll be disastrous if we happen to have eight babies and all of them have to have names starting with an E."

Eros glanced over at me mysteriously and said, "I don't think that will work either."

My eyes narrowed and my stomach seemed to do a weird flip because of how his ominous words sounded like an affirmation of the coming future.

I wasn't going to have eight babies… was I?

. . .

After lunch, Eros had left to patrol the borders and check on the progress of the homes that were being built by the pack members. Since the whole Hunters incident, Eros had been really on it about patrolling and keeping his territory secured.

There were nights when I woke up to go to the bathroom and found him missing from our bed just to go monitor the borders and check on the pack members. He'd actually gotten kind of obsessive about it. And I didn't know if it was a good thing or a bad thing. But, if that was what he wanted to do, then I wasn't going to stop him.

Sitting on our bed, I whipped out the new cellphone Eros gave me a while ago and tried to remember Anira's phone number from memory. Ever since she'd left the pack house, I hadn't heard anything from her, and it was making me wonder if she'd ever gotten home safely.

Although I knew that she was a strong, independent woman who could take care of her own problems, I couldn't help but worry and blame myself for failing to contact her earlier than this. If I hadn't been too caught up with everything that had happened previously, I would have probably remembered. But I hoped that she made it home.

After putting her number into the phone, I hit the call button and waited for her to pick up. If she didn't answer, I'd have to call Anira's parents to see if they'd heard from her, and I didn't really want to do that.

The first couple of rings continued until I was sent to her voicemail. I ended up calling her two more times, but no one had answered. As the minutes passed, I got even more worried.

After the fourth time trying to call her, I gave up and fell back on the bed with a frustrated sigh. Just when I was about to call Anira's parents, my phone lit up as Anira called me back.

As soon as I picked up, Anira's voice came from the speaker, "Hello?"

"Ani, it's me," I said quickly, in case she decided to hang up before hearing me out.

Anira was not a very patient person... and neither was I.

"Emi? Why in the hell are you calling me at three in the morning?" she asked, her voice raspy like she'd just woken up.

"What?" A bewildered look formed on my face as I pulled the phone down and checked the time to make sure I wasn't hallucinating. "Three? It's only one in the afternoon here."

"I'm not in the country. I'm taking a little break," she stated. An audibly long sigh, that I knew was accompanied by a roll of her pretty green eyes, could be heard.

"How am I supposed to know that? It's not like I did it on purpose," I replied, picking at my cuticle while putting the call on speaker. "Wait. Are you on your honeymoon with Wyatt?"

I was sure that the wedding was going to be at the end of the year.

Did I miss the wedding?

"No. There's no honeymoon because there is no wedding," she concluded adamantly, sniffling like she was trying to hold back her tears.

My brows quickly furrowed into a line.

"No wedding?" I repeated. "What do you mean no wedding?"

"The wedding has been canceled," she sniffled angrily.

My eyes narrowed as a dark thought made way into my head. "This doesn't have anything to do with Zanthos does it? Because, I swear, I will come after him with a sledgehammer and three torpedoes if he—"

"No, it doesn't. It has nothing to do with him…" There was an oddly long pause after that.

Even though I was tempted to say something else, I decided to wait for Anira to tell me what had happened.

"…I have cancer… again, Emi," Anira admitted rather solemnly. "They put a chemo port right under the skin by my collarbone. It looks disgusting, and I couldn't wear my off-shoulder wedding dress without looking like a zombie, so I had to call off the wedding. And you know what? I might die this time."

Although she tried to hide her emotions with a cold, toneless voice, I could hear the tremble in her words.

My heart dropped to the pit of my stomach.

"So what? You're just going to give up and die?" I asked, gritting my jaw to keep my emotions from coming out and making me bawl like a little child. Once the tears came out, it would be a crying fest for both me and Anira. And I didn't want to make it any more harder for her.

"I don't give up, Emi. I'm a fighter. Fighters don't fucking give up!" Anira exclaimed. The conviction was strong in her quivering voice.

Out of everyone I knew, Anira treasured her life too much to just lie down and die. She'd fight even if she had only one breath left. How else did you think she got through all the chemotherapy and cancer?

If I were her, I didn't think I would last half as long. I'd probably drowned myself in self-pity and died from overthinking and depression.

"What did the doctors say?" I inquired anxiously.

"They told me that there wasn't anything else they could do for me, that I didn't have very much time left. Three months tops. Three fucking months! Ninety-two short, lousy days! What am I supposed to do at this point? Order myself a coffin? Buy a plot of land at the cemetery? Rot in misery after drinking ten years' worth of alcohol?" she paused, her voice cracking as a sob broke to the surface, "No. No. I'm not going to do any of that. I haven't lived long enough, Emi. I can't die yet. I haven't married Wyatt and I haven't seen the kids we'd have together graduate from school and leave for college."

"You won't die, Ani. You're too strong for the reaper to come and get you. You'd probably kick him in between the legs and send him packing," I tried to joke. "What'd you tell the doctors when they told you that?"

"I said that I'd live longer than their great-great-great-great-great-great grandchildren."

"I believe it," I chuckled. "Well, I called to check on you and let you know that I'm going to give birth soon, probably to a litter of werewolves. If you want to come and visit me, you are more than welcome to… and if you don't, I don't really care."

She chuckled into the phone at my lame attempt to cheer her up.

"I'm going to come look at those 'werewolves' of yours. Don't you doubt it," Anira replied.

"I'll be waiting then." I bid her my goodbyes and wished her good health before turning off the phone.

Then, I sat there for nearly ten minutes to let her words sink in.

Even though I really wanted to go visit Anira and give her my support, I doubted Eros would let me leave the pack house with the Hunters out there and how overly pregnant I was.

The thought made the fake smile on my face wilt into this bittersweet expression full of sadness. I didn't even realize that I was crying from anger and how unfair life was.

*Why did they keep picking on Anira? She hasn't done anything to deserve this.*

I sighed, wiping off all the trails of tears on my cheeks and chin.

At this point, I could only pray that Anira was going to get through it like she always did. She had to.

After talking with Anira on the phone, I did some walking around the pack house to help digest all that food I ate and stop thinking about Anira's situation.

As I strolled past the dining hall, I noticed that there were a lot of pack members sweeping and cleaning the halls. From what I'd concluded, it was probably in preparation for the gathering with all the other Alphas and their packs.

Rora was standing by the front of the dining hall while pointing at some of the tables that were being cleaned. I guessed that she was in charge or something, because some people didn't look too happy following her orders.

Without another thought, I walked down the long winding hallway and into the dining hall where the gathering was supposed to take place.

"Hey, Rora! Is there anything I can help with?" I asked, waddling past a group of members sweeping the floor and making my way over to Rora.

"You're way too pregnant to be of any help," a rather familiar female voice interjected from behind me.

When I turned my head to look, Lia was standing in the back with her arms crossed over her chest. Her long blonde hair was pulled up into a messy high bun while her makeup was on point, like always.

The cat eyeliner was perfectly drawn on both of her eyelids, and the hint of highlighter made her face shimmer in the light. She looked way better than she did weeks ago.

Ever since that whole incident where Eros beat the living daylights out of her, I'd seen Lia twice. The first time I saw her, she was limping and her arm was in a cast, bruised from head to toe. But with her werewolf healing, she had healed up not even a week after that.

I had thought that Lia would avoid me because of that. But she had struck up conversation when she first saw me again, and it wasn't as awkward as I thought it would be, since she was willing to converse with me instead of ignoring me because of the whole ordeal.

Other than trying to make herself seem sinister and badass, Lia was not that bad to hang around.

"I'm sure I can do a thing or two," I tried to protest, although I knew it was a feeble attempt at this point.

"You're better off sitting and watching everyone. Who knows what would happen if one of us bumps into you," Lia replied sternly, lifting a brow as if she were daring me to make another protest.

"That's true, but—" I said, not willing to give up so easily.

Just because I was pregnant didn't mean that I was worthless and couldn't do anything. In fact, I'd seen pregnant women weightlifting and doing a lot more exercise than I had in the last ten years, and they were completely healthy and safe. Although I wasn't going to go and start weightlifting or Pilates, I wasn't going to sit around like a tub of lard waiting for the day I expired.

"No buts," Lia replied.

"But—" I tried to say.

"No buts," Lia stated in finality.

Before I could try to protest again, Rora started to giggle uncontrollably at our childish banter.

"Do you have something against pregnant women?" I asked, wondering why she was so adamant about me sitting down and staying put.

"No, but my mom had seven miscarriages before she had me, so you better have a seat," she replied, narrowing her lined eyes and daring me to do otherwise.

"…" My lips parted but nothing came out. I totally didn't know what to say after that. What was I supposed to say?

# CHAPTER 3

"We're going to sweep and change the table decorations, Emi. Just have a seat and chat with Lia." Rora giggled and headed off to help a pack member carry two giant vases and move it from the room. I didn't know if sitting here and chatting with Lia was a good idea because I had a feeling that she was going to say something to make me frustrated again.

"So... you're older than Rora right?" I brushed a stray lock of hair out of my face and tried to start a conversation with Lia to make the silence less awkward than it already was.

"Yeah." She glanced at me from the corner of her eye and tapped her acrylic nails on the table, waiting for me to continue.

"Have you met any Breeders before me? What I mean is, do you think there will be any Breeders at the gathering?" I looked over at Lia.

She glanced at me and didn't say anything for nearly ten seconds. And I suddenly got the feeling that there might not be any Breeders attending the gathering. For what reason, I didn't know.

"I don't think so..." she trailed off mysteriously, smoothing her bangs down with one hand.

"They haven't been born yet or something?" I furrowed my brows, trying to wrack my brain for a reason.

"Not quite..." she trailed off again. "They were targeted and killed rather violently by the vampires until they became extinct, not that there were that many to begin with. But, congratulations, you're currently the only Breeder alive."

Lia's shiny lips curled into a rather wide and canine-filled smirk.

"Oh," I squeaked in slight horror. "Well, that sounds... terrible."

"Before the peace treaty between vampires and werewolves, any Breeder that was discovered was immediately obliterated. But now, since there is a peace treaty, they won't try to come after you. So don't worry about dying just yet," she tried to reassure, though I wasn't going to let my guard down around vampires anytime soon.

"But what about their mates and the Sentinels? If those Breeders had children, shouldn't they—"

"Most of them were killed while pregnant and their mates were killed, too," Lia continued. My blood ran cold at the sickening notion.

"How could anyone be so coldblooded and kill a pregnant woman and her unborn babies?" I murmured in disbelief.

Lia shrugged her shoulders and said, "Probably some half-bloods. But don't worry, Alpha Eros will keep you safe. Look at how he beat the shit out of me and everyone else in the pack just to protect you."

My whole face deadpanned for a full minute and a half.

Eros sounded pretty abusive once Lia said that out loud. But then again, he was only doing that to protect me, so I shouldn't complain.

"I know he will keep me safe," I replied firmly.

. . .

As I combed through my extremely long and unruly hair, I contemplated cutting it when Eros came up from behind me and took the comb from my hand.

"Should I cut it? It's gotten too long now," I asked as Eros helped me comb out the rat's nest in the back of my head. Since I was getting impatient,

I was just dragging the comb quickly along to get it untangled, uncaring of all the hairs I'd ripped out in the process.

But every time Eros combed my hair for me, he was way more patient and did a much better job, so I preferred him combing it.

"We can cut it a little bit if you want," he responded, smoothing down the last section of hair he'd managed to untangle.

I had a feeling that Eros liked my long hair and didn't want me to cut it.

Ever since I started taking prenatal vitamins for the pregnancy, my hair had gone from elbow-length to pass my butt. And it had become a real hassle to shampoo, dry and comb. A really, really big hassle that I didn't have the patience to deal with.

"You know how to cut hair?" I asked, shocked.

I would be really surprised if Eros were able to do that too. He was already a master of multiple trades in my eyes.

"I can learn how to." Eros' warm blue eyes stared back at me through the mirror, and my heart melted into a giant, gooey puddle of mush.

"You don't have to. We can wait until after I give birth to get my hair cut in a salon or something," I decided, turning around to wrap my arms around his neck.

This action was a lot more straining than usual. Even when I wanted to reach up and kiss Eros, it was especially hard because my belly had become a roadblock between the two of us. Thank goodness it was only going to be another month before I pop.

Eros hummed a response as I smoothed down the dress I was wearing and glanced at the clock to notice that there was only thirty minutes left before all the guests would arrive for the gathering. Because I didn't have any dresses for special occasions, I'd ordered the one I currently wore through an online website. The dress arrived within two days—to my extreme relief—and fit my overly pregnant belly pretty well, albeit a little tighter than I'd like, but it would work.

The dress I'd picked was wine-colored and very long, dragging pass my ankles and on the ground. There were delicate lace details across the torso area and short sleeves, adding to the simple design.

As I glanced down at Eros' attire, hearts probably appeared in my eyes.

He was dressed in a fitted black tux and a white dress shirt with a wine-colored tie that closely matched the color of my dress.

Was it weird that seeing him dressed so handsomely made me a little aroused?

"You do the same to me. All the time, Emira," he whispered huskily, his lips brushing softly against the shell of my ear as he spoke. Then, his hot tongue languidly stroked across the sensitive appendage, and a shiver immediately ran up my spine.

I had to turn my head away to keep from throwing myself at Eros and messing up my dress and makeup.

"Oh hush, Eros." A hot blush crawled across my cheeks, and my heart started to beat rapidly in response to his teasing.

Eros' right hand pressed against my flushed cheeks, and he turned my head to him. As our eyes met, I could see the sparks of desire ignite inside of Eros' electric blue eyes, reminding me of how often I'd been receiving this hungry look from him. All it took was one glance at my pregnant belly before his cock was standing at attention, ready to enter my body and make love to me until I was a quivering mass of flesh and bones.

My fingers wrapped around his thick forearm just as he lifted my face up and tilted my jaw slightly to gain access to my lips. Then, he leaned down and kissed me slowly on the mouth, firmly rubbing our lips together until tingles scattered all across my face.

A pleased sigh purged itself from my mouth as I eagerly returned the kiss and parted my lips for his hot tongue to enter. Almost immediately, he deepened the kiss and plundered my mouth until I found myself breathless and lightheaded. It didn't take too long after that for me to become a boneless ball of goop. Somehow, Eros' kisses always managed to make me weak in the knees, no matter how many times we had kissed or touched.

"Eros, we're going to be late," I muttered against his lips, trying to pull myself away before we get ahead of ourselves.

I could already feel his thick shaft coming to life as it poked me in the stomach. But Eros didn't seem to give a damn because his mouth slanted over mine again and his tongue lazily lapped at my bottom lip before he nipped at the delicate skin with his teeth.

Instantly, I became wet between the legs.

From just one kiss.

*Damn it.*

"Eros," I muttered again, scratching at his sides to get his attention.

Eros sighed regretfully against my lips and finally pulled away to let me breathe.

As I glanced up at him, I noticed that my lipstick had transferred onto his lips and left a red spot on the corner of his mouth, too. It made Eros look ridiculous and was similar to the red lipstick on the Joker from the Batman movies I'd seen.

My shoulders shook as I tried to contain my laughter but found that I couldn't.

I giggled nonstop and had to grab a Kleenex from the box to help Eros get rid of the evidence on his face. Thankfully, the lipstick wasn't very hard to take off. If it had been an eight-hour, long-lasting lipstick then Eros would have been screwed.

"I have to go to the bathroom again," I said, quickly waddling into the bathroom to wipe myself off and fix my lipstick.

Speaking of lipstick, I remembered when I first met Eros I had applied almost four thick layers of it to make myself look as ugly as possible. If I still did that, Eros would have eaten almost half a stick of lipstick just from kissing me.

Could you imagine how gross that would have been?

. . .

The dining hall was packed, overflowing with people, most of whom were staring at my pregnant belly with interest and curiosity the moment Eros had led me into the room. It was like they were using laser vision to look inside of me and count all of the babies as they gossiped about it to their friends and family.

It was a rather creepy feeling that I eventually chose to ignore.

As I looked around the room, I realized the pack members had done a really good job of cleaning up the halls and dining area. I almost didn't recognize the room.

Although the walls and chandeliers were still the same, the floral bouquets on the table centerpieces, along with the cream-colored table cloths, made the room more bright and easy on the eyes. Even the walls were decorated with streams of curly ribbons and light-colored wisteria bunches. All the tables and chairs were lined against the walls so that the center was empty, making it easier for people to mingle and traverse without bumping into anything.

Eros led me to the front of the room where a group of females stood close together and chatted. Since he had informed me about the Cardinal Alphas and their powerful mates, I had already known a little bit of background information about them. But now that I was going to meet them face to face, it was a completely different matter.

Taking a deep breath, I tried to recompose myself because I was getting extremely nervous, and I didn't even know why. When we got closer, a female with fiery red hair and vibrant green eyes turned to us. She was dressed in a long black gown that fit her vivacious figure like a glove. The long sleeves were lacey and see-through, and the back was cut out to reveal her smooth, porcelain skin.

With a quizzical brow raised in amusement at my blatant appraisal of her, she said, "Ah, you must be the infamous Breeder. What a pleasure to meet you."

I could feel my cheeks heat up in embarrassment as her eyes stared back at me.

"And you are?" I asked, mildly mesmerized by the red-haired beauty and her glittering green eyes.

"I'm Maya," she replied shortly, her blood-red lips curving up into a small grin as she stared down at my rather pregnant belly.

"She's Alpha Xavier Thaeos' mate," Eros introduced, patting my hand to comfort me.

"Oh!" My memory was suddenly jogged at the words "Southern Cardinal Alpha."

A while back, Eros had said something about a sorceress going to extreme lengths to kidnap a Cardinal Alpha and had succeeded, to everyone's disbelief.

"You're the dark sorceress who kidnapped Alpha Xavier!" I exclaimed, my eyes wide open in amazement.

Maya smirked rather amusedly and nodded curtly in acceptance of my words.

"That would be me," she replied humorously.

Before I could say anything in response, Beta Toren came towards us. He greeted Eros and I before saying, "Alpha Eros, the Cardinal Alphas are already in the meeting room."

I didn't have to guess to know that Eros would leave me here to mingle and chat with all these powerful females so that he could go and have a serious meeting with all the other Alphas.

"I'll see you in a bit," I said, peeking up at him through my lashes.

Eros nodded and gave me a kiss on my temple. Then, he walked off with Beta Toren.

After he left, I turned back to Maya and the other Alpha Females with a wide smile on my face, greeting the woman with dark hair.

"My name is Ai. I am Alpha Cain's beloved," stated the black-haired and purpled-eyed female. She was dressed in a deep red dress with a white bodice that cinched her waist and sparkled prettily in the light.

I was told that Alpha Cain's mate was a vampire so I wasn't that surprised when I met her. But now that I was standing in front of her, I was suddenly reminded of the conversation I had with Lia about the vampires killing off all the Breeders.

A shiver ran up my spine at the thought, and I had to swallow the lump in my throat.

"My name is Emi," I stated, quickly brushing off the thought and trying to smile as nicely as I could. "You probably know this, but my mate is Alpha Eros."

She nodded her head and smiled back rather calmly.

"I'm Gemini, Alpha Deimos' mate," said a female with beautiful hazel eyes and shoulder-length auburn hair. I could hear the hint of bitterness laced rather deeply within her voice when she said that she was Alpha Deimos' mate. By the sounds of it, Gemini didn't seem too happy to be mated to Alpha Deimos. But I wasn't going to dig into it by asking and adding fuel to the fire.

Gemini was the youngest of the four females and looked to be sixteen or seventeen years old. She was dressed in a blush-pink chiffon dress that tapered around her waist and she had a pretty diamond necklace dangling from her swan-like neck.

By the way she kept glancing at the glasses of wine on the tables, I could tell that she wanted to get drunk but couldn't.

Since she was so young, I wondered if Alpha Deimos mating with her was even legal, but I wasn't going to straight out and ask her that question. It was too personal and inappropriate for such an occasion.

From what Eros had said, Alpha Deimos' mate was a human Moon Healer capable of healing anyone within the span of seconds. Even if your arm or leg had been chopped off, she could put it back together without leaving behind any scar or indication that the limb had previously been removed.

Though this was way too magical for my human mind to comprehend, I couldn't question it because my womb was also capable of doing a lot of unimaginable things.

After saying "hi" to her, I turned my gaze to the female with long snow-white hair and citrine-colored eyes, dressed in a white chiffon dress without sleeves.

"I'm Ara, Alpha Zander's mate," she stated, keeping her gaze on my face and not my pregnant stomach.

"Wait a minute, aren't you supposed to be in that meeting, too?" I asked Ara, suddenly remembering that she was also a Cardinal Alpha, a very powerful one at that.

"Zander, my mate, is going instead," she replied.

When I heard that her mate was Alpha Zander, I couldn't help but think of all the things I'd heard about him and his previous mate. He was the Alpha that had killed a bunch of werewolves and gone on a rampage when his first soulmate died. Ara was his second-chance mate and was one of the first Female Alpha's to exist. Truthfully, I really admired her.

"Crap like that bore her to death." Maya smirked. "She'd rather duel to the death inside of a locked cage than sit in a boring meeting with a bunch of ego-centric Alphas."

I nodded along, knowing that I wouldn't want to sit inside a room full of Alphas, either. That would be torturous, especially if any of them were like Zanthos or Alpha Jared. How Eros managed not to kill anyone was beyond me.

"How long is it before you are due?" Ara asked.

"I have a little less than a month to go," I replied, rubbing my stomach through the gown when I felt several kicks on the left side of my belly. The achy feeling wasn't unbearable, but could become pretty painful the longer the babies kicked against my ribs. Sometimes, it felt like they wanted to kick out my kidneys, my spleen, my right lung, my liver—about every organ in my body.

"Do you mind if I touched?" Gemini looked over at me with gleaming eyes, staring at my giant belly like I was some kind of present she wanted to unwrap. It was odd, but I wasn't bothered by it or anything.

"Of course not. You can go ahead," I replied, noticing how her hands started to glow with white light the moment I said those words.

Next thing I knew, she'd already settled her glowing hands onto my abdomen and started to feel around. I could feel heat like glowing sunrays scatter wherever she touched. It warmed my belly and made my entire body relax.

"Oh, wow! That's quite a few you have there," she muttered, eyes wide open, probably in shock at the number of babies inside of me. "One, two, three, four, fi—"

"Please don't tell me how many!" I exclaimed quickly, before she could count them all. "I get too anxious and stressed thinking about it, so I try not to know the exact number."

"Oops!" She covered her hand with her mouth. "I'm so sorry!"

"It's okay," I laughed, bursting into giggles because of her facial expression. "At least you didn't count them all."

She smiled sheepishly and said, "From what I felt, your babies are all really healthy and strong! Congratulations!"

"Thank you," I replied, smiling because of her affirmation of my babies' good health.

As I mingled and chatted with them, I started to feel quite out of place. All of these females felt powerful and much more useful than I was with their kick-ass powers.

Maya was a powerful dark sorceress.

Ara was a dominant Female Alpha. Gemini was a magical and amazing Moon Healer.

Ai was a pure-blood vampire who could kick some serious ass.

And all I was capable of doing was… breeding. That was it. Breeding.

I felt like all I was good for was popping out kids by the dozen, like an easy-bake oven popping out dozens of cookies every hour or so.

Why couldn't I have had some other amazing talent instead of this? Like telepathy or super strength or laser vision or… something?

At this point, my inner feminist was wilted down to nothing, and there wasn't anything I could do to make it better.

I sighed pitifully.

"Emi!" Rora called, waving at me to come over to where she stood by the open doors.

I quickly excused myself and walked away from the Alpha Females.

"What's wrong?" I asked, worried that something bad had happened while everyone was here, having a good time.

Rora shook her head to indicate that nothing was wrong, and my shoulders immediately dropped.

I didn't really know what to do if someone had decided to make a ruckus or if there were Hunters here to crash the party.

Could you imagine?

Because this would really be a good time to just kill everyone, drop a bomb, or raid the pack. Okay. I should probably not be thinking about that.

*Think good thoughts, Emira. Only good, positive, happiness-inducing thoughts.*

"Thank goodness," I breathed out in relief.

"Alpha Eros asked me to check if everything was okay and if you were hungry," Rora replied.

The smile on my lips widened and my depressing thoughts seemed to disappear at the knowledge of how thoughtful and caring Eros was.

"Everything's fine. And I'm not really hungry yet, I'll probably eat something later." I looked at the room of people as Rora and I started to walk around and mingle.

Just when we moved on to another pack, I saw Kent talking to a tall and lanky female with short red hair. His sleazy hands were all over her, and she didn't seem to mind his advances because there was a wide smile on her nude-colored lips.

My mood dropped at the thought of Alpha Jared and his pack.

"That's Alpha Jared's mate." Rora pointed at the female in red next to Kent, who was dressed in a revealing red dress that really showed off her ample cleavage and had a high slit that showed her long legs whenever she moved.

Jared's mate?

My mouth dropped open. If that was Jared's mate, then why was Kent feeling her up and slobbering all over her? Did he have a death wish?

"Is Alpha Jared here too?" I asked worriedly, hoping that Jared and Kent weren't going to ruin the party by fighting over Jared's mate.

Rora gave me a strange look and opened her mouth to say something but didn't. She floundered for the correct words to say before settling on shaking her head instead, causing her short curls to bounce lightly around her lightly made-up face.

"He's not?" My shoulders dropped, once again, at the good news.

"Alpha Jared was killed over a month ago," she whispered to me, trying to keep her voice low.

"Killed?" I squeaked softly in surprise.

Already? Who could have killed an Alpha like him?

"Who?" I asked.

Rora pointed her finger over at Kent's form.

I inhaled sharply and turned my gaze to Kent and the red-haired female.

That pack was really dogs eat dogs—er—wolves eat wolves, by the sounds of it.

After we both left the dining room, I whispered as low as I could, "Kent killed him?"

Although I was surprised at the news, I had a feeling that Alpha Jared would get himself into trouble one of these days with how he acted. But I just didn't think that it would be this soon.

"I heard that Alpha Jared was drunk when Gamma Kent challenged and defeated him."

"Drunk? Isn't that kind of like cheating?" I murmured in wonder.

"Well, he killed him, cheating or not. And that's all that counted in his pack."

# CHAPTER 4

Although I was relieved at the fact that Alpha Jared was no longer a threat, I still felt immensely uncomfortable at the knowledge of Kent being the new Alpha of the pack right next to ours. He was a merciless werewolf who'd wanted to kill me off since the beginning because of his brother's untimely death in the hands of Sanders and Amy, my ex-co-workers. And he probably still wanted to kill me.

I could still remember the anger and hatred that had leaked in waves from his eyes and his body as he nearly choked me to death and dragged me around by my hair. Had it not been for my Breeder mark, he would have mercilessly put an end to me, devoured my flesh, and swallowed my bones, like he'd said he would. There would be no saying what would happen to me if I were to ever fall into his hands again.

I shivered at the thought and raised my eyes to the bathroom mirror, staring at my pale reflection as I cleaned off the bit of makeup still on my face.

My severely swollen feet were killing me because of the long hours of standing on them, and I wasn't even wearing heels. The pain was worse than when I was inducted into the pack, mostly because of the extra weight I now carried. If I hadn't taken a break to go eat dinner, Rora would have had to carry me bridal style back to my room, which would have been a little embarrassing on my part. Her fragile body was less than half my size and her spindly arms did not look like they could carry my weight, though I was assured that it was possible. She was a werewolf. She could probably carry ten pregnant women all at the same time, just like Granny Ada could.

Shaking away the humorous image of Rora carrying me up and down the stairs, I tossed off my clothes and quickly took a shower.

As my belly grew bigger and bigger, I found myself having a hard time doing many things, like taking a proper shower, for instance. Because my arms had become seemingly too short, I couldn't reach the important areas of my body and washing myself had become more time consuming than it'd used to be. I couldn't wash the area between my legs without struggling past my massive abdomen and I couldn't wash my feet without kneeling. As for my hair, that was another struggle all on its own.

By the time I was finally done and semi-happy with how clean I was, I was huffing and puffing like I'd just finished a long-distance running challenge. And I was starting to sweat again. Ugh.

"Done?" Eros asked, walking into the bathroom just as I put away the blow-dryer. He'd already changed out of his outfit and taken a shower because his hair was still damp.

"Mm-hm," I hummed in reply, attaching myself to Eros and inhaling his relaxing scent mixed in with his usual fresh and clean body wash. My head settled against his chest and I rubbed my face against his collarbone, allowing myself to bask in his warmth. "How'd the meeting go? Good? Nobody made a ruckus?"

"Fairly good. No ruckus," he murmured, pressing his lips against the top of my forehead in a chaste kiss.

"Have you eaten yet? I had dinner earlier with the Alpha Females," I said.

"I just finished eating after all the Alphas left." Eros lifted me off my feet and carried me out of the bathroom before setting me down on the bed and taking a seat next to me. Then, he proceeded to take a look at my extremely ugly feet that had swelled into horrific balls of flesh and showed the deep imprints of the rim of my shoes.

A noticeable frown formed on Eros' face as he lifted both my feet onto his lap and started to massage them, making sure not to squeeze too hard. "I only hope that the pups can be delivered soon so—"

"You can see the pups sooner?" I chimed in.

He shook his head, " So that you don't have to suffer anymore, Emira. I hate to see you suffer like this."

My heart melted, once again, because of Eros' words. He'd always managed to make me feel like the most loved woman in the world... and I probably was.

A smile bloomed on my lips as I said, "I don't really think I'm suffering, Eros. Some pregnant women probably have it worse than me, yet they aren't as lucky to have you as their mate."

"I'm more lucky to have you as my mate," Eros replied.

My entire body sagged as he worked on my shins and ankles and travelled up and down my legs until he reached my feet. By then, he lessened the pressure and was a lot more gentle.

"Eros? I've always wondered this but... what did you think of me when we met for the first time?" I asked out of nowhere, as soon as the thought suddenly popped into my head.

"Be truthful," I warned, sending a sharp, hopefully threatening, glance at him.

After a long pause, he said, "I was very happy when I first saw you, because the moment our eyes met, I knew you were my soulmate."

"Not that. I meant about my appearance," I said, trying to hide my mischievous smile.

Eros cleared his throat, as if the words had become stuck and wouldn't come out unless there was some extra help. "I thought... I thought you were very hard on the eyes—but that's mostly because of your makeup."

"You're just sugar coating it, aren't you? I bet you thought I was hideous," I accused.

Eros stayed quiet, probably because he didn't know what to say to make it any better.

"I knew it!" I exclaimed, after the silence answered the question I'd asked.

At the nervous and guilty expression on Eros' face, I burst out into a fit of uncontrollable laughter. "I'm kidding, Eros. I know I looked like a train wreck when you saw me. I'd almost puked just seeing my own face. But I'm really surprised that you still want me after seeing me like that."

At that time, my face had way too many things going on. My makeup had melted in clumps, my lipstick had smudged into a crooked circle around my mouth, and there were dirty stains and dried vomit everywhere on my ripped clothes. It was unbelievable how he'd managed to overlook everything and even consider me as his mate.

"I will always want you, even when you aren't looking… or smelling your best."

Although I should be embarrassed about what had happened in the past, I wasn't. I was still laughing, hard, until the urge to pee hit me again, and I almost peed my pants.

"Bathroom," I choked out.

Eros was quick to pick me up and carry me to the bathroom.

When I finished my business and washed up, a yawn left my lips, and after that, it didn't take very long for my eyelids to come together.

. . .

Tree branches swayed in the strong wind as a brewing storm built. The air felt moist on my skin, and, in the distance, a bolt of lightning lit up the night sky in a brilliant and electric show of light.

Though I knew I was still in bed, covered from shoulder to toes inside a warm blanket next to Eros, I was mentally somewhere else. At first I thought I was dreaming, but everything felt too real to be a dream. From the chilly wind cutting across my cheeks and wildly ruffling the short strands of silken hair on my head to the tickling of the branches and leaves that slapped against my buff forearms.

It was a familiar feeling that made me believe I was seeing the world through Eros' eyes again, probably travelling through one of his many memories as I slept. Hopefully, this memory wasn't going to be very gruesome or melancholic, but I had a feeling otherwise.

The scenery soon became a blur as Eros swiftly ran through the dark forest at an inconceivably fast pace. He dodged all the random trees and animals in his way and jumped past any bushes or puddles that popped up. After running for a handful of minutes, he stopped and raised his face to the sky, tasting the air and scenting his prey, before continuing.

I didn't know how long he was running like that, but he eventually came to a stop right as a city came into view. Eros lifted his head, pausing for barely a second to smell the air again. Then, he ran even faster, trekking through the dark and racing through the empty streets at the speed of light, causing the scenery to become a complete blur.

When the scenery stopped spinning, Eros stood stock-still outside of a two-story brick house and peered into an open window at the side of the building, making sure to keep himself hidden from the people inside.

It was fairly dim inside of the house, and the only light came from the crackling fireplace at the far end. Though I couldn't completely see the two people sitting on the couch because they were facing the other direction, I felt as if I knew who one of them were just by the creepy feeling I got from seeing the top of her head.

"It's been months! Why the fuck do I have to wait in line after the Hunters to get those arms? I'm more important!" a terrifyingly familiar female voice screamed, standing up abruptly. Her emerald-colored eyes were wide, glistening in a way that made my insides burn with disgust and rage.

It was Candy.

The scientist whose hands I had mutilated in my rage and desperation.

When I saw her face, I was suddenly reminded of the traumatic experience I had inside of the government lab as the two ruthless and crazed scientists cut me open and tried to remove my womb and take my babies.

"You're going to get them soon. Just a couple more days," the male reassured, turning his head to look at Candy.

"That bitch ruined my life! I want her dead, buried six feet deep with those mutts of hers after I cut out all their organs and skin them!" Candy cried, as if she were in a maniacal fit. "I'll tear that bitch's heart straight from her chest and make her mutts eat it. I'll fuck her up real good. Then, I'll cut her body up piece by piece and dig out her brain before I kill her abominations."

As Candy ranted on and on about the ways she'd wanted to torture and kill me, Eros had already crushed the doorknob and opened the door, not bothering to keep quiet because any noise he made was covered by the sound of rolling thunder.

By the time Candy noticed that there was a person standing behind her and the male next to her, it was already too late.

Eros had snapped the male's neck with the tip of his thumb and tossed the lifeless body away with a flick of his mighty wrist. Anger was roiling off his body in waves, most likely because of Candy's statements.

After that, he came for Candy, who screamed and tried to scramble back but tripped on the couch and fell on the carpeted floor. Both of her arms were useless so she had no way of getting herself back up or crawling away.

"Who the fuck are you?" Candy questioned, as if knowing who really mattered when death came knocking on her door. Her face was extremely pale and sweat was gathering on her brows.

Eros didn't answer immediately. He stepped closer to her fallen form and looked down at her from above. "I'm the mate of the woman whose heart you want to tear out and father of the 'mutts' whose fur you want to skin."

Candy's face lost all color. She shrieked and tried to scoot back but Eros grabbed her shirt and tugged her up to her feet.

"Should I start with skinning you or digging out your brain?" he asked nonchalantly, as if he were talking about what he'd eaten for dinner or how his day had gone.

"Please, please! I didn't mean it! I was just… I was just…" she begged, trying to force out crocodile tears with a pathetic wail, but the scent of her lie was bitter and smoky like burning rubber in Eros' nose.

From there, Eros lost his patience. He lifted her higher with one hand, while the other hand dug into her chest and pulled out her beating heart. The organ throbbed in his fist, sputtering blood from the aortas and veins. Eros tossed her heart to the ground and stomped on it, making sure to ground his heel several times in the fleshy chunk.

Candy didn't even have the time to struggle. Her green eyes were wide open as if she were still alive, probably because her brain hadn't caught up with the fact that her heart was missing. But after a couple of seconds, her breathing stopped and her head flopped to the side, dangling on her stiff shoulders.

Eros threw her body away and quickly left the house, scenting the air through the streams of light rain that came down. As it rained, the many scents that had covered the air started to disperse and become trapped in the water molecules. Once all the scents were washed away, it would be almost impossible for Eros to find whoever it was he was trying to look for.

After he had gotten a trail, Eros immediately ran forward. And as he ran, the rain pelted harder and harder, washing away all the debris on the road along with the slimy coat of Candy's blood on his hand. It trickled down Eros' face and had him completely soaked in a manner of minutes.

When Eros stopped again, he was standing in front of an apartment complex that was probably five to six stories high. He followed the trail of his next prey until he came to a door with the numbers two-zero-six on it. And instead of crushing the knob like he had done earlier, Eros knocked this time, like a true gentleman, once then twice.

After a minute, the familiar bald-headed scientist, Scar, opened the door, smelling strongly of cheap whiskey and stale beer. Behind him was a very dirty apartment full of empty beer bottles, food wrappers, used soda cups, to-go containers filled with squirming maggots, mold, and smelly clothes.

I mentally heaved at the condition of the old apartment, but wasn't that shocked when I saw Scar at the door. I had a feeling that Eros would be after the other scientist that had hurt me after he had killed Candy. Eros had probably memorized the scent of them both on my skin when we were in his cave, waiting for the moment to track them down and kill them.

As Scar opened his mouth to talk, Eros had grabbed a hold of his throat and pushed him backward before stepping into the disgusting apartment and closing the door. Scar tried to fight back, but it seemed as if he didn't have very good control of the robotic arms attached to the stumps of flesh left on his shoulders. Not that him being able to control the attachments would have made any difference, especially when he was fighting against someone as strong and superior as Eros.

With one hand tightly wrapped around Scar's throat, Eros completely cut off Scar's airflow and kept him from speaking a single word, because he didn't want anyone to hear the incursion and call the police.

Although Scar struggled and kicked Eros hard several times in the leg, it didn't hurt at all and felt like a light tap, when in actuality, it wasn't. If it were me being kicked like this, I would have lost a kneecap or broken a bone.

Once again, I had to reiterate that being a human was extremely tough.

Eros didn't speak a single word to Scar. Instead, he chose to quickly end the pitiful male's life. He ripped out Scar's throat and caused blood to fly everywhere. It splattered on the floor and stained the walls in a rather macabre and surreal way, creating a really vibrant murder scene for whoever was unfortunate enough to discover it later.

With that last scene, I was pulled back to reality and out of Eros' memory.

As I lay there in bed, warm and safe, I could hear the rain pelting against the roof and walls, could hear the thunder roar loud and ferocious. My heart was pounding in my chest as my brain continued to work, showing me image after image of the gruesome murder scenes I had just witnessed.

I couldn't believe that Candy was still planning revenge, planning my death and my babies deaths.

But then, what did I expect from a crazed psycho like her? Not repentance or shame for her past actions, that was for sure.

With a frustrated sigh, I rolled over, thinking of all the terrible things that could have happened to me and the babies if Eros hadn't taken care of the both of them.

What was I thinking when I just demolished her and Scar's hands and left them there to be saved?

I opened my eyes and turned my head to the bathroom, hearing Eros' light footsteps as he came out, toweling his wet hair. Suddenly, I realized that he must have just gotten back from "taking care" of Candy and Scar because it was still raining cats and dogs outside.

"I-I was too softhearted," I whispered, clearing my throat lightly when my voice cracked from my tumultuous emotions. "I should have taken care of her when I had the chance, instead of making you do the dirty work, Eros."

"It's alright, Emira," Eros murmured, sitting down on the side of the bed. "I'm more than happy to do the dirty work for you. Any time."

As Eros stroked my back and hair comfortingly, a thought abruptly came to mind.

"Eros… did you sanitize your hands?" I asked, glancing at his hands to check if there was any residual blood.

Eros chuckled, nodding.

# CHAPTER 5

Staring out of the open window, I glanced at the passing scenery and brushed a strand of flying hair out of my mouth. Since there were barely a handful of days left before my due date, Eros and I thought it would be a good idea to get settled in his den before the occasion approached.

Even though the cave brought back some ugly and horrific memories, I wasn't too against the idea of staying with Eros inside of it. But I was not going to suffer like I did the last time I was in this cave. I think I'd been traumatized enough. If it wasn't for Eros and his customs, I would never think of delivering my babies inside of a cave far away from civilization. And though I wasn't too sure how all this would turn out, I trusted that Eros would keep me and the babies safe.

"We're here," Eros said as Gamma Sergio stopped the car and hopped out.

Eros opened my car door and helped me out of the seat before leading me into the cave. Almost immediately, I noticed that the cave wasn't extremely dark like it had been previously. There were several round light bulb covers hooked on the rocky surfaces of the wall, lighting up the entire chamber. Against the right side of the cave was a large bed that looked rather soft and comfortable and a French door refrigerator. And across from the bed was the pile of furs I had lain in previously.

The cave looked a lot cleaner and more livable now.

"Do you think it's too late to add a bathroom?" I asked, suddenly remembering the most important thing that I had forgotten.

This made me panic because I couldn't imagine crawling to the corner or going outside to relieve myself right after giving birth. What was I going to use to clean myself? Leaves? Could you imagine how painful that would be?

"Already one step ahead of you, Emira. The members finished the bathroom last week." Eros patted my arm reassuringly and led me towards the back where a new room had been created.

The floor had been tiled and there was a brand-new shower with glass doors to the left. On the right was a fancy gold-rimmed white sink, a white standing cabinet, and the toilet paper holder. Farther in the back of the room was a big tub.

At the sight, I felt as if life had been completed now, just because there was a bathroom and toilet paper.

"Wow. I love it, Eros," I murmured, pressing a soft kiss on the side of Eros jaw before standing back to admire the nice bathroom.

"I'm glad you like it. Is there anything else you want in the den?" Eros asked.

I shook my head and said, "I think that's it."

"If anything comes to mind—" Eros said.

"—I will let you know." I smiled up at Eros.

After I tested out the toilet, the bidet, and the sink, Eros helped me out of the bathroom and sat me down on the bed in the main room of the cave. When I turned my head to look out at the opening of the cave, I saw Rora and Granny Ada with a basket in her hand. From the sweet and delicious smell that was already starting to come my way, I knew that Granny Ada must have brought me something to eat, like how she always did.

"We've brought you some pie and zucchini cookies," Rora announced, rushing over to my side as Granny Ada slowly followed, smiling widely.

"My favorite!" I exclaimed, watching as Eros dragged a table out from the middle of nowhere and set a couple of chairs around it.

Granny Ada placed the basket on the table and opened the lid, and the scent of delicious desserts immediately filled the cave. My mouth suddenly filled up with saliva, regardless of the fact that I'd eaten a very big meal before Eros and I had even gotten into the car with Gamma Sergio.

Just the knowledge of how I'd turned into a black hole these last couple of months made me realize that I was going to have to work a lot of this weight off after the pregnancy. Albeit this weight gain was good for the babies, it was bad for me.

"How have you been feeling?" Granny Ada asked, watching me waddle over to the table and take a seat with utmost difficulty.

"Fairly good," I replied, taking a bite of the zucchini cookie.

Rora and Granny Ada took a seat as Eros left the cave, probably to go get the rest of the items out from the car and talk to Gamma Sergio, who had stayed outside of the cave the entire time. I wondered if Gamma Sergio was prohibited from entering the cave because he was a male whose scent could cause Eros' instincts to go haywire, thinking that there was an intruder. I wasn't too sure, but that was my best guess.

"Try the pie, it's delicious," Rora encouraged, picking up a cookie and munching on it.

"I know it is. Granny Ada always makes the best food. I don't know what I would do without you, granny," I said, turning to Granny Ada and giving her a wide, appreciative smile. "Thank you."

Granny Ada smiled until her eyes crinkled into little crescents. "I'd cook for you any day, Emi."

. . .

"Just a little farther. Then, we'll go right back to the den," Eros said, holding my hand as I waddled alongside him. This would have been a beautiful image if it weren't for my enormous feet and gigantic belly.

I was hot like hell, sweating cats and dogs, and quickly running out of energy.

Though the idea of long walks in the sunset with Eros was supposed to be romantic and all, in actuality, it was rather arduous and painful because I was carrying three large watermelons on my belly as I walked. Every step I took was beyond tiring, and I was panting for breath like a water buffalo crossing a river. And we hadn't even been walking for ten minutes!

If walking a lot wasn't good for delivery, I wouldn't have let Eros persuade me into getting off my butt and on my feet.

I sighed under my breath and clutched on to Eros' arm like he was my lifeline, while trying to keep myself from whining or protesting because of how much my feet ached.

"Eros?" I called.

"Hm?" Eros turned his head to look at me, casting a shadow over my face from the orange sun in the distance.

"What are we going to name the babies?" I asked. "I haven't come up with any names yet..."

"I've come up with some. What do you think of Roy?" he suggested.

"Too boring," I replied, not really digging the name.

"What about Ria?"

"Like diarrhea?" I gave Eros a wide-eyed, semi-grossed out face.

Eros went silent.

I coughed awkwardly and said, "Sorry."

After a moment, he continued, "Then how about Bernadine? Ollie? Myrtle?"

My brows furrowed tighter and tighter at the names Eros came up with.

The names all felt as if they were from the people in the 1800s in England. I had nothing against British names but I just didn't want to name my daughter Myrtle or Bernadine. I wanted something pretty sounding and meaningful, something unique and cute.

"What in the w—Eros! Those names sound so... old," I exclaimed, wrinkling my nose.

"These names were pretty popular back then," Eros replied, chuckling. "You know, my father wanted to name me Giles instead of Eros."

Giles?

What in the actual hell?

"What made him change his mind?" I asked.

"My grandmother hated the name so she suggested Charles and Eros. My mother and father liked the latter name and decided to name me Eros."

"I'm glad they did. I like the name Eros a lot better, too." I nodded my head, thankful to Granny Ada for the thousandth time. That lady had a very steady and wonderful head on her body. "My mom originally named me Annie, you probably know this already, but do you like Annie or Emira better?"

"You. I just like you, Emira. No matter what your name is," he answered, tucking a loose lock of hair behind my ear.

Eros always made me fall right back in love with him. Over and over again.

*I mean, I've never fallen out of love with him but he always reminds me of how much I love him. Not that I'd forget but... oh, never mind.*

Why was it that the more I explained myself the worse it became?

"Really?" I smiled from ear-to-ear and stared at him with glistening eyes filled with emotional tears. "Eros."

"Hm?" Eros stopped in his tracks for a second.

"I love you," I said, wrapping an arm around his waist and hugging him tightly.

"I love you, too." He smiled.

• • •

After that "long" walk, we headed back to Eros' den. Since I was still covered in sweat I decided to take a quick shower before I became too lazy and sleepy. But just when I washed my private areas and my legs, I realized that I needed to shave. Again. Those darn prenatal vitamins I took didn't just make the hair on my head grow faster and longer, it also made all the other areas grow faster, too. Since shaving had become quite impossible for me, I had to enlist Eros' help, like I had been doing these couple of months.

How did anyone expect me to shave myself when I couldn't even see what or where I was shaving? I didn't want to cut myself.

"Need help?" Eros called from outside the door.

"Yes, please," I replied, knowing that he'd heard my piteous wailing about unwanted hair and shaving and had come to my rescue before I could call out to him, like he always did.

Eros opened the door and came in. Afterward, he went straight over to the white cabinet and grabbed some shaving gel and the two separate razors I'd used for my legs and the area in between.

Albeit I had been extremely embarrassed when Eros first helped me shave, I didn't feel that way as much anymore, probably because I was so used to being naked in front of him now, like he said I would.

After carefully drying my feet on the bathroom mat, I walked out of the shower and pulled on a bathrobe, trying to keep myself from slipping and falling. From there, Eros helped me sit down on a chair he had brought into the bathroom.

He kneeled in front of me, and I couldn't keep myself from staring at his handsome face as he applied the shaving cream on my legs and started to remove the overgrown hairs.

The razor was quite sharp, and I'd cut myself several times before, but every time Eros shaved me, he'd never nicked me even once. He was always so careful, making it nearly impossible for me to do a job as good and clean as him.

It made me feel a little insecure sometimes, but the feeling was rather fleeting, because he'd chase them away before it even meant anything.

"You know you're perfect, don't you?" I murmured, admiring my view of Eros' handsome face and strong hands doing such delicate work.

"Of course." His electric blue eyes glanced up at me and a dazzling, wicked smile nearly blinded my vision.

He cleaned off the razor and lifted my right leg onto his thigh, slowly working his way up. When he was done, he cleaned the razor and washed his hands in preparation for a more intimate shaving.

I pulled the robe apart and separated my thighs before tilting my hips upward, staring at my big belly because that was the only thing I could see. Sadly.

"Ready?" Gleaming blue eyes looked up at me.

I hummed a reply, feeling Eros' warm, long fingers spread the shaving cream on my mound. The ever-existent sparks immediately erupted, and I had to clench my stomach and teeth to keep from making any unnecessary noise as the pleasurable sensations gathered, making me wet with just one touch.

No matter how hard I tried to keep myself from getting aroused, I could feel my juices start to trickle out and mix with the shaving cream Eros had applied. Although I couldn't see, I could feel the sharp razor slowly brush against my skin and Eros' hot breath fluttering on my belly and thigh. And I got all hot and bothered. Again.

I couldn't wait until this pregnancy was all done and over with. At least by then, I'd be able to do everything myself and not have to endure this kind of pleasurable torture.

Eros looked up at me, his beautiful blue eyes dark and mesmerizing as his nostrils flared, and I knew that he could smell my arousal. A hot blush quickly collected on my cheeks and spread all the way down to my neck.

"Don't move, Emira. I don't want to cut you," he said, one hand settling on my thigh to keep me in place.

"I'm trying not to… but you make it hard," I voiced, feeling lightheaded all of a sudden. "You know what your touch does to me."

"Don't tempt me, Emira." Eros breathed in sharply, his hand shaking when he quickly finished up and pulled away. As he tossed the razor onto the sink and washed his hands, I could see the large tent in his dark pants from the corner of my vision.

"What me to help with that?" I grinned sheepishly up at Eros.

Eros shook his head and sighed pitifully.

• • •

After lunch and a walk around the den, I took a little cat nap and found myself brought back to life, that was until this sudden pain I'd never felt before developed in my lower abdomen and built in pressure like menstrual cramps, but ten times worse. I couldn't get myself to roll out of bed or call for Eros. My entire back hurt and my inner thighs did too.

Though I had to go to the bathroom really bad, I was afraid that I was having pre-labor contractions and could end up delivering my babies into the toilet, if I weren't careful. That would be horrific and I would never forgive myself if it happened.

But what was I going to do?

Lie here and wet the bed?

*No, I'm not going to do that,* I decided.

With a pained groan, I grabbed the headboard and used it as leverage to pull myself up, hesitating between going to the bathroom or not. I felt like I was in between a rock and a hard place. But I had to go to the bathroom because I didn't want to pee myself and sit in it. I'd done that before and it was not a good feeling.

When I managed to get upright and on my shaking feet, Eros came in from the lip of the cave and immediately appeared in front of me.

"I really need to go to the bathroom," I panted as he helped me up and into the bathroom.

I didn't dare to sit on the toilet because of my strange fear of giving birth on the toilet seat, so I decided to pee standing up. My legs were shaking and my heart was pounding rapidly, probably in timing with the terrible contractions that were giving me the sweats.

After I finished and cleaned myself off, Eros helped me out of the shower.

"I think you're going into labor, Emira. I just called Khanh to come over." Though Eros' face was rather calm, I could feel his anxiety and nervousness just from the way his hands shook as he held me to him.

It was amazing that Eros was able to tell all this when I could not. Being that this was the first time that I was pregnant, I wasn't too sure what the signs were and it made me really nervous. I didn't want to be a bother and make Khanh come here for nothing, that would be quite embarrassing.

"I think you're right, Eros. My water just broke," I said, feeling warm liquid gush uncontrollably out from between my legs and on to the tiled floor.

Damn it. Why couldn't my water break when I was in the shower? Now there was a nasty mess on the floor someone had to clean. And that someone was most likely to be Eros...

*Sorry, Eros.*

"Khanh is on her way. She'll probably be here in around three minutes," he reassured.

Eros helped me wipe my legs down and got me out of the bathroom. He carried me over to the piles of fur on the floor and placed me gently down, before he kneeled next to me and held my shaking hand, trying to comfort me the best way he knew how.

As I lay there in pain, I couldn't help but become nervous, thinking of what was to come.

My mind was whirling almost one hundred miles a minute with unnecessary thoughts that weren't even relevant to the situation, like usual. But after a few seconds of deep breathing and seeing that Eros was just as nervous as me, I calmed down and lay my head back on the fur to look at the rocky ceiling, feeling beads of sweat collect on my upper lip, nose, and forehead before dripping down from my temple to wet my neck.

The pain was still coming and going, sometimes hurting badly in my core before settling down to a dull ache accompanied by a rippling sensation in my lower belly. When the pain was bad, I felt as if I would burst into tears, throw up, or poop. But I didn't really have the energy to do any of that. Though I'd read that some women have puked or did the number two during delivery. I just hoped that I wasn't one of them because that would be very gross.

As my brain came up with more distracting and disturbing images of what my birthing would look like, Khanh came into the cave with Rora on her trail, holding a giant white case, probably filled with items required for my delivery.

"Hi, Emi," Khanh greeted.

"Hi," I greeted back, shakily, with a smile that didn't really reach my eyes.

"Let me go wash my hands and set up." Khanh grabbed a bag from her case and went into the bathroom. By the time she was done sanitizing and setting up, I was already dead exhausted just from the pain in my abdomen and vaginal area.

I hadn't given birth yet and I felt like giving up already.

Noticing my pained expression, Khanh kneeled in front of my spread legs and asked, "Would you like to have an epidural?"

*Epidural or no epidural?*

That was the real question I'd been mulling over the last few days, yet I still had no clue if getting an epidural was a good choice. There were pros, like no pain at all during delivery, and cons, like having back pain when the weather was cold for the rest of my life, if I were lucky enough to hit that jackpot.

After a moment to catch my breath and think of all the pros and cons I'd read online, I shook my head and decided to go without.

I would endure this pain to remind myself of the trials and tribulations related to unprotected sex… well, unable-to-protect sex, if that made any sense.

*Because, you know, Eros' semen is stronger than the average condom.*

At least that was what I was going to say until I forgot what this pain felt like and hopped into bed with Eros, again.

"No, thank you," I croaked, wondering why I was torturing myself like this when I could have just taken the easy way out. But that wouldn't be me if I did.

"Okay. Let me check to see how much you've dilated," she said, pushing my legs a little wider to get a better view.

At this time, I felt glad that Eros had helped me shave just before all this went down.

Khanh checked with gloved hands and nodded her head, "We're good and dilated. You can start pushing now."

I'd originally thought that it would take a long time to dilate because of what I'd read online, but I was glad that I didn't have to walk around to get myself even more dilated. That would be way more agonizing, especially because of this pain coursing through my entire body.

# CHAPTER 6

I'd been holding back the urge to push a couple of minutes earlier in fear of messing up the procedures. But now that it was time to push, I felt like I was too tired to. My arms and legs felt like overcooked jelly and my brain felt too sluggish to command the rest of my body to do anything.

With a deep inhale of breath, I tightened my muscles and forced myself to push as hard as I could. I wasn't too sure how long I could do this with all the babies I had to push out, but I knew that I had to. No matter what.

This felt like an out of body experience, and I soon lost the ability to think or keep any thoughts other than to push and push and push. The veins on my hands were popping up, so I knew that the ones on my forehead were probably swollen with how much effort I was putting in.

Heaving a deep, pained breath, I continued to push as Eros used a towel to wipe off the sweat trickling down the side of my face. My body felt like it was no longer mine and my vagina felt like it was being torn apart and cut into tiny little pieces. It hurt so badly that I was crying with my eyes closed, begging for it to be over soon, begging for enough strength to finish.

Though I felt like screaming at the top of my lungs, I didn't want to hurt the three occupants in the room with sensitive hearing. So I stuck with clenching my teeth tight and swallowing down all the angry screaming that was bubbling up my lungs.

Eros noticed that I was clenching my jaw and grinding my teeth so he rolled a small towel into a log and had me bite on it to keep me from chipping a tooth and swallowing it.

After a couple of minutes of pushing with everything I had and crying like a river, something was gradually pulled out of my body, but I didn't dare to look because I feared that I would faint if I saw what had come out.

*'Eros,'* I wailed inside of my head.

*'I'm right here, Emira. I'm right here,'* he replied, wiping off the never-ending sweat coming from all over my face and neck, along with the instinctual tears of pain that wouldn't stop falling from my closed eyes.

*'Eros, you're never going to put it in again,'* I threatened through the mind-link I'd rarely used since Eros was with me twenty-four-seven now.

Eros chuckled under his breath and patted my hand.

*'I'm not kidding,'* I said through gritted teeth, trying to hold back a scream of pain.

*'I know, Emira,'* he answered, wiping my stream of tears with his thumb and forefinger.

From the corner of my eye, I saw Khanh set down a ball of black on some thick white towels and had to do a double take.

*What is that?!*

*Oh my g—*Khanh set another one down right next to the first squirming black ball of fur. And just the sight of the wet fur made me want to pass out right on the spot.

*I think I'm going to be even sicker than I already am.*

Khanh kept taking one out after another, and I was almost too shocked to feel any pain as I pushed myself to remain conscious throughout the entire process.

*How many are there?!*

I nervously glanced over at Eros whose gaze was entirely focused on me and how I was doing instead of the black squirming balls Khanh was continuously extracting from between my legs. I didn't dare to look at the increasing amount of babies being placed on the towel. So instead, I kept my focus on Eros and our intertwined fingers, locked and laced together like they were born to be that way.

As the time dragged on and Khanh called for me to push one last time, I thought that I was on the brink of shutting down. My brain felt like it was completely melted into a pile of goo, while my vision slowly became black in the corners.

At this point, I was scared that if I fell asleep bad things could happen to the babies still left inside of me, so I had to force myself to continue.

My face had become deathly pale and sweat was raining down my skin and wetting my nightgown in patches on my chest and underarms. From where I lay, the warm liquid that had stained the towel underneath my butt and abdomen started to become cold against my skin, especially because of the slight draft that was circulating in the cave.

Holding back a shiver, I gritted my teeth and clenched my hands hard in order to use the last of my energy to finish this delivery. Though my labor didn't last hours or days like some poor, poor women, I felt as if it were a lifetime that had passed. Three lifetimes, to be exact.

Any longer and I might have to ask for a Snickers break and continue later. Ha. Ha. Ha. I was kidding. My hallucinations were probably kicking in.

"We're all clear, Emi. You did a great job," Khanh said as she cut off the umbilical cord connecting me to the last baby.

I gave her a weak, probably tired and ugly, smile and tried to force myself to stay awake instead of giving in to the darkness. My breath was coming out in pants and my vision was bleary. I was drained. Completely drained. Not even food could make me feel any better.

But I wanted to see my babies, at least one glance at all of them before I let myself get carried away by the darkness. Eros knew what I was thinking so he moved out of the way to let me take a look.

At the sight of all the babies, I couldn't help but force myself to count, wanting to confirm that there weren't thirty-eight babies like I had deliriously thought. Because if there were… I would probably be sobbing myself into a coma.

One... two... three... four... five... six... seven... eight ...ni— Good gods! There were nine wet balls of black fur spread out on the stained towels, waiting to be cleaned as they squirmed and kicked each other.

Looking at all of them, I couldn't really see a difference. They all looked the same in their wolf forms. Same black fur, same little claws, same raised snout, and same closed eyes. I couldn't see a face to give a name to, and I couldn't help but think that this was a lot more difficult than I'd originally thought. Because nothing came to mind. Not even one name.

*What in the world are we going to do?*

. . .

Turning to my sides, I stared at the nine wolf pups lying next to me on the clean pile of fur, squirming around to find a better position and climbing on top of each other like a dogpile. Though I wanted to touch them all, the bottom half of my body still hurt and moving was way too tedious for me to attempt anything.

Even going to the bathroom had become a hassle. Because every time I peed, the stinging pain from the tear on my vagina became extremely unbearable. My urine felt like acid whenever it washed over my swollen and red wound, and I literally teared up when I was sitting on the toilet seat, deciding if I should try to pee slowly or as fast as I can. Because, either way, it didn't make the pain any less intense.

But since it wasn't a bad tear and was starting to heal, Khanh said stitches weren't necessary and would be a lot more painful to put in and take out.

*Thank the gods.*

Just the thought of having my opening pierced by a needle and sewn back together was enough to make me cringe and cry in my sleep. Truthfully, I'd never been much of a needle person. If I ever had to get a shot or have my blood drawn, I never looked and always held my breath.

Tossing the thoughts aside, I touched the baby closest to me as softly and delicately as I could, trying not to startle the little guy too much.

Under my fingertips, his black fur felt very soft and silken because he'd been given a bath to clean off all the birth fluids and blood on him. Compared to the other eight pups, this little babe was the smallest, probably only two or so pounds. He had his belly up in the air and legs all splayed out, lying like a human baby, while chewing on one of his paws with his toothless gums.

"Hi there, little guy," I cooed, stroking his extremely soft little belly with the pads of my fingers.

After my words, he wiggled his little paws and continued to chew on himself, as if he didn't hear what I had said, which was probably true because his hearing hadn't quite developed yet. According to what Eros said, his hearing would probably get better in a couple of days.

Raising my eyes, I glanced at all the other babies who were curled around each other and settled on their bellies. There was a thin film of semi-see-through skin that covered over their eyes and made them look like they were sleeping, but I knew otherwise.

Some of them were still squirming around, trying to kick and flail their little arms and legs in all directions.

Albeit I had given birth to them, they didn't look anything like me. Instead, I vaguely realized that they looked exactly like Eros in his wolf form. From the black fur down to their paws and muzzles. They were his copy.

As I looked at them, I wondered if they were going to stay in their wolf forms forever or change into their human forms later on in their lives.

"When do you think they will be able to open their eyes?" I asked, glancing at Eros, who was busy attaching the legs on to the crib he was putting together.

He'd already finished six and still had three to go.

Poor him.

*This is what happens when your pullout game is weak*, I thought jokingly.

"Most pups open their eyes after a week of being born and will be able to change back and forth into their human and wolf forms within the span of two to four weeks."

My eyes widened.

"They'll change into little human babies?" I asked, surprised and a bit happy at the news. How awesome was it that I would be able to see what they looked like in both forms?

Eros nodded. "Yes. But it will be inconsistent until they are strong enough to remain in their human forms without shifting back into wolves. And the time period varies between each pup."

"That's so awesome! I thought they were just going to stay like this until they became adults or something. Not that there's anything wrong with that," I said sheepishly, turning my gaze back to the pile of pups all nestling against each other, except for two, who were nibbling and chewing on each other's faces with their gummy mouths.

It was kind of cute and gross at the same time because the amount of saliva coming from their mouths was quick to wet both their furs and the fur underneath them.

*They are probably very, very hungry,* I thought to myself.

But that in itself was another problem.

How was I going to feed them?

*Think about it. I only have two nipples and there are nine babies.*

Two and nine would only call for unnecessary pain and make my nipples suffer. Literally.

If I had been born with eight or ten nipples like other canines, this would have been a much easier job. But wait, why would I want that many nipples?! How would that even look on a human body?!

The image procured by my brain was not something I was interested in. Not at all.

As I was having a panic attack over the thought, I could hear Eros chuckling to himself on the other side of the cave as he set the last crib onto its four legs.

"I didn't mean to laugh, Emira. It's just that your thought process always amuses me," he confessed, standing to full height and brushing off the invisible dust on his pants.

"I'm glad that you find my thoughts amusing," I replied, my voice deadpan.

Eros chuckled again.

"Is there any way that you can block my thoughts?" I asked.

"Yes, I could…" Eros drawled. "But I don't really want to."

I glanced at him and pouted.

Though I had learned how to block my thoughts from Eros a long while back, I'd quit doing it after the first two times because it was too straining. For me, a person who liked to think too much, it was difficult to keep up a mental barrier all the time. I got lost in my thoughts way too easy and the barrier would slip away, so I decided not to bother with it. And I'd thought that it would be best for our relationship if we were to be brutally honest with each other. After all, there was no point in keeping secrets from Eros, the man whom I loved with my whole heart.

"Eros, are we supposed to put diapers on them?" I asked, worried that the pups might do the number one or the number two on the fur, more so the latter than the former.

"Khanh gave me some newborn diapers before she left. Let me grab them." Eros picked up a handful of little white diapers on the table and came down on his knees beside me. If I hadn't looked up videos and made Eros watch them with me, I would never have known how to put a diaper on a baby.

Since I'd never had the chance to touch or see a baby in the flesh, this was going to be a totally new learning experience, full of trials and errors. I had a gut feeling it would be chaotic.

"Do you want to try it?" he asked, turning his beautiful blues to me.

I shook my head and watched as he lifted the first little pup and lay him on his back on top of the diaper, making sure to put the little tail through the hole on the back. Then, he pulled the front of the diaper up and held it down to put on the two tabs. After watching Eros do this effortlessly, like everything else he'd ever done, I was given the oh-so-familiar feeling of immense awe and appreciation. He was so reliable… so …perfect.

*What can't Eros do? Is there such a thing?* I thought to myself, picking up a diaper and setting it down to help Eros speed up the process. Then, I decided to try myself, realizing that this wasn't as hard as I'd thought.

Once we were done putting diapers on all of them, I realized that there were seven boys and two girls.

"Do you want to try to feed them?" he asked, helping me up into a sitting position before handing me a baby. I cautiously cradled the baby's head in my arms and held it against my chest.

In the beginning, I didn't even know how to hold a baby. I was completely clueless and didn't know where my hands were supposed to go. But now that the pup was in my arms, my motherly instincts kicked in and I felt completely at ease, staring down at the bundle of joy in my arms. I didn't know how other mothers felt holding their child, but I felt completely overtaken by love and happiness.

The moment I held the baby against my aching chest, he kept rubbing and nudging his head into my breast, like he was searching for a source of food that he knew was coming closer. I unbuttoned the sleeping gown I was in and pulled the fabric down my shoulder to expose my naked breast. Though I was a little nervous with Eros watching, I chose to ignore his heated gaze and watched as the little pup finally latched on to my nipple and started to suck.

At first, it felt really weird and ticklish because of the fur brushing against my areolas, but I endured the entire process and continued to feed the rest of them. By the time I'd finished feeding all the babies, my nipples felt like they were going to fall off. Literally. The entire nipples and areolas were sore and red and achy, regardless of the fact that I kept switching the babies from the left nipple to the right nipple. At this rate, I didn't think that I was going to last an entire day of breastfeeding.

*What am I going to do when their teeth comes in?*

Because, from what I knew, wolves had very, very sharp and pointy teeth. Breastfeeding a wolf with teeth would be like asking to have my nipples bit off. And, unlike my magical womb, I doubted that my nipples would grow back.

*I don't want to be nippleless.*

I sighed.

How in the world was I going to survive this?

*Okay, Emira. Let's take this one step at a time. Don't panic. Panic will only make it worse,* I told myself.

I sighed again.

Other than that problem, there was also the problem of taking too long with one pup that the others were forced to starve until it was their turn. It took almost twenty to thirty minutes per pup so the last one had to wait quite a while before feeding, which was terrible. I didn't want any of them to starve, but I only had two nipples. This meant that Eros and I had to find another solution to this problem.

If Eros were able to lactate, then we'd have four nipples to work with.

At the awry thought, I laughed to myself.

"Does it still hurt?" Eros asked, placing the last baby into her crib before coming to sit by my side.

I nodded my head and gave him a pitiful look. "I didn't know that breastfeeding would make me this sore."

Eros' brows furrowed before he walked into the bathroom. When he came back, he was carrying two carefully folded wet towels.

"I'll go out and get some cold compresses later, but for now, we'll have to make do with this," he said.

I nodded my head and undid the button on my gown again, hoping the cold towels would be able to make this uncomfortable feeling go away.

As soon as my breasts were freed from the cotton fabric scratching them, I felt a little bit better, but I didn't want to go naked inside the cave all day. What if someone came in unexpectedly?

"You can go topless all day if it makes you feel better, Emira. If anyone were to come close to the cave, I will tell you," Eros said, helping me lie back before he slowly lay the cold towels on my breasts.

I shivered uncontrollably as goosebumps formed all over my body.

"Okay," I replied, feeling a little better now that the cold was taking away a bit of the soreness on my nipples.

# CHAPTER 7

I'd been breastfeeding for two days, and I'd come to the point where I wanted to call it quits. But I couldn't, because I didn't want to feed the babies formula. It was said that if a baby drank breastmilk growing up, he or she would be a lot healthier than the babies who didn't. So, I didn't want to give up. But I was suffering. Physically and mentally.

Though my healing was quite a bit better than the average human, it still couldn't combat the constant soreness accompanied by breastfeeding. Every couple of hours I would agitate the nipples by repeatedly feeding the babies, and it was not something that I could control or stop.

After suffering and contemplating the situation, I looked online and found that I could just use a breast pump to take out all of my milk and feed it to the babies that way.

From what I had read, this was a fool proof method that many mothers utilized. So I was assured that it would work for me, too. And if it didn't, I could just go back to the regular old nipple-to-mouth technique.

After I had purchased a breast pump online and had it shipped as fast as it possibly could to the pack house so Eros could go get it, I knew that I'd made the right decision because using the breast pump was convenient and a lot less painful. I could also feed more babies at the same time, making sure that none of them were starving for too long. The only thing I didn't like was the clean-up, but I was fine with that since Eros helped me clean and sanitize the equipment after every use.

Once I had filled up all the bags with milk, I was extremely surprised that my body had managed to produce enough milk to feed at least twenty human babies. And I hadn't even had a single cup of milk for over a week now.

As a child, I'd always thought that a pregnant woman would have to drink tons of milk to produce enough of it to feed their children, but, thankfully, that was not true. If it were, I would have had to drink gallons of it to produce this much milk, and I couldn't imagine drinking a gallon or more of milk a day.

I cringed at the thought.

That was way, way too much milk.

"The pups are so cute," Rora said, calmly brushing one of the babies' fur with her pointing finger, while staring at them with sparkling eyes full of awe. "They look just like Alpha Eros!"

"They sure do." I nodded my head repeatedly in response.

Rora and Granny Ada had come to visit us today for the first time after I'd delivered the baby and had been helping me and Eros feed them. Apparently, only two people feeding nine babies was very difficult, because we had to keep them upright when feeding, which meant that we had to hold them up and put the bottles in their mouths at the same time.

While Eros was able to feed two babies at once, I could only feed one. My reflexes weren't as fast as his to catch a baby if he or she were to slide off from my lap while I had the bottles in my hand. So I wasn't going to risk it.

But now, with Rora and Granny Ada's help, we were able to feed a lot more pups at the same time, leaving two to three of them to chew on their paws until they were next.

"It's been a really long time since I have seen this many pups," Granny Ada stated, smiling warmly as she fed the baby in her lap. "I think you've broken a record, Emi."

"Really?" I glanced at Granny Ada, who nodded her head along with Rora. "For what? Having the most babies at the same time, without an epidural?"

"I don't know about human babies but you've given birth to the most pups in one pregnancy," Granny Ada explained.

"—And they all survived!" Rora piped in. "This rarely happens for anyone in our pack."

I lowered my eyes and mulled over the last of Rora's words.

Though I had been told that she-wolves had a hard time conceiving and keeping their children, it was much harder to hear now that I had seen my own babies and felt the connection we shared in such a short time. I was unable to imagine any mother having to say goodbye to their babies right after giving birth to them, or even losing them way before they delivered.

The imagery was much too heartbreaking and cruel. And for this to be a recurring event was just heart wrenching. But I didn't know any way to stop this from happening. All I had was a super womb, not some magical abilities that could help with that problem or bring people back to life, even though I wished I did.

"Now if we can have some more pups running around the pack house..." Granny Ada murmured wistfully.

"More?" I repeated, bewildered. Nine was already a lot. I couldn't imagine having more than this. "Not from me, I hope. Nine is already enough. I don't think I will be having anym—"

"Oh, nonsense! It's too early for you to be saying that. Once you get to seeing all your little pups grown up, you'll be wanting many, many more," Granny Ada chided. "That's how I felt when all my pups left the nest. It gets very lonely at that point. And you'll be wishing you could have more little pups to keep you busy."

My mouth opened and snapped closed. Although my mind was telling me to refute her insane claims and call it impossible, I knew that she might be right because who knew what the future would bring. I surely didn't see myself mated to a werewolf or having wolf babies back when I was still working at the lab or in high school. But look at me now, mated to a wonderful man and a mother to nine beautiful babies.

*It's unbelievable how much my world has changed,* I thought to myself. *But I wouldn't trade it for anything.*

"You're right. It's too early to say that," I finally said, choosing to respect her wise opinion, just in case I was proven wrong in the future. "I guess we'll just have to wait and see."

If Eros and I were to have any more children, it would have to be a long, long, long way from now. And by that, I meant decades from now. A time when I was either drunk or had forgotten what delivering a baby felt like.

*I guess this means that Eros is going to have to go back to a life of celibacy, like before he met me. Poor him.*

Eros sent a look my way.

. . .

Off in the world of sleep and lying next to Eros in the wonderfully soft bed in our den, I suddenly heard something that sounded like a puppy yipping or growling, several puppies all at once, inside my head. At first, I thought the babies were making the noises, but as I looked at the cribs, I noticed they were all asleep.

*What the heck is that?*

"Eros. Eros!" I turned to face Eros on the bed, looking at his peaceful face until his lashes quivered and his blue eyes opened to look at me.

"Did you hear that?" I sat up in the bed and glanced around at the entire cave.

"Hear what?" he asked, his voice groggy from sleep.

"The growling and yipping," I replied, hoping that this wasn't just all in my head.

Eros shook his head, his brows wrinkling. He turned his gaze to the pups before saying, "Do you still hear it?"

I nodded my head. "Do you think it's ghosts or something?"

Was I imagining things or were there ghosts? Because if there were ghosts, I was going to get my ass and my babies asses out of here as fast as I possibly could. Ghosts and me did not go well together. I'd rather sit in a pool filled with worms and frogs than stay in a room with a ghost.

No matter how friendly that ghost was.

"It's not ghosts," Eros replied.

I breathed out a deep sigh of relief and said, "Thank goodness."

"I think you are hearing our pups talk," he continued.

"Talk? Our pups?" I repeated in disbelief.

*What in the world?*

"So you don't hear any of this growling?" I asked again, just to make sure.

"No. I believe that your connection with them allows you to hear them, even when they are sleeping."

"I bet you would understand them. All I can hear are growling and screeching and whining," I said, frowning at the thought. "Too bad I can't understand the language of wolves."

This was a little scary to hear when in the middle of sleeping. If only they would talk to me during the day and not during the night.

"I wonder what they're dreaming about," I murmured, yawning but unable to go back to sleep because of the voices in my head.

"Probably something good," Eros said.

I turned my gaze over to the clock and noticed that it was already feeding time for the babies, again, which meant that I wasn't going to get any sleep any time soon. I sighed under my breath and glanced pitifully at Eros, who was already getting out of bed and heading over to the fridge. He pulled out a handful of milk bags and poured them into nine clean bottles to reheat.

As he busied himself, I buried my face into the pillow and stifled a yawn that threatened to come up, trying to treasure the warmth of the bed for another second or so, before crawling out of the covers.

"You can rest, Emira. I'll feed them," Eros said, popping the bottles into the microwave one by one.

I shook my head and said, "It'll be faster if I help."

After waiting for the bottles to cool down to the right temperature, I whisked the first sleeping baby from her crib and roused her from her sleep. Then, I set her on my lap to start the feeding process. Her mouth was downturned, probably because I was bothering her when she was sleeping so well, but it had to be done.

I propped the baby on the crook of my arm and placed the bottle against her mouth. Even though she was cranky, she immediately took the bottle and started to suck, drawing the milk quickly like she was extremely hungry. Out of all the other babies, this one really valued her sleep. Every time I woke her to feed her, she was always quick to finish her milk so that she could go back to sleeping. She also slept a lot more than the other babies.

"Slow down a little. You're going to choke," I murmured, lifting the bottle away from her mouth for a few seconds so that she could breathe in between her feeding. The moment the nipple left her mouth, she licked her lips and looked like she was ready to head back to the realm of sleep. But before she could, I placed the nipple back in her mouth, stopping her just in the nick of time.

By the time I was done feeding her, Eros was still feeding the two babies in his lap.

*Three down, six more to go.*

*Hurray.*

. . .

Every day for me now consisted of staying up at night to feed the babies every couple of hours, changing diapers, and rocking nine babies to sleep. And I didn't really know if I liked this change or not, especially because the lack of sleep was making me cranky.

But as for Eros, he was okay with not sleeping for days and nights. Though I knew this, I didn't want him to be the only one taking care of the baby. Parenting was supposed to be a combined effort.

So, instead of letting him do everything, I chose to stay up with him to take care of the babies, who seemed to be quite rambunctious during the middle of the night and asleep during the day. Not that I could really sleep through all the yipping they do now.

Ever since that first day, they started to become a lot more active verbally in my head and physically in real life.

"Your sister's here with Zanthos," Eros said, handing me a wet rag to wipe off the droplet of milk dripping down the side of the baby's mouth.

"Anira *and* Zanthos? What a surprise," I said, turning my head to the door. Just as my eyes caught sight of Anira's bright green ones, a small smile formed on my lips.

She was wearing light blue skinny jeans, a nice pink turtleneck that matched the pink beanie on her head, a warm wooly coat, and black heeled boots. But not one bit of curly blonde hair was in sight. Sadly.

"I'm here to see those babies, Emira. Where is my little niece or nephew?" Anira greeted and asked as Zanthos and Eros stayed by the front of the cave to talk.

"It's nieces *and* nephews," I corrected.

"Nieces and nephews? What do you m—?" she asked, slightly confused. Then, she saw the nine cribs to the side of the bed and completely came to a halt, almost causing Zanthos to bump into her.

"Holy shit!" she exclaimed. "Excuse my language. But how many are there?"

"Nine," I replied.

"Nine? You had nine freaking babies? How the hell is that possible?" Anira's eyes became the size of saucers and her mouth gaped open in extreme disbelief. I myself would never have believed that nine babies all came out of me, but they had. So that was that.

"Yup. Just five days ago," I said nonchalantly.

"You say it like it was that easy to have nine freaking babies all at the same time. Did you have a C-section? Epidural?" she asked.

"No and no. I had the plain-o natural birth with no epidural," I said, quite proud of my accomplishments.

"Are you insane, Emi? Oh my God," she gasped, her eyes almost bulging from their sockets. "Your down there must be like mashed SpaghettiOs with a side of ketchup."

My face deadpanned for a second and a half, and I had to control my chortling in case I startled the kids. "My down there is completely fine. It's already healed back up."

"I sure hope so," she murmured, crossing her arms over her chest as we walked over to the cribs. "Anyway, what's their names? You've come up with the names, right?"

Anira only asked that because she knew how much of a procrastinator I usually was. Except this time, I'd procrastinated past the due date.

"Of course, we've come up with names. What kind of parents do you take us for?" I joked, sweating bullets while glad that Eros and I had come up with all the names yesterday. We'd brainstormed whenever the babies were asleep for these last five days. That was how long it took us when we sat down to do it.

If Anira knew that it took us this long to name all the babies, she would never let me live it down, not even when she was eighty years old and in a wheelchair. And if it were her who had nine babies, she would have had the names picked before she'd even gotten pregnant. Anira was just that fast and organized with everything she did.

I led her over to the first crib and said, "This is Silas, he's the first one to come out."

"Cute," she commented, nodding her head.

"This is Erik. He's usually very calm and collected."

"Cute," she said, again, while stroking the soft skin on the inside of his paw.

"He's Nicholas. He likes to chew on the others."

"Cu—" she tried to say.

"Can you not make the same comments?" I wrinkled my brows.

"What do you want me to say? They all look alike. And none of them look like you," she said, speaking the obvious.

"They actually look like Eros in his wolf form," I admitted.

"Really? Well… they're cute and all but there's way too much fur," she admitted, chewing on her glossed lips as if she had wanted to keep herself from saying that but couldn't.

"They're werewolves. And their father is a werewolf. What did you expect?" I said, raising a brow at her.

She crossed her arms over her chest again and said, "This wasn't exactly what I'd expected. That's for sure."

I glanced at Anira's face and bit back a laugh after recognizing that sour expression.

"Oh, admit it already! You're jealous, aren't you?" I grinned at her.

"I *am* jealous. Just a tiny bit," she continued, "You're here with nine little babies while me and Wyatt…" Anira glanced at Zanthos. "Well… you know."

I raised a brow and turned my head to look at Zanthos, who was busy talking to Eros about something, but I knew the both of them were listening to our conversation. And though I wanted to ask what was with the look she sent Zanthos, I didn't.

"They'll be changing into human babies in a couple of weeks."

Anira probably thought the babies would come out looking like regular little human babies since she'd never seen Eros in wolf form. Because if she did, she would have known that they were the carbon copy of their father.

I shook my head at her and continued to name the rest of them, hoping I didn't get them wrong. For some reason, it was hard for me to remember them all because I hadn't gotten around to using their names very often.

If I had put name stickers on each of their cribs, it would have been a lot easier. "This one is Noah and this is Ace and this little one is… is… um…"

*Damn it.*

I forgot what this little babies name was.

*How horrible of me!*

Anira raised a defined brow at me and pulled her beanie lower over her forehead, hiding the semi-bald head I knew she was sporting instead of her beautiful and luscious golden curls I'd been jealous of since childhood.

"Cillian," Eros said from the other side of the room, proving that he and Zanthos had been listening to us talk with their superior hearing.

"Cillian. This one is Cillian. And this little one is Darius." I pointed at the crib right next to Cillian's. "And finally, these are my two baby girls, Wren and Kyra."

"Finally some girls! I thought all you had were boys, which would have been mighty disappointing for me. But two out of nine is ridiculous. What kind of odds are those?" Anira scoffed. "There should have been more girls!"

"Two is better than nothing. And it's not like Eros and I can control which gender will come out," I piped in, gesturing for her to take a seat over by the table.

Anira shrugged and pulled out a chair before plopping down into it.

"Is your chemo port still in?" I asked, grabbing a plate of precut fruit, two bottles of water from the fridge, and four forks before taking a seat across from her.

Anira shook her head, stabbing a piece of strawberry, and said, "No. Not anymore…"

I cocked my head to the side at her words and really looked at Anira, carefully analyzing her from head to toe.

Although her hair was gone and she was very pale now, there didn't seem to be too much of a difference in the her before cancer and the her after cancer.

*This is different.*

Usually, Anira would look like a walking skeleton within a week of starting chemo. She dropped weight really fast. Her cheeks would hollow in and her eyes would be adorning dark bags big enough to make it seem as if she hadn't slept in centuries. Even her skin would be dry and flaky, bruised and red within a matter of days.

She didn't look very sickly this time, and it was making me wonder if she was taking chemotherapy. Because if she were on chemotherapy, she wouldn't look this cheerful and energetic.

"Are you still on chemo?" I picked up the fork and forked a piece of watermelon to put into my mouth.

Anira shook her head and chewed on another piece of strawberry.

"Why not?" I asked, extremely worried that she was giving up instead of fighting for herself and her life.

# CHAPTER 8

"I'm getting better without it," she replied, looking me straight in the eye. From her steady words and clear green eyes, I could tell that she wasn't lying to me. But I was still very worried and suspicious.

"Are you sure?" I asked.

"Yes. The doctors say that the cancer is going away... by itself," she said, turning her gaze away from me, as if there were something she didn't want me to know.

My brows wrinkled and my mind whirled with the possibilities, but I couldn't figure out what was missing in this equation. Then, I glanced over by the lip of the den and caught Zanthos' eyes.

I had a feeling this all had something to do with him, yet I didn't know what. But if Anira was getting better, I wasn't going to question it and make her uncomfortable. I just wanted to know what was going on with her and Wyatt and Zanthos. I was so, so curious. Because it looked like there was something crazy going on, but I wasn't going to ask her with Zanthos standing there looking at us with those sharp hawk eyes of his. It creeped me out. He creeped me out. Still.

"Okay. As long as you're getting better. If anything happens, just call me. You know I'll always pick up, even when I'm in the bathroom," I said, joking again.

"I will. And ew. Don't call me when you're in the bathroom," she replied, smiling until I could see her pearly whites.

Sometimes, it was really hard to see when someone was in pain when they had such a bright and beautiful smile imprinted on their lips and looked at you with such clear and bright eyes. It was hard to tell. But I hoped that Anira was as happy on the inside as she looked on the outside. Because I really didn't want her to suffer.

"Ready to go?" Zanthos asked, walking over to Anira.

Anira nodded and stood. "I'll come back and visit you later, Emi."

"Have a safe trip back home. I'll call you when I get the chance." I glanced back and forth between her and Zanthos, swallowing down the questions that wanted to crawl up my throat and out of my mouth. Curiosity did kill the cat, after all.

*Don't do it, Emira.*

"Hi, Emi," Zanthos said, smiling widely, as if we didn't have any bad blood between us, when in actuality, we did. And it was him who had started it.

I looked over at Eros, who had also come into the cave, and immediately felt a lot safer.

Ever since Zanthos came into the cave, I hadn't spoken a single word to him, but that didn't stop him from coming close to me or my children. And I didn't like that. I didn't like that one bit.

"The pups are beautiful," Zanthos complimented, trying to strike a conversation while in the presence of Anira. He was probably trying to look as friendly and nice as possible in an attempt to get to her.

I narrowed my eyes at him.

"Thank you," I said curtly in a well-mannered-even-though-I-still-don't-forgive-you kind of way.

*I hold grudges and he probably knows that by now.*

"I'll take Ani home and come back to have a chat with you and Eros. Hopefully, you'll welcome me back," he said, still smiling.

I turned my eyes to Eros and tried to send him a why-is-he-coming-back look, but Eros only shrugged his shoulders.

"Of course," Eros said, because I didn't want to say another word to Zanthos in fear that my emotions would get the best of me and curse words would come out instead.

. . .

By the time Zanthos had dropped Anira off and come back to the cave, the babies were awake.

Instead of going straight to Eros, who was playing with the babies, Zanthos came over to me and sat down in the chair across from mine. I sighed to myself and turned to him, trying to get this "chat" over with as quickly as possible.

"What did you want to talk about, Zanthos?" I asked, pushing a bottle of water over to him while trying to maintain my calm and not punch him in the face, because I'd been holding in this feeling for close to a year. And at some point, I had a feeling that it was going to break out and grab a hold of Zanthos' throat like a vice and never let go. Never, never let go.

"I just wanted to apologize for everything that I'd done before. I'm sorry. I'm really sorry, Emi," Zanthos said, losing that smile he'd kept on his lips when Anira had been here.

Zanthos apologized to me.

*Me!*

I was in shock. Immense shock. Because I'd never seen this day coming. But then, a thought came to my mind and made my overwhelmed emotions come to a halt.

"Are you apologizing because of Ani? Just to get on her good side? Because if you are, it's not necessary." I narrowed my eyes warningly at him.

"No. This has nothing to do with Anira." Zanthos looked quite sincere, and this made my anger kind of falter. "I wanted to sincerely apologize to you for being such an asshole in the past. I took my anger out on you when you had nothing to do with it. What's between me and Eros shouldn't have been pinned on you. But I guess I was too miserable to see that so I wanted to make you and Eros miserable, too. And for that, I'm sorry."

I frowned.

At least Zanthos was mature and man enough to actually apologize for his mistakes. Because an apology coming from someone with an ego twice the size of the moon like him was probably very hard to come by. And I was going to relish and bask in it as long as I could.

"I know you're probably not going to forgive me, but I just wanted to get that off my chest."

I nodded my head, agreeing with what he'd just said. "Well, you thought right."

"I guess I still have a few centuries ahead to get your forgiveness," he joked.

"Good luck trying, Zanthos. Good luck trying."

. . .

After waiting day by day to see the colors of my babies' eyes, I finally got to see them on the seventh and eighth day. The first to open his eyes was Darius while the last to open her eyes was Wren, the one who valued her sleep more than playing and eating and basically everything that didn't have to do with napping or sleeping. No surprise there.

Darius had blue eyes.

Silas had blue eyes.

Noah had blue eyes.

Wren had blue eyes.

Nicholas had blue eyes.

Ace had blue eyes.

Erik had blue eyes.

Kyra had blue eyes.

Cillian had blue eyes.

They all had blue eyes. And when I saw that, I was mildly concerned that none of my genes had registered and that I had now become a copying machine only good at printing out carbon copies of Eros.

*What the hell, womb?*

*Why don't any of my children have brown eyes like me or a mixture of my eyes and Eros' eyes?*

I knew that Eros' genes might be pretty dominant. But damn. I didn't see anything of mine in the babies. And here I thought that blue eyes were recessive genes while brown eyes were dominant... dominant my ass!

*It's fine. It's fine, Emira,* I told myself, trying to calm down and not freak out over something that I couldn't control. *At least Eros is handsome because then the babies will all grow up to be good looking and have beautiful blue eyes that can just take your soul from you.*

"Their eyes are all blue, Eros," I said, pouting up at him. "I don't think any of them look like me."

"Their eyes might change colors in the future," he said, trying to comfort me.

"Really?" I was a little skeptical of that.

"Mm-hm. Once they get some sunlight, their eyes will probably become a different color," he reassured.

"But this blue is so beautiful, though," I said, changing my mind now that I knew their eyes might change. "It's just a tad bit lighter than yours, but it's so pretty."

Eros chuckled and said, "You can't make up your mind again, can you?"

I grinned up at him. "You know I can't."

Eros shook his head.

As I looked over at Silas and Erik, I noticed that they seemed to be emitting a weird golden light from their little bodies. The glow surrounded them and looked like it was expanding in size, almost blinding me with its intensity.

"What's happening to Silas and Erik?" I asked, startled by the sudden glow radiating off them. Though I knew that it probably wasn't something bad, I was still kind of worried. Because this was not a normal occurrence, at least not for humans anyway.

"They're shifting," Eros answered, wrapping his arms around my waist and propping his chin against the top of my head.

We both watched as all the black fur and tail gradually diminished, almost like they were being drawn back into the babies' body, until soft, pink skin covered them from head to toe. Cute little paws became tiny little hands and feet, while little noses and pink mouths replaced their snouts and maws.

When they finished shifting into their human forms, I was in awe at how incredibly cute they were. And my hands itched to touch their soft skin and play with their silken black hair.

Without further ado, I reached out and stroked Silas' left cheek, flushed from his little nap. The texture of his skin was so much different than mine. It was so much softer and made me feel like I was touching a ball of mochi.

"He's so soft," I murmured, watching Eros stroke Silas' dark hair with this adoring look on his handsome face. Just watching Silas nudge his head into Eros' palm made my heart flutter with warmth and immense satisfaction.

*This is what family feels like. My family,* I thought.

"Thank you, Emira," he said suddenly, smiling widely, lovingly at me.

"What are you suddenly thanking me for?" I gave him a confused look.

"For allowing me to be the father of our pups, for choosing me as your mate, and for making me the happiest man alive." Eros pressed his warm lips on my forehead in a soft, tender kiss.

My eyes immediately lowered. I wrapped my free arm around his waist and leaned into his body, letting his body heat wrap around me like a second skin.

This was where home was for me. Always.

"If that's the case then I'd have to thank you for being a wonderful mate and a wonderful father, for always comforting me when I'm down, and for making me believe in love again. Thank you, Eros. I don't know what I would do without you," I said softly, feeling my eyes burn as the waterworks started rolling again.

"Don't cry, Emira," he murmured, leaning his head down to give me a kiss, but I quickly placed my fingers over his lips.

"Not in front of the babies," I said, turning my head away.

Eros sighed pitifully and pressed a kiss on my temple instead.

Though I felt bad for cutting him off, I couldn't help the grin that blossomed on my lips.

. . .

After staying in the cave for a little over a month, Eros and I decided to head back to the pack house when the babies were able to sustain their human forms without shifting uncontrollably back into wolves. Now that my entire body was back to normal and the area in between my legs was as good as new, I thought it was time to get out of hiding and go back into the real world again.

With the help of Sergio and Qian, the pack Gammas, Eros and I packed all the cribs, diapers, baby essentials, milk, clothes, and infant car seats into the SUVs before fastening all the babies into their appropriate seats. And since there were nine of them, we had to split the babies into two vehicles, making me wonder if we should get one of those twelve-passenger vans. That way, we wouldn't have to use two cars if we ever needed to travel somewhere. But then again, Eros said that the Gammas needed to go everywhere with us since it was dangerous for us to travel without guards.

"Are we almost there yet?" I asked, getting sleepy from the music playing in the car.

"Almost," Eros said. "Probably in another fifteen minutes or so."

I rested my head against his shoulder and closed my eyes, hoping my dress didn't wrinkle from sitting too long in it.

Since we were heading back to the pack today, we'd decided to do a little party to introduce the babies to the pack because everyone had been so excited about seeing them.

Granny Ada, Rora and some pack members had helped get all the party supplies, food, and decorations. I'd told them I wanted to help. But since I couldn't leave the babies, they didn't let me. In the end, all I was in charge of was dressing myself and the babies and showing up at the party.

I didn't know how others usually felt about not putting in any effort or helping towards this kind of thing, but I felt really guilty, especially since it was a party for my babies and I was the mother.

At the thought, I grimaced and decided I would try to help the pack more in the future, like I should as the Alpha Female.

"You've already helped out, Emira." Eros' comforting words cut through my thoughts.

"Have I?" My brows wrinkled, and I tried to think of the things that I had done for the pack since I'd become a member, but couldn't really come up with anything. All I'd done so far was get pregnant and have nine babies. Nothing to contribute to the pack. Well, not in that sense anyway.

"You've contributed nine times." Eros shot a look at the babies behind us and smiled.

"That doesn't count," I huffed, realizing what Eros was pointing at. "What I meant was helping around the pack."

"You'll have plenty of time to help out in the future. Don't worry about it," Eros said.

"You're right," I said, lifting my head off Eros' shoulder to notice the wad of brown hair sticking to his white shirt. My nose wrinkled, and I frowned, reaching over to pick off all the strands of brown clinging to Eros' shirt with magnetic force.

After giving birth to the babies, I'd gradually noticed that the drain would get clogged with balls of my hair whenever I finished showering. And when I'd comb my hair, handfuls of it would be stuck to the brush.

I was going bald on my head and not in the areas I wanted to be bald in. Sadly, this was even worse than when Kent had torn out a handful.

It scared me a lot to know this, so I'd searched online and found that postpartum hair loss was a common occurrence for mothers. This meant that I would have to deal with this for another six months to a year before my hair growth would become normal again. I just hoped that the hair loss wouldn't be too noticeable, or else I'd have to start wearing a hat around the house. And I could imagine how ridiculous it would be for me, especially in the summer.

*Why in the world does all this crazy stuff happen to women?*

From all that time suffering while carrying a baby to the birth pain and the crazy hair loss and so on and so forth. Hopefully men had it this hard. Because if they didn't, that would be totally unfair.

"I'm going bald, Eros. Your mate is going bald like the bald eagle mixed with a naked-mole rat!" I exclaimed rather dramatically.

After my words, I heard the Gammas chortle and try to choke down their uncontrollable laughter, but it was coming out regardless of how hard they tried.

"Go ahead and laugh, Sergio. Because when your mate gets pregnant and gives birth, she's going to lose all her hair like me. And then she's going to make you pick up all the fallen strands and make a wig for her to cover her head. And by then, you'll be crying," I joked, glancing at the burly male in the driver seat.

"I wouldn't mind, Alpha Female. If my mate could get pregnant quicker, I'd be happy to make her a hundred wigs," he replied, grinning.

"I think she's going to soon, but trying harder on your part is required," I said.

Being in the pack for a while now, I'd heard Gamma Sergio say one too many times that his mate was the sole problem in their quest for conception, so I couldn't help but make a comment on it, hoping he'd stop blaming her for something she couldn't control.

"Oh, damn." Gamma Qian all out guffawed, slapping his knee repeatedly. "Serves you right for always saying it's Ashley's fault ya'll don't have any pups yet."

"It's actually proven that she-wolves—" Gamma Sergio tried to say.

"But just her trying isn't enough. As with anything in your relationship, you both have to make the effort and not put the blame on one another," I said, feeling like a relationship therapist all of a sudden.

Eros chuckled next to my ear.

"I'll take your advice to heart, Alpha Female," he said, giving in.

"Good to hear, Gamma Sergio." I smiled at him through the rearview mirror.

. . .

"They're so adorable!" Rora's friends all cooed, staring into the cribs with stars in their eyes.

"Thank you," I replied, smiling at Ciara and Jeanne before stuffing a fork of spaghetti into my mouth and chewing. After swallowing, I said, "They can be a handful sometimes."

"I can imagine. With this many, it's probably very hard to handle," Ciara said. "Are you guys going to get a nanny?"

"I don't think so. Eros and I can handle it at the moment. If, in the future, we can't, we will probably consider finding help," I paused to take a sip of my sweet tea, "It's just hard to find someone you really trust. You know?"

Ciara and Jeanne nodded.

"You guys should try the spaghetti, it's to die for," I commented as Rora came back over with a big plate of spaghetti and stuffed garlic bread.

Ciara and Jeanne glanced over to the food table and bid me goodbye, powerwalking over to the long line of pack members.

Every time Granny Ada made food, everyone in the pack knew to stand in line and get their plates ready before it was all gone. Though I'd had the honor of always eating Granny Ada's food, it wasn't common around the pack house because everyone was open to cooking their own meals.

The kitchen was very big and was shared among all the members living in the pack house. Everyone else who had a house of their own made food in their own kitchens, so any party with Granny Ada helping was always a blessing. Really. It was. And I planned to appreciate her for as long as I could.

"Homemade bread is always the best bread," I sighed blissfully, taking another bite of the garlic bread. This time, the steaming cheese was pulled out and was worth the burn on my tongue. It was so delicious that I needed another one.

# CHAPTER 9

Looking around the room, I saw Eros coming towards me so I had to set the garlic bread down and wipe my hands and lips with a wet wipe. Then, I stood and brushed the crumbs off my floral dress.

Everyone sitting at the tables had already gotten the chance to take a look at the babies and get their food, so I knew that Eros was going to introduce our children to the pack now. As he came over and held my hand, the pack members stopped talking and turned their attention to us, even going as far as to drop their forks and sit with their backs straight.

"First off, I would like to thank Granny Ada, Joyce, Angie, Meredith, and Rora for putting together this whole celebration and cooking us a wonderful meal. Second, I would like to thank everyone for coming. And third, I would like to thank my Alpha Female for giving us hope and a reason to celebrate today," Eros said, his deep voice booming across the room. "As you already know, a month ago, my mate gave birth to nine strong Sentinels. And today, I would like to introduce you to my pups. Starting from the oldest to the youngest. This is Silas, Erik, Nicholas, Noah, Ace, Cillian, Darius, Wren, and Kyra."

Squeezing Eros' hand, I smiled brightly and glanced at the nine cribs lined up next to each other. I didn't know how Eros was able to tell which one was the oldest and which one was the youngest, but I was glad he knew which was which. Because I was not good at telling them apart.

It had already been a month and I still had a really hard time deciphering the babies. If it wasn't for Eros putting them back into the cribs after they were done playing with each other, I would have them all mixed up and in the wrong cribs.

*I'm bad. I know. But I can't help it.*

Before I could delve into another thought, the crowd cheered and applauded and brought me back to reality.

Eros led me back to where I was sitting before and let me get back to my meal while he went off to talk to Alpha Xavier, who had come to the celebration without his mate.

By the time I got back to eating, Rora was already done with her plate and grabbing another heaping of ribs with mashed potatoes. She was tiny but she was quite the eater.

"Try the ribs, Emi. It's so tender and full of flavor!" she exclaimed, dropping a rib on my plate.

"I wish I have the stomach to try everything on the table," I said, jabbing the rib with my fork and cutting some of the glistening meat off. From the corner of my eye, I saw Lia holding a plate of ribs and seasoned fries. I waved her over to sit with us.

"Just try a little bit of each. Don't make yourself sick," Lia said, setting her plate down before taking a seat.

I nodded my head, eyeing her fries as I decided if I should go get some after I finished my plate.

"Have some of mine," she said, picking up her plate and pushing some fries on to mine before I could say anything.

"You don't have to do that. I can go get some on my own," I said, even though I was already shoving some fries into my mouth and chewing in complete happiness.

"You didn't get any ketchup?" I asked, my eyes sweeping across her plate.

"No. They're already seasoned perfectly," Lia replied, popping some into her mouth.

"They are, but ketchup always makes things taste better," I said.

"I don't really care for ketchup." She took another bite of the fries before digging her knife into the ribs.

"What?!" My eyes widened in disbelief. "What do you use then?"

"Ranch. Mustard. Anything not ketchup."

"Wow. I haven't really met anyone who doesn't like ketchup. You're the first," I said, shrugging it off and going back to my spaghetti and garlic bread.

"It's my pleasure being the first." Lia grinned widely, before she started eating the ribs.

When I was done eating and chatting and everyone in the pack had gotten the chance to take another look at the babies, Rora and Lia helped me take the babies back to our room. It was a little time consuming to go up the stairs with the cribs but we managed to do it without asking for more help.

"I'm going to go walk some of this food baby off," Lia said.

"Me too." Rora nodded her head, rubbing her flat belly.

"Thanks for helping me bring the babies up. I'll see you later!"

"See you later," they both chimed, closing the door behind them.

"I ate too much," I muttered to myself, groaning in slight pain.

In a way to help myself digest faster, I decided to give the babies a bath before letting them nap. Though I had a hard time in the beginning trying to bathe them, I did a lot better now after I got the chance to practice repeatedly every day, and my fear of hurting them or dropping them or getting soap in their eyes was completely erased from my mind.

While filling the babies' tub with warm water and grabbing a little towel to wash them with, I left the door open and took quick glances at the babies to make sure that nothing happened.

When I was done, I took the tub out of the bathroom and set up all the products I needed before grabbing the first baby from his crib and undressing him to start the bath. I always started with Ace because he didn't like bathing and was super fussy during the bath. It was like he was a cat and not a wolf, though I wasn't too sure if wolves liked bathing or not.

By the time I was done bathing him and his eight siblings, I was pooped, like I always was after wrestling them for over an hour and repeatedly changing the water for each child.

I took a deep breath and wiped the sweat off my brows. Just as I sat back on the bed, my cell phone rang and I saw "Anira" pop up on the screen.

"What's up, Anira?" I said, my muscles tensing up for an unknown reason.

"I just called to chat with you. Do you have any free time?" By the sound of Anira's voice, I didn't think anything bad had happened, so the sudden stress and anxiety that filled me immediately dissipated into thin air.

"Always for you," I said, grabbing some toys for the babies to play with while I talked to Anira.

"I know you're really curious about what has happened with Wyatt and me, so I'm calling to fill you in… if you still want to know," she said.

"Of course, I want to know!" I exclaimed, almost too excited for my own good. "So, what happened? Are you still getting married or has it been permanently postponed?"

"No. I'm not getting married anymore. The wedding's been canceled. For good. Wyatt and I broke up—on good terms—after I got cancer again," she said.

"But then, why are you with Zanthos? Is he blackmailing you? Because, if he is, I will have Eros kick his a—" Just the thought of him threatening Anira made my blood boil. That son of a—

"No, no. He's not blackmailing me…" she trailed off and stopped talking for a moment.

"So, to put it simple, you're with Zanthos now," I stated for her.

Without an ounce of hesitation, she said, "Yes."

"Do you like him?" I was really surprised that it was so easy for Zanthos to get to Anira. Because, from what I remembered, Anira hated his guts after he'd forced his mating mark on her. And she'd really wanted to come after him with some silver bullets. So how did he do it?! How did he manage to change her mind?

"…Kind of," she said slowly.

"Kind of?!"

"We're still in the trial period. If it doesn't work out then I'll just break it off with him," she said, as if it were something so easy and simple.

*It's not that easy to get rid of a werewolf who's your soulmate. No matter how you think you can, you really can't. It's impossible and probably dangerous,* I thought.

What in the world made Anira think that breaking off a bond with a werewolf was just as easy as breaking up with someone?

I'd thought that she must have done her research before jumping into things with him. But now, I wasn't too sure if she knew the consequences of her actions just yet, and I really didn't know how to break it to her.

"It's not as easy as you think to get rid of a werewolf, Anira. I hope you have done some research," I warned. "And I don't know if you know this or not, but, a while back, Zanthos had me kidnapped and peed on and sent off to a foreign country because of some problems he had with Eros. He really made me suffer physically and mentally for weeks."

"I know. Zanthos told me about that," she paused, "He also said that he was deeply regretful for putting you in the middle of that, Emi."

"And you're siding with him on this?" I knew I sounded really petty, but I couldn't help it. Anira was my sister, wasn't she supposed to be on my side? Especially when I was right?

"I'm not siding with anyone on this, and I'm not asking you to forgive him either. I'll just let you guys figure it out," she said, sounding exasperated already.

"Has he marked you? Because if he has, then—" I said, changing the subject before I let my anger get the better of me.

"I know what I'm doing, Emi. I can handle this," she replied, evading my question and making me completely apprehensive of the situation.

Since the last time I saw her, I wasn't able to see her neck because of the turtleneck she wore.

But now that I was thinking this over, I realized that she must've been trying to hide her neck from me, trying to hide Zanthos completed mating mark.

And if what I thought was correct, then that meant that Zanthos and Anira had mated… and she only "kind of" liked him. Eek.

I frowned and said, "Alright. If it makes you happy to be with him, then I won't say anything more. But don't say I didn't warn you if things go south."

"I know. I know. I won't let it get to that point. Besides, Zanthos… he's a lot different than what you think. Once you get to know him, he's a really kind and considerate guy."

Wait. What?! Zanthos? Kind and considerate? What was Anira on?

I took a deep breath and exhaled away from the phone, before I could blow up into a million, billion pieces.

"If you say so," I said as calmly as I possibly could. "Now that I think about it, I'm glad that I haven't told you what to do or who to choose because things would have been ugly for me. Especially when we fight over it."

Anira laughed and said, "I'd never blame you for that."

"Uh-huh. Like I'll believe you," I said, pulling a small stuffed toy out of Noah's mouth before he choked on it.

"For real, Emi. I really wouldn't."

"I'm still not going to believe you," I joked.

. . .

Today was an off day for me since Granny Ada wanted to stay with the kids and help me watch them.

I was originally just going to take a walk around the pack house to get some exercise in, but after Lia and Rora invited me to watch them train, I decided to go do that instead.

Since I'd never been to their training rooms, I wasn't too sure what to expect. But when I got there, the training rooms turned out to be training land, because they didn't train indoors, regardless of the weather. Instead, the area used for training was a small arena that was free of grass and trees. The ground was covered with grey-colored dirt and was extremely solid, like cement, but still retained a bit of bounce to it.

"Do the other pack members train here too?" I asked, looking around to see that the entire area was as empty as could be. Not even a ghost was in sight.

"No. This is just one of the smaller training areas," Rora explained, blocking Lia's arm with her forearm in an extremely easy way. If it were me, I had a feeling that my bone would have shattered into deformed pieces never to be put back together again. "Alpha Eros and the warriors train in a different training ground about fifteen minutes from here."

"Oh. That explains why this whole place is empty," I muttered, taking a seat in the chairs lined up a little farther from the center where Rora and Lia sparred.

"Can you guys teach me how to spare?" I asked, taking off my jacket and putting it down on the chair. Learning how to defend myself would be good for any kidnapping incidents in the future. If I could at least learn the basics, I would feel more secured and prepared for anything that came at me.

But hopefully I didn't have to use any of this knowledge. Because, after my previous experiences with being kidnapped, I was always very cautious of going anywhere with anyone I didn't know, and, sometimes, even people I did know. I didn't want to be the leverage that the government had over Eros and the pack.

"You? Are you sure?" Lia asked, sizing me up by glancing up and down my body with a questioning look on her face.

"Yes, I'm sure," I replied, my voice full of confidence.

"I don't think you're a good candidate for this," Lia said truthfully, shaking her head at me like I was a major disappointment, like I was not a worthy student.

"Don't judge a book by its covers, Lia. Though I may look small, I'm pretty strong." Jokingly, I put my arms up and tried to flex to show her my muscles, if they were even considered that.

"Then, prove it. Because I really don't believe you." She grinned wittily and beckoned me to come over with a quick motion of her index finger.

All of a sudden, I felt as if I had walked into her trap, like I had asked her to beat me up instead of "sparring" with me.

*Well, shit.*

"I want to learn the basics first. We can leave the sparring for another time," I said, not really interested in getting a beating from Lia or Rora.

"Of course." Lia nodded her head, chuckling at me, probably because of the scared look on my face. "With your beginner level, you won't be able to spar yet."

I pouted and walked over to Lia before standing still.

"First, we'll start with stretching. Just follow my lead." Lia started doing some of the most basic stretches, and I followed them rather easily because I'd done this before back when I was still taking yoga classes.

"Okay. I can do that," I said, bringing my arms over my head and stretching.

After the warm up, she had me run laps around the arena. And I tried to run as fast as I could, but by the second lap, I was already lagging behind and regretting my life decisions faster than you could say "onomatopoeia."

"Running is not my thing." I huffed and puffed, losing my breath and feeling so out of shape. But after imagining there were Hunters behind me, I'd managed to make four laps before falling into my chair. "Is there something else we could try? Something that doesn't involve running?"

"That's pathetic, even for a human, Emi," Lia said, shaking her head.

"Not really, I've seen worse," Rora interjected.

"Thanks, Rora." I wiped the sweat off my brow and was too tired to think of a comeback.

"You'd have to work on getting your body into the best condition before we can start sparring lessons. That'd take maybe six months to a year if you're consistent."

"Okay… Is there something else that's easier and can be learned right away?" I asked, grabbing a tissue from my pocket to wipe my entire face.

While I was breathing hard and sweating like a pig, Lia and Rora were still crisp and clean, even after they had sparred with each other for over an hour.

"What about target shooting? Maybe you're better at that?" Rora suggested, handing me a water bottle out of nowhere.

"Ooh. That sounds like fun. What am I shooting with?" I asked excitedly, taking a sip of the cool water.

"This," Lia answered, handing me a silver gun that looked a lot lighter than it actually was.

By the time I had it in my hand, I figured that it must've weighed at least a pound or two. If I had this in my pocket while running from the enemy, I would have totally lost my pants in the process. And what a sight that would be.

"Is there anything lighter?" I didn't think I would last really long holding this gun upright with my flabby arms.

Lia and Rora both shook their head and led me over to the shooting range a little farther from the arena.

"Most guns weigh the same as this one," Rora explained.

"Oh," I replied, watching as Lia and Rora set up the targets several feet away.

Truthfully, I'd never shot at anything before in my life. And the closest I'd come to a gun was probably the plastic toy guns I had as a child, nothing that could shoot real bullets or kill anyone. Though I didn't really know if I wanted to kill someone or not...

"This is how you load a gun and cock it." Lia proceeded to show me the entire step of loading, unloading, and loading the gun again before cocking it.

I was quick to pick up on how to do all that within a matter of minutes. The only thing I struggled with was cocking the gun because my hands were getting sweaty, making it harder for me to pull the slide back.

"You're good at this," Rora complimented, smiling widely at me with a hint of relief in the depths of her pretty eyes.

I was pretty relieved that there was something I was good at too.

"Thank you." I smiled back, grabbing the ear protection and safety goggles from Rora. I put them both on.

"Remember to always keep your gun down until you plan to shoot or else you can misfire and kill a lot of innocent people," Lia explained, showing me how to stand properly to keep myself from falling back or hitting myself in the face from the recoil. "Now try hitting that first target. Make sure to hold the gun tight. Not too tight that your hands start shaking, Emi. You're not going to hit anything like that."

"What do you mean tight but not too tight?!" I gave Lia a bewildered look.

"Here, let me show you."

I placed the ear protection back on my head as Lia took the gun and stood properly. Then, she pulled the trigger and hit the target on the little red dot like a professional sniper.

"Okay. My turn!" I exclaimed, squinting my eyes and focusing on the bullseye. When I took my shot, I was a little surprised by how the gun forced my arm backwards in the aftermath.

"Did I get it? Did I hit the mark?" I asked excitedly.

"No. But you almost hit that poor squirrel in the back," Lia said, pointing at a tree a little farther away from the target.

My expression fell and disappointment filled me, but I was quick to pick myself back up and take aim again and again and again and again.

After what seemed like a hundred shots, all three of us came to a conclusion. And that conclusion was: I had no hand-eye coordination. None whatsoever. Though I wanted to hit the target, my hand just didn't want to do what I told it to. And I was endangering the forest animals with my terrible aim, especially that poor squirrel who'd almost gotten shot by me.

Other than the target shooting fail, Lia and Rora also showed me some defensive moves for if anyone came at me or tried to grab me. I learned that a lot faster than the gun shooting, but I wasn't any good at it.

Maybe Lia was right about me not being cut out for this.

# CHAPTER 10

By the end of the day, I was bruised all over. There were blue and purple spots all over my arms and legs from when I tried to block Lia's "attacks" and from when I tripped over my own two feet and fell on my face. Twice.

"I should probably get back to the babies before Granny Ada goes nuts trying to keep them occupied," I said, noticing that the sun was still up.

I had thought that a lot more time had passed, but it hadn't.

*I guess that's what happens when you do the one thing you hate most.*

"It's still really early. We can get some lunch in town and go window shopping before you go back to the pups," Lia suggested, looking at her wristwatch.

I grabbed my jacket from the chair and put it on before saying, "In town? There's a town close by?"

"Wessville. It's just ten minutes from here," Rora replied.

"I don't think Eros will let me go. He thinks it's too dangerous for me to go anywhere without supervision," I said.

Rora and Lia glanced at each other, probably laughing at me on the inside.

"I think he won't mind if we have the Gammas with us. Come on! It's just like ten minutes from here. If anything happens, Alpha Eros would already be there in a second."

I glanced at Rora, who nodded her head, before saying, "Let me go ask him and see if Granny Ada is okay with watching the babies for a bit longer."

. . .

I'd thought that it would be a lot harder to get Eros' approval, but it wasn't. As long as I was safe and had the Gammas watching me, just in case things go bad, he wasn't going to restrict me from going anywhere too far from him.

As for Granny Ada, she was having the time of her life with the babies. She was actually happy that I was giving her the chance to be with them longer, which really surprised me and made me wonder if all grandmothers were this way. But I wasn't going to question it or ruin her fun, so I took a quick shower and headed out with the girls for a fun afternoon in the town.

"I thought we decided on wearing skirts and a nice blouse?" Lia said, looking at my blue jeans and black t-shirt ensemble, the usual for me whenever I went out anywhere.

"I chickened out last minute and went with jeans instead," I said sheepishly, flashing her a guilty smile.

Lia was dressed in a rather tight black skirt that had a slit pretty high up her thigh and a nice halter top that really hugged her breasts and waist, leaving a little bit of skin to show in between where the skirt and halter top were supposed to meet.

"I like your outfit," I complimented, hoping that would calm her.

"Thanks," she muttered.

"Are you guys ready to go?" Rora said, coming down the hall.

When I saw her outfit, I burst out laughing. Not because it was funny or anything, but because Rora was also wearing jeans and a t-shirt that had the phrase "I'm not shy. I just don't like you." on it.

"Why am I the only one in a skirt while you're both in jeans? Did you guys plan this?" Lia asked, whining.

"We didn't plan on it," I chuckled, shaking my head. "Did you chicken out too, Rora?"

Rora nodded her head and giggled.

"Whatever. Let's just go," Lia grumbled, stomping her feet as she walked.

I sent Rora a wide grin and followed her out of the door.

At the front of the house, there was a black SUV already waiting along with the two Gammas Eros had appointed to accompany us into town today.

"Alpha Female," the two Gammas greeted, nodding their head at Lia and Rora, who nodded back and smiled.

"Hi, Sergio. Hi, Qian. I hope we're not wasting too much of your time," I said back, smiling at them as I got into the car.

"Not at all, Alpha Female," Gamma Qian said, getting in the passenger side while Gamma Sergio got in the driver side.

. . .

"The Pho here is so good," I sighed, taking my last sip of the beef soup and feeling as if my world had been brought back to life.

For me, Pho was always a good choice when it was cold outside. And other than chicken noodle soup, it was the second thing I always went for whenever I had a cold and needed something warm to make me feel better.

*Never fail. It always works like a charm,* I thought.

"Is everyone good and ready to go?" Lia asked, wiping her mouth with a napkin.

"I'm ready," I said, leaning back into the chair to catch my breath because I had eaten way over my limit and now felt kind of nauseous. Though I'd ordered a medium bowl of Pho, I also had four spring rolls, two eggrolls, some of Lia's stir-fried noodle, and two cups of Vietnamese iced coffee, because one cup was never enough. Though I regretted eating all that at once, I would probably do it again if I had the chance.

*I don't ever learn my lesson when it comes to food.*

"Me too," Rora replied, popping the second half of her fortune cookie into her mouth and chewing rapidly like a little squirrel chewing on its acorn.

I picked up the bill and made it over to the cashier before Rora or Lia could ask to pay. That was the least I could do for all the help they'd given me so far.

After I'd finished paying, we left and decided to go window shopping for a bit to walk off some of the food we just ate. But just as we walked to the first shop and were about to enter, someone tapped on my shoulder and made me go into alert mode immediately.

*Oh, crap,* I thought. *Not again.*

"Emira? Is that you?"

Hearing the slightly familiar voice I hadn't heard in almost twenty years, I turned my head and came face to face with one of my old high school classmates, Bennet Mathias Miller.

"Hi, Bennet. It's been a long time," I greeted. "How have you been?"

"Pretty good. How about you?" he asked.

"I've been really good," I replied casually.

"We'll go in first and look around," Lia said, giving Bennet a long glance as Rora opened the glass door and held it for her.

"Okay." I nodded my head and watched as they went into the shop.

"You look really good. It's like you haven't aged at all, like the older you get, the more you age backwards," he praised, smiling warmly like he always did back when we were still in high school.

"Thank you. You look really good, too." I smiled back.

Although Bennet had aged quite a bit since high school, that rugged and handsome face of his hadn't changed too much, because I could still recognize him with just one glance.

His hair was still that dirty blonde that bordered brown and his eyes were still as hazel as ever.

The only differences were the fine lines by his eyes and the start of a receding hairline at the top of his forehead.

I had a crush on Bennet throughout all the years of high school, starting when we became partners for a science project in ninth grade and ending when he left for college with his girlfriend.

He was a really popular guy who was friendly and outgoing, willing to help anyone who needed his help and willing to become friends with everyone, including me. And that was probably why I felt bad for crushing on him. He only wanted to be friends while I was just being creepy and daydreaming about marrying him one day.

If it weren't for his then girlfriend, Lucy Bardot, I would have embarrassed myself by confessing my infatuation for him like a fool during the last year of high school. But now that I thought back on it, I was really glad I didn't have the courage to tell him I liked him because I would've been sporting an ugly, bruised face for graduation after Lucy Bardot got done with me. Speaking of Lucy Bardot, she was a pretty sporty girl who'd gone through years of competitive swimming and wrestling, so I knew I had no chance when it came to beating her in a fight or beating her for Bennet.

"Do you live in town?" I asked.

"Yes. I moved here two years ago to coach at the high school."

"Oh, wow. I didn't know you coached!" I made a surprised face, as if I didn't know this already.

"I originally wanted to be a cop but coaching called to me more. So I stuck with that major instead. What about you?"

"Me? I…" I trailed off, not really wanting to talk about being a scientist for the government or my current unemployment and stay-at-home-mom status.

"Bennet? Are you done yet?" a woman in her late fifties called from the parking lot, cutting me off just as I was about to reply.

"Almost," he replied, turning back to me. "That's my mom, she's here to visit for a couple of days. You remember her?"

I'd only met his mom once back in ninth grade so trying to put a face to her name was very difficult, at least for me anyway.

I shook my head truthfully and said, "You better go before she waits too long."

"Wait, Emira! Next week there's a little reunion in town with some of the girls and guys from our class. Do you want to come?" he invited.

"Reunion? I thought it was going to be back at the old high school. Did they decide to change it?" I asked, confused.

Everyone in our class should be turning thirty-eight this year, and the reunions were always held every ten years from when we graduated. I'd received a little email online about it months ago to pick a location and pay in advance to book a spot. But I never went to the class reunions because I didn't have any friends there I wanted to reunite with, so I never replied to the emails. That was what I always replied with when anyone from school asked. But in actuality, I got really nervous when it came to meeting up with people who'd seen me grow up or made fun of me during the four awkward years of my life. I'd rather live without it.

"It's not *that* class reunion. Some of our classmates that live around here wanted to meet up and chat before then. It'll be really cool if you came," he said.

"I'll think about it," I replied.

Before Bennet left, I ended up giving him my phone number so he could text me the location and time of the reunion, in case I decided to go.

But I had mixed feelings about going to any reunion or meeting up with people who I really didn't know anymore. It was like meeting familiar strangers. We'd all grown up and done our own things, so it was just going to be awkward trying to reconnect what was already lost. At least that was what my philosophy was.

*Bad philosophy. I know.*

"Who was that guy?" Lia asked, her brow raised as I walked into the antique shop and saw the both of them standing at the front waiting instead of looking around.

"That was Bennet, my old high school classmate. He just came by to say 'hi' and invite me to a class reunion," I explained.

"Really? With the way he was looking at you, I thought you guys used to date or something," Lia teased, grinning and wiggling her brows at me with this look on her face that I couldn't really describe.

"We never dated. We were just friends in school. Nothing more than that," I said quickly.

"I was just kidding. What are you panicking for?" she continued to tease.

Rora giggled at my misery.

"I'm not," I denied. "I just didn't want you to misunderstand."

"Now you sound even more suspicious..." she trailed off, rubbing her chin.

"Okay. Fine. I used to have a crush on him back in high school. But nothing ever came of it."

"I knew it!" Lia burst out laughing before she finally changed the subject to save me from the embarrassment.

As we left the shop to venture through the other ones, the topic of food came up again.

"Next time you come to town, you have to try Raymundo's taco truck, Emi. The tacos, flautas, and tortas there are everything! My mouth is watering just from talking about it," Lia exclaimed, smacking her lips.

"We just ate, Lia," I said, trying to hold my laughter in.

"That's my fast werewolf metabolism talking," she said.

I laughed out loud, wishing I also had that fast metabolism.

"There's also a really good Indian restaurant on Kingston avenue," Rora said, pointing towards a building to our left. "Their chicken tikka masalas and tandoori chickens are great. And their samosas, too!"

"Are there any Thai restaurants here?" I asked, not willing to search on my phone. "I've always had a spot for Thai food in my belly. Especially for the Tom Yum soup and the Pad Thai and the mango sticky rice. I can go on forever."

Other than Thai food, Moroccan food was another favorite of mine. But it was just so hard to find a restaurant like that close to the home I used to live in. If I ever wanted the food, I'd have to drive for two hours, and I'd driven far for food before. I would still do it again if I had to.

"Yes, there is. And they even deliver straight to the pack house." Rora nodded.

"Really?! I didn't know that. If I did, I would have been calling in orders every day. Maybe I can treat Granny Ada to some Thai food this week instead of having her always cook for us. But then again, does she like Thai food?" I pondered to myself.

"Granny Ada isn't very picky. She's always in for trying new things. I think she will like it," Rora answered.

"What about you, Lia? Do you like Thai food?" I turned to Lia.

Lia shrugged her shoulders and said, "I don't know. I've never tried it before."

"Never? All these years and you haven't tried Thai food?! You don't know what you're missing out on!" I exclaimed. "I'll have to order some to the packhouse and have everyone try it!"

Since Lia was hundreds of years old, it was insane to me that she hadn't tried out every single cuisine on the planet. If I had lived that long, I would've tried everything. Everything. Especially all the food from Africa, because it was so good and there was so much to try.

What was the point of living that long and eating the same things over and over again?

"You need more flavor in your life, Lia," I said.

. . .

When we got home, I was already tired and my legs were killing me. They were shaking from all the exercise I had suddenly chosen to force on them. But I still had to take another shower to get rid of all the sweat and dirt clinging on my body, before I could get into bed and call it a night.

Granny Ada still had the babies so I needed to go get them. But when I was about to go find her, Eros came into the room. And just from his body language, I could tell something was up. His shoulders were stiff and his jaw was tight, like he was biting back from saying something that wasn't very nice. And if I was correct, then whatever he was upset with had to do with me talking to Bennet and giving Bennet my phone number.

Though I looked calm on the outside, just sitting there at the edge of the bed dangling my feet like there wasn't a care in the world, I was actually freaking out.

A part of me wanted to apologize, screamed at me to make Eros feel better, while the other part wondered why I had to apologize when I didn't really do anything wrong. So why was I feeling so guilty and at fault?

It wasn't like I still had feelings for Bennet or was thinking of ways to cheat or anything.

*I love Eros too much to even think of that, to ever think of doing something so terribly cruel.*

But I couldn't brush his feelings aside just like that. I needed to be considerate of how he felt and ask him if he was okay with it.

As Eros strolled out of the bathroom and sat down next to me on the bed, I said, "I was invited to a reunion with some of my classmates. Do you think I should go?"

I was trying to tentatively talk about the sensitive subject matter without giving a name.

"If you want to go, you are free to, Emira. Go relieve some stress and have fun," he said, wrapping an arm around my waist to lift me up on his lap.

"Can you go with me?" I asked, hoping that he would because that would beat going by myself.

"Not this time. We have training till late this whole week and next week," he said, pressing a kiss on my temple.

"Are you mad at me, Eros?" I murmured, kissing his jaw softly while inhaling his masculine scent.

Eros shook his head and said, "I'm not mad."

"You're not jealous, either?" I glanced up at him, trying to see if he was going to tactfully deny it or not.

"I am jealous. If I weren't, that would only mean that I didn't love you, that I didn't care. But I do care, Emira," he confessed, always choosing to be honest with me no matter what. And that was one of the things I loved most about him. "Although I don't like you talking to him, I don't want to be controlling and restrict you from doing what you want to do. I respect you, Emira. I trust you."

Hearing Eros' words, I didn't know what to say. I was so touched, so choked up with my own emotions that my mouth opened and closed a couple of times, but not a single word would come out.

"I just wished that I had seen you in your younger years and had made memories with you the way he had," he said softly, kissing my brow.

"You've made better memories with me, Eros. One hundred times better. One billion times better. Plus, you don't want to see me in my younger years. Really. You don't," I stated. "I was really ugly back then."

When I was in ninth grade, I had severe acne on my face, my back, and my chest. And in order to hide it, I cut thick bangs on myself and kept it that way for a majority of the school year. I also never wore anything that had straps or showed cleavage because I was scared that people would see the acne and judge me. Those years were truly the darkest years of my life. I was super depressed and lacked confidence because of how people perceived me and because of my family situation. It took me quite a while to get out of the shadows of my thoughts and my depression.

*Though some people say depression is not an illness and it's not real, it is. It can eat away at you and destroy you the same way a deadly virus can. Because the mind can be a very powerful and lethal weapon. It can either save you or it can kill you.*

"You were probably very cute," he said.

"I wasn't," I stated, not even joking. "I was really awkward and depressing to be around. And even if you were to know me when I was in school, you wouldn't have been able to date me, Eros. I'd be too young for you."

If Eros were to come into my life at that point, he would have made me into a hormonal and emotional wreck. I'd be too caught up in him and his good looks and his wonderful personality to even care about my studies or graduating high school. And, to be honest, Bennet Mathias Miller would have just been Bennet Who? in my dictionary when my eyes caught sight of Eros-hot-as-hell-Hall.

I was dead serious about that.

My inner teenage fangirl would have thrown Bennet out of the window and worshiped Eros on a pedestal inside of a shrine I'd hand built out of recycled wood and clay and painted pink to show the color of my love for him. Yes. I was that crazy as a teenager.

# CHAPTER 11

"I would have waited. You know I would," he replied, rubbing his nose along the column of my throat before leaving soft, wet kisses on the sensitive skin.

Just his hot breath fluttering against my neck was enough to make the sparks race across my skin and make my entire body tremble and give in to him, like it always did when we got intimate.

I had a hard time holding myself together after that.

My nipples hardened, my breathing became labored, and I was becoming a wet mess between the legs. Again. And Eros hadn't done anything more than kiss my neck with those sensual lips of his.

*I'm screwed,* I thought, finding myself helpless to his kisses.

"Yes, I do. I know you would have," I murmured breathily, catching his arm with one hand to steady myself while tipping my head slightly to the left to allow him more access to my neck.

But before he could do anything else, I found myself pulled back to reality when the thought of a wriggling sperm meeting a helpless egg popped into my mind. I felt like I'd been electrified, and I immediately grabbed a hold of Eros' wandering hand.

Could you imagine me getting pregnant again and giving birth in five or so months? I cringed every time the thought came to mind.

It was like a wrecking ball, destroying any thoughts of getting intimate with Eros. And I didn't know how to get past it. Because if Eros and I did the dirty, I'd probably have eighteen or twenty babies and life would be very painful. Very, very painful.

Though I didn't know how Eros felt about becoming celibate again, I was too scared to ask. I felt like I was torturing him, a very strong and virile male, by forcing him back into a life of celibacy.

But what was I to do? I didn't want to get pregnant again.

"Eros, we shouldn't. We really shouldn't," I squeaked out, getting more and more anxious as the seconds ticked by.

Eros chuckled and seemed to become amused by my sudden panic.

"It's not funny," I said, trying to be convincing when it became harder and harder to keep my thoughts together.

"Eros, do you think birth control would work on me?" I blurted suddenly.

Since I had a super womb, I wondered if taking the pill would have any effect. Although my mind was already saying "no," I was still hopeful that there was a way through all of this.

"I'm not too sure. But I don't want you to take birth control, Emira. There are too many side effects that I'd hate to see you struggle with."

"It'd be worth it," I murmured, kind of disappointed that the only option was now out of the question.

"There'll be a way, Emira. Don't worry about it. I'll figure it out." Eros patted my back. "But for now, we can still do a lot of things without penetration."

My eyes bulged.

"No penetration?" I echoed, unsure of what he meant. "Then how are you going to feel good? I want you to feel good, too."

"There's a way to make the both of us feel good," he chuckled, sounding as convincing as ever.

"Really?" I murmured.

"Mm-hm," he hummed.

Before I could say another word, my phone pinged and indicated that I had a new message. Since it was just within hand's reach from where I sat in Eros' lap, I leaned over and looked at the screen to see that Bennet had texted, '*If you decide to come to the reunion, we're meeting up at six on Saturday at the Longhorn Steakhouse in town.*'

Why Bennet? Why did you have to text me right now of all times? And why couldn't I have just ignored the text?

I wanted to facepalm.

"I'm sorry," I said, trying to be considerate of Eros' feelings without being too obvious.

Eros picked up the phone and tossed it directly onto the nightstand, without looking away from me. The phone made a thumping noise when it hit the wood but stayed relatively still where it had been thrown, showing how precise Eros was with everything he did.

If it were me who had done that, my phone would have bounced off the wood and hit me in the face or the screen would have shattered when it hit everything not the nightstand, because I knew I would have missed by a mile.

"I trust you," he repeated again.

After that, Eros was back to kissing my neck and jaw and lavishing my body with irresistible sparks and tingles. His hot hand slid from my knee up to my thighs and gradually pushed the fabric of my dress higher as it went under the skirt.

While one of his hands found purchase on my clothed left breast, the other hand was busy tracing the outline of my underwear with the pads of his fingers, teasingly fluttering over the wet spot every now and then.

I swallowed down my saliva and didn't have to look at a mirror to know that my cheeks were flushed and my eyes were hazy with pleasure. I couldn't think straight because every expanse of skin he'd kissed hummed with satisfaction and became heated with desire. It was like he was the fire that consumed me and I was the moth that couldn't deny the flames. I wanted him to burn me and I didn't care if I died doing it.

Eros pulled off my shirt and tossed it away before undoing my bra and throwing it off somewhere too.

As the cold air in the room glided against my skin, I shivered and tensed my body, feeling Eros' heated body close in on me.

After removing my shirt and bra, he cupped my breast again, weighing it in his hand and squeezing the rounded globe that had grown in size since the last time he'd fondled it. This time, the feeling of skin on skin made the sensations much more intense than it had been before.

Eros kneaded my breast roughly, grinding his palm against my sensitive nipple until I whimpered and trembled like a leave flailing in the wind.

As his left hand worked my breast, his other hand continued to tease the skin by my inner thigh. He ran his fingertips across the soft skin barely two inches from my core but wouldn't move any closer to where I really needed his touch.

"Eros, please," I whined, arching my hips into his hand, trying to get him to do something, anything.

Eros picked me up off his lap and deposited me on the bed, before he tossed off his shirt and kicked off his pants.

My eyes hungrily devoured the sight of his broad shoulders, hard abs, and thick cock, watching as the swollen shaft twitched under my intense scrutiny, as if it were greeting me in its own way.

*It's just too bad we can't put it to good use today,* I thought regretfully, not even realizing how bad I found myself aching for his swollen cock. I missed the sensation of him filling me to the brim, of my body straining to consume his engorged member.

Eros smirked at my hungry expression before he trapped me underneath his body and bent his head to kiss the expanse of my face.

He pressed a soft, delicate kiss on my eyes, my nose, both of my cheeks, and my chin, avoiding my lips for the first time and making me pout.

When he moved to pull back without kissing my lips, I reached out and cupped his face in my hands, pulling him down so that we were eye to eye, brown to blue.

"I want a kiss," I said, licking my dry lips in anticipation.

"Then take it," he replied, smirking at me again.

After his words, I leaned my head up and took what I wanted.

As our mouths firmly sealed together, I felt extreme relief, felt as if all of my tension was fading away with just one kiss. My tongue left my mouth to probe Eros' lips, gliding across the seams before dipping into his mouth to explore the inner orifice.

After a moment of me initiating the kiss, Eros finally responded. His mouth slanted against mine as he put a pillow under my head to give me the extra leverage I needed, keeping me from straining myself just to kiss him.

His hot tongue slid against my teeth and the roof of my mouth, sending a pleasurable sensation through my body as he deepened the kiss and devoured every inch of my lips like a starving man.

The slick and slippery fight between our tongues felt extremely good, but after a while my mouth started to get tired and the tip of my tongue became sore as he sucked on it for too long.

When Eros broke away to let me breathe, he licked our combined saliva off the corner of my mouth before kissing a trail down my chin and neck.

As he got to my collarbone, he bit the skin around it and lathed it with his tongue, leaving behind red imprints of his teeth. And it didn't take long after that for his hot mouth to circle my breasts and suck on the skin around my nipple.

The sensation of wet, moist heat made goosebumps form all over my body.

I suddenly felt like a budding flower that had finally been watered. It felt so good that I didn't want him to stop, that I wanted more and more.

Eros rolled my nipple around with his fingers on one side, tweaking the pebbled tip until it ached and hurt and felt so good all at the same time, while his tongue licked across the other nipple once, sending a string of undeniable pleasure straight down my core.

Just him playing with my breasts was making my lower abdomen clench and build up with pressure.

I was so wet already, so ready for him.

"Do you like that?" he asked, his fingers plucking my erect nipple as if it were some kind of instrument. As his breath fluttered against my left nipple and chilled the wet tip, I bit out a moan and arched my back.

"Yes," I breathed, unable to catch my breath as my thoughts became too foggy to comprehend.

Eros slowly pulled my skirt down and kicked it off the bed before his fingers hooked on the elastic band of my underwear to drag it off. As the cotton fabric separated from my body, I could see a string of my juices stretch out before snapping.

For some reason, Eros groaned at the sight, as if it had turned him on even more, and opened my thighs to look at the wetness gleaming in the light as it trickled down to create a moist spot on our white comforter.

Eros always liked looking down there before, during, and after we had sex. It brought him immense pleasure to see how we became one, how my opening swallowed his cock every time he entered, and how he filled my body with semen until it came dripping out of my entrance. The sight always turned him on more than anything.

At first I'd been extremely embarrassed and didn't want him to look, but now, I got used to it and didn't mind anymore. As for my human modesty, it had left me for a long time now.

"Oh," I gasped as Eros sucked my puckered nipple into his mouth and chewed lightly on the tip, dragging me back from the realm of my thoughts.

That talented mouth of his switched from one side to the other and lavished both breasts with adequate attention, forcing wave after wave of pleasure through every nerve length in my body.

I melted on the spot when Eros' other hand found its way back between my legs and trailed over my bare mound to soothingly rub circles around my lower lips, setting my entire body on fire. Each time he made one full circle, he would press down roughly on my clit and squeeze in time with his wet mouth sucking hard on the tip of my breasts.

By the time five circles had been made, which was less than a minute, I found myself pushed over the edge of an intense orgasm.

I choked out a whimpering moan and came hard enough that my vision went white for nearly three seconds. My entire body shuddered and my inner walls fluttered, tightening around what should have been in my body, plundering my depths.

"So soon?" he asked, raising his head to look at me with glowing blue eyes filled with hunger and desire.

I panted for breath and felt my cheeks burn even hotter.

His fingers hadn't even made it inside of my body and I'd already came.

"I haven't even gotten to the main course yet," he said, smirking sensually, pinning me down with a hot and mesmerizing gaze.

I shuddered.

"Main course?" I cleared my throat.

"Mm-hm," he hummed in reply, letting me calm enough before dipping his middle finger in between my folds to coat the length in my nectar. Then, he caressed my clit in an up and down motion and curled his finger until it barely dipped into my entrance. After that light stroke, he removed his finger to start again from the top.

Electric energy traveled up and down my spine. And the maddening friction was almost unbearable as it left my legs feeling numb and my opening burning with delicious heat.

Eros planted a chaste kiss on my breast and then kissed his way down my belly until his head was in between my open legs. He kissed my mound once before opening his mouth to suck on my clit.

"Oh... Harder, please," I moaned, clutching on to the pillow with both hands.

Eros' mouth took place of his fingers. He held my hips down and drank from between my legs, his tongue lapping at my opening over and over again. As he swallowed my juices and probed my entrance, mimicking the actions of love making with his tongue, I was pushed back up the hill and towards ecstasy.

"I bet you're as tight as when we first made love," Eros murmured over my mound, his fingers slowly rubbing my slick opening in a circular motion. "Do you want my cock, Emira?"

I moaned thickly.

I loved it when he dirty talked because his voice was so deep and raspy, so full of lust and desire, that it always left me even wetter and hungrier for him.

"Yes. Yes! I want it so badly," I moaned, arching my back to get closer to him and forgetting that I really shouldn't be wanting his cock right now. I didn't even know what I was saying anymore.

Eros grinned.

He kissed my inner thigh twice and then suddenly pushed two fingers in as deep and as fast as he could.

I gasped and tensed, and my entire body bowed in response.

"You're even tighter," he panted as his fingers entered all the way inside of me, until only his knuckles were left.

Eros pumped his fingers into me at a fast pace as his mouth reattached itself to my clit. He sucked and bit the sensitive nerve bundle before comforting it with his hot tongue, forcing me to squirm desperately as I felt the pleasure build behind my eyelids. My spine stiffened in response to the stimulation.

"Eros…ah…" I moaned, my mouth wide open as I gasped for air, feeling like I was going to touch the sky soon.

As his hands and his mouth worked my heated flesh, it didn't take very long for me to reach my second orgasm. A rapturous cry purged itself from my throat as I tensed and then shuddered, losing sense of my surroundings.

Eros pulled away from my clit but left his fingers inside of me, slowly easing them in and out to prolong the pleasurable feelings. By the time I came down from my high, I could barely move my legs.

"What does it taste like?" I breathed, looking at my glistening cream on his lips and chin.

Eros didn't answer immediately. Instead, he leaned over and kissed me, spreading my own juices into my mouth.

Though I'd found this gross in the past, I didn't think that way anymore. Because if Eros was willing to swallow it and didn't find it gross, why should I be afraid to taste it?

As I licked his tongue and lips and chin, I couldn't taste anything. And I didn't really get why Eros liked it so much.

"It's sweet and fragrant, mixed in with your unique scent," he replied, licking his lips while looking at me.

My brows wrinkled but I didn't question it, instead I let my gaze trail from his face down to his weeping cock, dripping creamy liquid down from the tip.

*What are we going to do about that?*

"Now it's your turn, Emira," he said, wiping his wet fingers on his thick member and trying to coat his penis in my cream.

As he rose to his knees, a hundred thoughts raced through my head on what it was he wanted me to do. But regardless of my lack of knowledge on this subject, I'd be willing to do anything for him.

"What do you want me to do?" I asked, watching as he leaned forward and grabbed a hold of my arms.

Eros pulled me up into a sitting position and turned us over until I was sitting on top of his waist with my knees on both sides of him.

I gave him a confused look and pulled my hair back over my shoulder.

*Did he want me to ride him?*

"I'll show you." Eros lifted me up a bit to readjust his shaft until it was pressed against his navel. Then, he set me down on it, making sure that my opening was on top of his thick cock.

The heat coming off of it made my lady bits quiver. And almost immediately, my juices seeped from my body and coated Eros' lower belly and layered itself on his hard and thick cock like never before. I trembled uncontrollably as Eros grabbed my ass and moved me forward and back until I got the idea of what he wanted me to do.

As he panted and groaned huskily beneath me, I realized that this was the true position of power. This was what I needed in my life.

"There you go. Just like that," he panted, lying back to let me work myself on top of him.

In fear of falling, I planted my hands on Eros' toned abdomen to steady myself as I ground against him, rubbing my swollen folds along the venous phallus and using my juices to lubricate our skin. Every time my opening slid across his cock, I could hear the wet and sticky sounds loud and clear, echoing in my head and making me even more aroused.

Albeit this didn't scratch the itch in the right place, it still kind of scratched it.

After a few minutes of steadily gyrating myself on top of Eros, the sparks and the friction made my belly tighten as another orgasm built, sucking the breath and energy out of me. I tried to hold it back by lifting myself up and changing the angle so that his cock would stop rubbing against my clit, but I still became a quivering mess as another wave of sparks forced me to come again and again.

Yet Eros hadn't come. He was still as hard as steel against my wet folds. And I had a feeling that I was torturing Eros more than helping him because of my sensitive body and low stamina.

"I'm sorry, Eros," I panted, cheeks flushed red as I became a boneless mass that couldn't sit straight no matter how badly I wanted to get back to business.

"Let's try a different position then," he said, lifting me off him to reposition me onto my hands and knees.

With one hand gripping his long length and stroking, he pushed my legs together before inserting his shaft in the space between my thighs.

"Squeeze your legs together for me," he said, pumping his hips to drag his cock in and out.

The mushroom tip ground against my opening several times before sliding up and across my clit. The frictional sensation returned and was just enough to push me closer to the edge.

Unable to hold myself up, I set my head on the pillow and reached a hand down between us to squeeze and stroke the tip of his length every time he entered.

The time seemed to crawl as the sound of Eros skin slapping on mine rang in my ears.

After another thirty minutes, Eros finally came, panting heavily and grunting his release as his body tensed for a split second. His hips slammed roughly against my butt as his shaft ejaculated in between my thighs, all over my stomach, and under my breasts.

If I'd looked down, my face would have been covered in it too. I breathed a sigh of relief and pushed the front half of my body up. As I made a move to roll around, Eros' member hardened again and was back to rubbing against me until he came time and time again.

By the time we were done, I had semen running from the crack of my butt down in between my folds and from my bare back down to my stomach and breasts.

# CHAPTER 12

"I'm really sorry for wasting your time, again." I apologized sincerely to the four Gammas inside the car as I got out and stepped on the cement. "I'll try not to take too long. I know you guys probably have better things to do."

"Oh no! Not at all! We actually volunteered to take you," Gamma Qian laughed.

"You did?" I asked, surprised.

Why in the world would anyone volunteer to wait on me?

"Yes!" Gamma Chandni and Gamma Sebastian agreed at the same time.

"Training has been kicking our asses lately. Taking you today is giving us a little time to rest and slack off," Gamma Sergio explained.

"Oh! Well then, I'm glad you guys can come along." I smiled at them before closing the car door and strutting over to the restaurant's double doors.

Just as I was about to touch the doorknob, I pulled back and turned straight around to go to the car. When Gamma Chandni noticed that I was coming back towards them, she rolled the window down and asked, "Did you forget something, Alpha Female?"

"No. I wanted to invite you guys to come in with me. Come on in and get something to eat while you wait for me." I opened the car door and peered at them from the outside, gesturing for them to come with me.

"We can protect you from here, Alpha Female. If anything goes wrong—" Gamma Chandni said.

"No, no. Come in. I've got Eros' card, and he'll be treating you to really good food tonight. And don't tell me you've already eaten like the last time because I know you haven't, Gamma Sergio," I said, grinning at Gamma Sergio like a mischievous cat. "And I'll feel safer if you guys are in eye sight."

"Alright. If Alpha Eros is offering to treat us all, then we can't really refuse now, can we?" Gamma Sergio said, opening his car door and hopping out with the rest of the Gammas.

The five of us walked into the restaurant before we were greeted by a waitress by the door.

"We'll be over at that table, Alpha Female," Gamma Sebastian said, pointing at the table their waitress was leading them to.

I nodded my head and looked around the restaurant before spotting Bennet, who was waving at me, and my old classmates sitting together at a really long table. From all the heads sticking up around Bennet, there had to be at least twenty people who had shown up for this little "reunion."

As I came closer, I noticed that the only seat open was next to Bennet, which was fine by me because I didn't really want to sit next to someone who I didn't recognize or get along with. That would be hell for the next hour or however long this dinner was going to be.

"Hi," I greeted, turning my gaze to Bennet, who was smiling widely at me with twinkling hazel eyes and straight white teeth. His hair had been combed back and his stubble had been shaved clean, giving him a rather fresh and young look compared to what I had seen of him the other day. As for his clothes, he had chosen to wear a black short sleeved polo and a pair of grey slacks, looking rather classy but casual at the same time.

"I'm really glad you could make it, Emi," he said, pulling my chair out for me to sit down.

"Me too," I said, a little freaked out by his gentlemanly gesture and what it could actually mean. Hopefully, I was wrong.

"Look who made it *late* to the party," said a rather snarky voice I'd recognize from a mile away.

Katelyn Wilson.

Also known as Katelyn-the-rich-and-bitchy-Wilson by almost all of my high school classmates. That nickname was given to her by Josh Wallaby, a popular football player who she'd dated and dumped in the span of three months, after she transferred to my high school in the tenth grade.

Her father owned a bunch of companies and only moved to the little town I lived in to inherit some more money from his dying father. And if I remembered correctly, Katelyn had also dated Bennet for a couple of months before he got with Lucy Bardot. She'd dated him for almost six months and used him like he was her chauffeur and nanny, before she dumped him for an exchange student from Germany.

I felt very bad for any man whose path crossed with Katelyn because that in itself was a place in between hell and quicksand.

*Either way, you will never get out.*

But, judging by the big rock on her ring finger, the woman was married to some poor man willing to deal with her bad attitude and never-ending demands. Whoever he was, I prayed for his poor soul.

"Good to see you too, Katelyn," I said sarcastically, tempted to roll my eyes at her for calling me out, yet again. This was such a common occurrence back in school. If she wasn't bullying someone, she was never happy. *Never.*

"I don't know if I can say the same," she replied, picking up her wine cup to take a little sip.

If I had known that Katelyn was coming, I wouldn't have bothered showing up.

"Drop it, Katelyn. We're all here to have a good time, not start a fight." Gianna, one of the honor roll students from my class, stated.

"A good time? We would have been having a good time if you'd chosen that nice French restaurant instead of this dump," Katelyn argued, setting her cup down.

"Everyone here is having a good time, except for you, Katelyn. And like I told you, not everyone can afford that restaurant you recommended."

Gianna looked like she was going to punch Katelyn in the face but didn't because this reunion was about making good memories and not bad ones.

"Whatever," Katelyn spat, turning herself away from Gianna.

"I'll go tell the kitchen to bring you your plate, Emira," Gianna said to me, before she got up out of her seat to go find help.

"Thank you," I said, trying to keep my eyes off Katelyn, who was frowning so much that her wrinkles were starting to show through her makeup.

Everyone at the table made small talk to get rid of the awkward atmosphere Katelyn brought, but I knew that she could never be easily brushed off like that.

As I looked around the table, I only recognized four other people, along with Katelyn and Bennet.

"What's your secret, Emira?" Abeline, one of the girls who used to be in band with me, asked.

"My secret? What do you mean?" I raised a brow in confusion.

"You don't look like you've aged a day. I just want to know what you use or what doctor you visit, because I really need it!" Abeline exclaimed. "My wrinkles are getting worser by the day!"

"They're not even that noticeable," I said, shaking my head.

"That's because I get fillers and Botox every six months. If not, I'd look like a grandma because of my four ornery children. And my hair may look fine now, but I have to get it colored every two months to keep all the white from showing!"

I glanced at her black hair before looking away.

"I feel your pain, but I don't really have a regimen. I just use whatever is available at the supermarkets."

How could I tell her that I was just born this way? I didn't have a need for Botox or fillers because my face was never-changing. She'd probably think that I was being conceited if I told her that.

"Me too," Bennet chimed in.

"You look good for your age too, Bennet," Abeline complimented politely.

"Thanks, Ab," he said.

As the three of us talked, I couldn't help but notice how Katelyn kept looking at my hands and smirking like she knew some secret about me just by staring at my fingers.

"Still not married, Emira? Or are you divorced like Bennet?" Katelyn asked, bringing the whole conversation back to me.

Everyone at the table turned their eyes to me and I was put back on the spot, like always.

"You're not still single, are you? God. We're like thirty-eight. Two more years and you'd be like the forty-year-old virgin," she joked, laughing hysterically like it was something super funny.

While I didn't think her little joke was funny at all, the two women sitting next to her, Kiesha and Janelle, were also laughing at me, along with some of the other people sitting at the table trying to cover it up by putting a forkful of steak in their mouths or drinking beer from their cups.

My blood boiled.

From the corner of my eye, I saw the Gammas looking like they were ready to come over and take Katelyn away, but I shook my head at them and mouthed, "I'll handle this myself. Don't worry."

Just the thought of them having my back was an amazing feeling.

"Stop. Just stop, Katelyn," Bennet stated, frowning deeply.

"It's fine, Bennet," I said, before turning to Katelyn, "I'm married, Katelyn."

"Really? I didn't see a ring so… did you forget to wear your ring or are you guys saving up for one?" Katelyn smirked.

*This bitch*, I thought, feeling like she needed a wakeup slap dealt by me on both sides of her face.

Apparently, Katelyn had the knack for making my blood pressure skyrocket.

But now that she'd pointed it out, I realized that I didn't have a wedding ring or band compared to all of the females at the table. I was the only one sporting bare fingers and wrists because I just didn't care for embellishing myself with bracelets or other accessories.

"Katelyn, can you just shut up for a second?" Bennet exclaimed, ready to get out of his seat.

"Who are you trying to play knight in shining armor for? She's married, Bennet. Oh, I forgot, didn't you crush on her in high school? When she was so gross and full of acne?" she taunted.

"Bennet didn't have a crush on me. Stop making things up," I said, clenching my jaw as anger filled me.

"He used to have a little crush on you when we were dating. Why'd you think I dumped him?" she retorted, crossing her legs and looking at me with this I-am-mightier-than-you look.

My mouth fell open and my eyes became as wide as the plates on the table.

I turned my head to look at Bennet, who acted like he didn't hear what Katelyn had said, but by how red his ears were getting, I knew her words were true.

*Well, damn.*

I finally knew where Katelyn's unwarranted anger and bullying came from now. Who would have known that Bennet was the cause of this bad blood between me and her? I surely didn't.

As far as I could remember, Katelyn had never liked me. I was poor, not very fashionable, and my family background was a mess. I was not someone she'd wanted to associate herself with, and she let me know that every chance she got. At first, I'd tried to get on her good side so that she would stop bullying me, but that didn't work. So I just learned to ignore her and stay out of her way.

But the more I ignored her and didn't fight back, the worse she got, especially after she started dating Bennet and bossing him around like she owned him. When Bennet wasn't around, she'd make snarky comments about my hair being too greasy, how gross my acne was, and how I looked like a walking skeleton.

It was too bad that I was too much of a scaredy cat to tell Bennet about it. But then again, I didn't think there was anything Bennet could do to help. She was just too mean and rude and bigheaded.

"Katelyn, stop or you're going to have to take yourself outside," Gianna threatened, coming back with the waiter and my plate of steaming hot food.

I took a deep breath and stayed put, trying to stop myself from doing something I would not regret to Katelyn's face.

"Don't listen to her, she's crazy," he said, embarrassment coloring his face.

"She's only taking it out on you because she's going through another divorce," Abeline whispered.

"Another one?" I repeated, trying to eat my food as quickly as I could so that I could get the heck out of here before I really contributed to ruining this reunion.

"I think this is her sixth one,' Abeline continued.

*Sixth?*

I cringed at the thought of getting married only to become divorced six times. I wouldn't have even bothered with getting married after the second or third time.

If an average person were to get divorced that many times, they would be financially unstable just from paying for court fees, attorneys' fees, and so much more.

Unless they married rich each time and walked away with half the fortune. But, unfortunately, that rarely happened.

"Have you seen your mom recently?" Abeline asked, trying to change the subject.

"No. I haven't talked to her in more than twenty-five years," I replied.

We only lived thirty minutes away from each other but my birth mother had never made the effort to visit me from when I had been adopted till now. And I wasn't about to visit the woman who considered me a bother to her and her boyfriend.

"I saw her when I went to visit my parents. She's still with that guy from the motorcycle club. The one that has a history of criminal records and jail time."

"Is she?" I asked on a whim, not really interested in my birth mother's new love ventures.

I had enough of caring for her. She'd taken herself out of my life so there was no reason for me to get involved in hers.

"She is. I think she's getting married to him in June. Are you going?"

"No. It's not like I'm invited or anything. I just heard the news from you. Otherwise, I would have never known." I took a sip of my water and set my fork down.

"So, what does your husband do?" Bennet asked, still looking crushed after I'd said that I was married.

"He works in construction," I said slowly, kind of hesitant about putting Eros' information out there.

Saying that Eros worked in construction wasn't really a lie because Eros did own several construction businesses in the region. But I didn't want to tell Abeline and Bennet that because I felt as if I would be bragging and rubbing it in their faces.

"Is your husband coming tonight?" Janelle asked from across the table, as if she were interested.

"No, he's not. He's still working," I answered, although I didn't really want to talk to the person who'd laughed at me a couple of minutes ago.

"On a Saturday night?" Katelyn interjected, rolling her eyes incredulously at me, like I was lying to everyone at the table. "Come up with a better excuse than that."

My mouth opened and closed with a click.

"Just tell everyone here the truth. You never got married. You have no ring and no man. It's as easy as that," Katelyn scoffed, acting exasperated for no reason whatsoever. "Stop lying."

I really didn't get Katelyn's thought process. Why was she so bent on making me look and feel bad when I'd never done anything to her? It wasn't like Bennet and me were together for her to keep harassing me like this.

"And how do you know all this?" I asked, shrugging my shoulders to get rid of the building tension.

Regardless of saying our nuptials in a church or not, to me, being mated was the same as being married. I was a taken woman and I didn't need a ring or a certificate to prove it. Truthfully, Eros' feelings for me could never be measured by a measly ring worn on the finger.

"I just guessed. But by your reaction, it's true, isn't it?" Katelyn seemed so sure of herself, so smug that it made me want to slap that haughty look off her face.

"No. It's not. Just because I don't have a ring doesn't mean that I don't have a man, Katelyn. Because—look at you, you have a ring and where are all of your husbands?" I said, taking a jab at her divorced status.

Everyone at the table laughed, and this made Katelyn narrow her thickly-lined eyes at me, as mad as a bull at the rodeo.

"At least I've been married, unlike some loser who will never know the taste of a man," she spat.

Oh, that was it, that was the last straw. I was up to my neck in it with Katelyn.

"You know what, Katelyn. You haven't changed one bit. Once a bitch always a bitch," I said, wiping my mouth off with my napkin before pushing my chair out to stand.

Although I'd eaten half of my plate of pan seared steak, roasted potatoes, and broccoli salad, I couldn't taste anything other than anger, and I couldn't control it any longer.

"What did you call me?" she screeched, scrambling to her feet as her neck went red from her fury.

"A bitch. I called you a bitch, Katelyn. You're immature and full of yourself and you're probably never going to change. I pity the fools who marries your ass," I said.

After all these years, I'd finally said the things I'd wanted to say to Katelyn's face, and it was a very mighty and uplifting feeling, like I'd just relieved twenty years of stress and tension.

Katelyn opened her mouth to retort but I was one step faster. I said, "Just shut up. Don't talk to me. I'm tired of playing nice with you while ignoring your rude comments about my personal life. As far as I'm concerned, you can just go and fu—"

I choked on the rest of that word when my eyes caught sight of Eros entering the restaurant, looking like a whole meal in his black dress pants and white dress shirt with the sleeves rolled up to uncover his strong forearms. His hair was still wet, probably because he'd taken a quick shower before coming here to get me, and his eyes were smoldering hot, glistening like pools of icy blue, as they ran up and down my body.

*Hot damn.*

Eros was looking finer than aged wine sitting in a bucket of ice waiting to be tasted by me. Thoroughly.

*I swear, just one look at him and all that pent-up anger is gone. How does that even happen?*

"I thought you were still training," I said, my eyes trained solely on Eros and his masculine visage.

"I got done a little earlier and decided to come pick you up," he answered. "Are you ready to go?"

"I'm more than ready to," I sighed.

"Aren't you going to introduce us?" Katelyn asked, fixing the ring on her finger.

"No. I'm not introducing my husband to you of all people," I replied, not even bothering to look at Katelyn as I talked.

After I bid my goodbyes to Bennet and Abeline and Gianna, I took my purse and didn't turn back. I was very relieved to get myself out of that awful situation. There was no way I was going to go back. No way in hell.

As we left, I heard Kiesha's husband say, "He's no construction worker. He's the owner of Hall & Co. Corp..."

Then, Katelyn was screeching like a banshee as she got in another fight with Gianna. Over what? I didn't care.

"Eros, if I ever say I want to go to another reunion, remind me not to," I stated as we met up with the Gammas and paid for their meals.

Eros chuckled and said, "I'll make sure to remember that."

"Ugh. I can't believe I even came. It was totally not worth it," I grumbled, attaching myself to Eros' arm for warmth as we left the restaurant.

As we got into Eros' car, I pulled my phone out of my purse to look at the new text messages I'd just received. When I saw it was from Bennet and Abeline, I didn't bother to open them, knowing that it was probably some kind of apology on Katelyn's behalf.

I put my phone back in my purse and leaned my head against Eros' shoulder.

*Note to self, changing stinky diapers and spending more time with the babies were worth way more than this stupid reunion.*

# CHAPTER 13

These last few weeks had been dragging by now that Eros was always training with the warriors of the pack and preparing for the extensive battle to come. He would always leave bed before the sun even came up and he would come back home by the time the babies and I were already asleep.

I barely saw him anymore.

Though I really missed conversing with him and seeing him, I knew that what he was doing was crucial and necessary, that I shouldn't be distracting him with my whining about his absence. His pack needed him and so did his kind.

As for me and the babies, we could wait. Since we were useless in this fight and couldn't really help with anything, we had to remain safe and healthy in a way to keep from being a burden to Eros and the rest of the pack.

At least I had the babies to keep me busy. Otherwise, I didn't know what I would do with myself.

"Kyra, let go of your brother," I scolded, reaching out to scoop Kyra off the ground before she could claw off Ace's leg. At her sudden removal from Ace's body, she made a growling noise in the back of her throat and was baring her nonexistent canines at me. But when her bright blue eyes met my stern brown ones, she finally settled down and whimpered as if to say that she didn't do anything, like she always did when I caught her chewing on one of her siblings.

I grabbed a little towel off the nightstand and was quick to walk back over to the pile of babies crawling all over each other, and it had only been two months since they'd been born.

Most of them had started sitting up when they were only a month and a week old. At two months, they looked like they were preparing to walk now that they were already able to crawl and climb on things.

Although they hadn't quite said anything more than gibberish and growling, I had a feeling they would start speaking full sentences in very little time. And that was crazy to me, because I was hoping that I'd see the babies in baby form for a long while. Yet at this rate, I didn't think that was going to happen. Maybe Sentinels' grew differently than the regular werewolf, like Rora, who still looked like a teenager when she was actually over one hundred years old.

How else could I explain their extremely quick growth patterns?

I sighed, dabbing at the drool coming from Erik's mouth and checking the color of his eyes. Even though Eros said that their eyes might change color in the future, nothing had really happened to any of them other than Wren, who had golden little specks sprinkled in the center of her blue eyes. Her eyes were very pretty, but it wasn't anything close to mine.

After a moment of sitting there and wallowing in my thoughts, I wrinkled my nose and turned to the pile of hands and feet and said, "Okay. Which one of you pooped? I know one of you did it."

Of course, none of them answered me with anything other than gummy smiles or drooling gibberish, so I had to pick them up one by one and smell them.

So… it wasn't Kyra… or Darius… or Wren…

After lifting Noah and Nicholas, I finally found the culprit. It was Nicholas.

I set him aside and waited for him to be done with his business before I cleaned him up. And by the time I'd finished tossing the diaper into the pail, at least a handful of them had also pooped and were grinning at me with twinkling blue eyes and toothless gums, except for Cillian, whose teeth were already starting to come in.

One by one, I wiped and washed their butts before sitting down next to the lot, thinking that life had become a lot harder now with nine always-hungry-and-always-pooping babies.

*'M… Ma…Ma.'*

What was that?

I had to do a double take when I heard those words in my head. One of the babies had spoken to me in English and now I had to hunt them down and see which one it was.

*Great.*

"Did you just talk, Darius? Or was it you, Silas?" I asked, leaning over them and inspecting each and every one of their faces, but had no luck whatsoever.

"Mama. Mama," I said, hoping that one of them would repeat it. Yet after five minutes of absolute silence, I gave up and decided to figure it out next time. Because if he or she spoke once, they would do it again.

As I got up to put the towel away, Granny Ada knocked on the door and said, "I've come to see the babies, Emi."

"Come on in," I called, tossing the cloth onto the nightstand before grabbing Ace to see if the scratches on his legs were very bad. Though there were some red welts here and there, I didn't see any blood or any open cuts. If I hadn't trimmed off Kyra's nails the other day, this would be a totally different scene.

"How are my little pups doing today?" Granny Ada cooed, coming to sit on the mats inside the little playpen.

At the sight of her wide smile, the relief melted off my body in waves. I could finally go to the bathroom and finish up some business!

"Can you watch them for a bit, granny? I'm going to take a shower and freshen up," I said, trying to get some time in to take care of myself before I was left with the kids for another eight hours or so.

Now that all the babies could crawl, it was a lot tougher to keep track of all of them. I only had two eyes and watching all nine of them at the same time was torturous and impossible. If I managed to keep two from fighting each other, another one would be trying to climb the bed or crawling into the bathroom. It was just one thing after another.

At this point, I kind of hated how fast they'd grown and wished they'd go back to lying in one spot again.

"Sure thing, Emi," she replied.

With her approval, I quickly grabbed some clothes and made my way into the bathroom.

Even though I really wanted to have a nice and long soak inside of the bathtub, I couldn't do that while Granny Ada was out there handling the adventurous babies. So I quickly used the toilet and took a shower before getting out to towel dry my hair. I usually blow-dried my hair, but the babies didn't like the noise it made and would startle and break out into hysterical, screaming sobs.

*Towel-drying is better for my hair anyways. Less damage and split ends,* I thought, trying to persuade myself into giving up another thing for the good of my children.

When I got back out, Granny Ada was wrestling with Kyra, who was trying to slap Ace's face with her foot.

*What is with these two babies?!*

"Kyra is always fighting with Ace," I sighed regretfully, picking Ace off the floor before he started screaming.

From all this work picking up and putting down the babies, my back had been in extreme pain, along with my arms. And I couldn't help but notice that they'd all been gaining weight pretty rapidly.

"Is it normal for them to grow this quick?" I asked Granny Ada.

She nodded her head and said, "It's very normal. The Sentinels are built to progress in weight and height and develop faster than the regular werewolves. So we need to enjoy them while they're in their baby stage as long as we can, before they grow taller and look like little adults."

As if reminding herself, Granny Ada whipped out her smartphone to snap pictures of each baby.

Ever since the babies had been born, Granny Ada had given herself the task of documenting every day of their life.

If she wasn't taking pictures, then she was taking thirty-minute videos of them.

I'd also taken some pictures of them myself, but I gave up after a while since Granny Ada was always sharing her pictures with me. It was kind of pointless when we had the same photos.

"Eros' birthday is coming in a couple of days…" I paused, "and I was thinking of throwing him a surprise birthday party with all the pack members to take some edge off their training. What do you think?"

"I think that's a wonderful idea, Emi! Eros hasn't celebrated his birthday in over six hundred years!" she exclaimed.

My eyes almost bulged from their sockets.

*Six hundred years of no birthdays?*

Well, if I really thought about it, I could kind of understand why he would get tired of celebrating his birthday.

For someone over nine hundred, celebrating a birthday only told you how much older you were getting and it could get a little repetitive and tedious.

But this year, I wanted to do a little something for him. Something special.

Because Eros was always doing something for me, so I wanted to put a little effort in and make him feel happy.

Since he had a ton of money and everything he'd ever need, I decided to make the gift instead of buying it. And the gift had been coming along very well, other than some mishaps due to being too rusty on my part.

I just hoped that Eros liked it. But if he didn't, I had a second, backup gift prepared, just in case. I had a feeling that he'd like the second gift way more than the first.

"Do you think it will be a problem?" I asked, worried that I would disrupt their training plans too much.

"I don't see a problem. In fact, I think it'd be good for them to get a little rest."

I smiled. If Granny Ada thought that, then I should probably be safe.

*Now, I just have to think of a way to keep Eros from knowing about it.*

Too bad that was a lot easier said than done.

. . .

This was the first time that I was keeping a secret from Eros, and I was succeeding.

I had to always have the mental barrier up so that he couldn't read my thoughts or go through my memories. Since we hadn't been conversing or seeing each other much due to his training schedule, this hadn't been as hard as I thought it would be.

He hadn't asked me anything about keeping the barrier over my thoughts, but I knew it was probably killing him right now. I just hoped he thought that I was mad at him for having no time for me and the babies or something. That would make keeping this secret a lot easier.

Just the thought of successfully surprising Eros was making me feel super giddy. It was unbelievable.

"Emira, are you sure you know how to bake?" Lia teased, slowly washing her hands by the sink while giving me this questionable look.

"Yes! I'd baked a lot with my grandmother when she was still alive," I said, repeatedly stirring the cream cheese mixture in my bowl with a metal whisk.

Since the last time I'd found myself feeling worthless and not being any help to the pack, I thought that I should at least help cook some of the food with the pack members this time.

While Rora, Lia, and I were here cooking, Granny Ada was watching the babies.

I wanted to give her a little break from cooking since she was always in the kitchen doing something for Eros and me.

*But isn't it crazy that it takes three people to fill in for Granny Ada in the kitchen?*

If you asked me, I didn't really think three people were enough. We needed at least seven more helpers. At the moment, there were us three and three other ladies, most of whom were much older and looked to be in their fifties.

"If you say so." Lia shrugged her shoulders and grabbed the bag of lettuce to start on her salad. "I just don't want a stomach ache."

"You're not going to get one, Lia. I've been watching Emi cook. She's done a clean and fantastic job," Helda, one of the cooks in the kitchen, said. She looked almost as old as Granny Ada and had short, curly white hair and deep brown eyes.

"She's just joking," I said, trying to cover for Lia. "Right Lia?"

"Of course," Lia replied, smiling widely, innocently at Helda, who just shook her head at our antics.

Although we're always arguing over something or bickering like children, I really liked Lia. She was very truthful, almost to a fault, and she always had my back when she wasn't instigating things. Other than the being in love with Eros thing, she was a pretty cool chick.

"The heat in this kitchen is making my makeup melt," Lia whined, turning to grab a paper towel to pat the sweat off her forehead.

"Like the Wicked Witch of the West, except she melts from water and you're melting from heat," I added.

While Lia was in charge of preparing the salad for the salad table, I was in charge of the desserts, which were two types of cake and mini fruit pizzas, and Rora was in charge of the ham and cheese sliders and the coleslaw.

As for Helda, Doris, and Esther, they made the shredded barbeque sandwiches, mashed potatoes, corn, baked penne pasta, and seasoned the gigantic amount of raw meat that was always readily available at any gathering in a werewolf pack.

I'd already finished putting the cakes into the oven along with the sugar cookie dough for the fruit pizzas, so I was just working on the frosting and the toppings before I cut all the fruits into pieces to decorate the pizza.

By the time Rora and I were done with everything, Lia was still struggling with washing her greens and preparing everything, so we decided to help her assemble her salad. When we were done with all the food prep and setting up the dining hall, I was quick to hop back to the room to take a shower and get myself dressed.

I bought a really pretty deep red dress in town the other day, with the plan to wear it to the party today. The dress itself was strappy and the straps crisscrossed in the back, revealing half of my back to the public, while the V-neck dipped down a little in the front, revealing a tiny bit of the cleavage area.

When I first tried it out at the shop, I didn't think it looked too bad, probably because of the yellow lighting in the dressing room and Lia's egging. But now that I was wearing it again, I felt as if I were too pale for the dress, that someone a little tanner would look better in it. And I was having all sorts of second thoughts on wearing red for the first time. But I didn't have a backup dress, other than an all-black one, so I had to stick with this dress instead.

Once I'd tied the bow properly on my dress and wore my nude-colored sandals, I quickly curled my hair into loose waves and applied some light makeup that enhanced more than covered. Then, I left the room and walked to the dining hall to wait for Eros to come back.

When I got to the dining hall, I spotted Lia standing next to Rora and the babies and wearing a sexy, all-black dress with pretty silver jewelry to jazz out the whole ensemble.

While I was afraid that black wasn't too cheerful, Lia was rocking it. *Damn it.*

I should have just worn the black dress.

"Alpha Eros is coming right now," Rora said, waving me over to her.

I didn't know who was in charge of leading Eros to the party but I hoped they hurry, because I was really hungry.

"Kyra, stop biting your sister," I said, lifting Kyra away from Wren, who was dead asleep and didn't even care that her arm was being used as a chew toy.

"She's teething," Granny Ada said, handing me a chew toy she'd just finished cleaning.

"I think they all are," I said. "Except for Wren."

It'd only been a day or two since Cillian's teeth started coming in before I noticed that the rest of the babies were starting to grow teeth, too. And with the teeth came cranky, fussy, angry, feverish, screaming babies that needed to be pacified throughout the day. It was non-stop now, and the only one able to sleep through all the crying and screaming was Wren, who I didn't think would wake up even if her butt were on fire.

After I thought that, everyone around me went quiet, and Eros and a bunch of the pack members came into the room.

"Surprise!" everyone screamed, blowing on their party blowers.

"Happy birthday, Alpha Eros!"

"Happy birthday!"

"May all your wishes come true!"

Once all the greetings were done and over with, all the pack members were quick to get started on the food. Some lined up to get the raw meat while others went for the cooked items.

"Happy birthday, Eros," I said, leaning up to kiss Eros on the cheek.

"It's been a long time since I've celebrated my birthday," he replied, wrapping a strong arm around my waist before taking Kyra from my hands.

"I know. Granny Ada told me about it. But I wanted to make it different this year," I said. "I wanted to make you feel special, just like how you make me feel special."

"Thank you, Emira." Eros pressed a chaste kiss on my brow and smiled so wide I could see his beautiful white teeth.

"You're welcome," I said, peering up at him through my lashes while smiling like an idiot.

# CHAPTER 14

The party went beyond expectations. Everyone enjoyed the food and had joined the blackout bingo we'd prepared afterwards.

Originally, I'd only thought about doing lunch, but Lia had suggested playing some games for prizes and it sounded like such a great idea that we picked a couple of games for everyone to enjoy.

After about two hours, everyone was quick to disperse to go on with their day. I was going to take the babies back but Granny Ada waved me off so that Eros and I could spend a little time together.

I felt bad leaving the babies with her again, so I'd told her I would take the babies back later today, but she told me she was going to keep them tonight.

After making sure she was okay with watching them the whole night and she had all the supplies she needed, I walked back to my room to wash my face, brush my teeth, floss, and gurgle mouthwash.

As I looked in the closet to find something to change into, Eros opened the door to our room, and I remembered that I hadn't even given him his present.

"Thank you for planning the party for me, Emira," Eros said, as soon as he closed the door behind him.

"Were you surprised? Did you think I was mad at you the whole time?" I asked, a little giddy at having managed to fool Eros for once.

After a little pause, he said, "I knew you weren't mad at me. Because if you were, you would have locked the door and not let me into our room."

Since Eros had avoided the first question I asked, like he always did when he didn't want to answer truthfully in fear of hurting my feelings, I was given the feeling that he hadn't been surprised. At all.

"You didn't know about the party the whole time, did you?" I narrowed my eyes as Eros came closer to the closet.

Though hesitant, he nodded.

"But how? I was so inconspicuous about it! I even kept my thoughts all locked up," I whined.

"I guessed." Eros shrugged his shoulders, unable to hide that little lift on the corner of his lips.

"Guessed? Well, you guessed right," I grumbled, extremely disappointed at my failed surprise.

*This is what happens when you are too confident and your mate is way too smart for their own good.*

"I knew about the party, but I didn't know what your present was," he stated.

"Really?"

Eros nodded.

*At least there is still an element of surprise left,* I thought to myself, trying to salvage what was left of my tattered hopes.

I turned away from Eros for a second to grab the neatly wrapped blue box off the bed.

Then, I handed it to him.

"Happy birthday, Eros. I hope you like it," I said, smiling.

As Eros ripped open the wrapping and the box to pull out the items, I said, "You have everything already and I didn't know what to get you... so I knitted you a hat and a pair of socks. You'll be able to use them now since it's still really cold outside."

I was very rusty now that I'd given up knitting for so long and didn't have my grandmother to fix my mistakes when I dropped a stitch or twisted the stitch.

After a lot of messing up and fixing, I'd finished the socks and hat just in time for his birthday.

Originally, I'd wanted to knit him a full sweater, but I was on a time crunch and feared that I would not finish it in time. Knitting a hat and a pair of socks were much easier than knitting a shirt or a sweater and wouldn't be as challenging for me, either.

*Maybe I'll knit him a sweater next year. Or wool underwear.*

I laughed at that thought.

That wouldn't really be a good gift idea because Eros would be itching for a whole day if he wore the underwear. And he'd probably wear it just to make me feel like he liked the gift, all the while suffering inside of his pants but unable to say anything about it.

*That'd make for a good April fool's joke,* I thought, *though I wouldn't really make him wear it. I'd just give it to him and see what his reaction would be.*

"Thank you, Emira. I really like it," he said, smiling warmly and staring at me with an adoring look.

"Try it on," I urged, eager to see how he looked in them.

Eros first pulled the dark gray hat over his head of ink-colored hair before he tried on the long socks.

"Does it fit good?" I asked nervously, twisting my index finger back and forth.

"Yes," he said, pulling the items off to put them back into the box. "It fits perfectly. I'll start wearing them tomorrow."

I sighed out in relief.

"Of course. Look at who made it?" I grinned, feeling quite proud of myself, yet again for the Nth time today.

Eros chuckled and shook his head at my antics.

"I have a present for you, too," he said, pulling a little box out of his pocket, like a magician, and holding it out for me to take. The box was dark blue and was around two inches wide and two inches long, and just seeing it made my heart thump wildly in my chest. I felt like I already knew what it was.

"It's supposed to be your birthday, Eros. You didn't need to get me anything," I murmured, even though I was already reaching a hand out to get the box.

*I'm telling you, any woman who sees this box would have it open in two seconds flat. Me included.*

My fingers tripped over themselves and trembled like mad before I managed to open the box.

Almost immediately, my breath stuck in my throat as I saw the beautiful ring and band lying inside.

The diamond in the center of the ring was just the right size and wasn't outrageously big like the ring on Katelyn's finger. And along with that, there were tiny little diamonds on both sides, swirling around in a beautiful pattern halfway down the ring.

"It's beautiful!" I smoothed my fingers across the band and the ring, touched beyond words.

"You've always conformed to my traditions, so I didn't want you to miss out on yours. It's the least I can do as your mate and—hopefully—your husband," he paused, as if to let the words sink in, "I want to marry you, Emira."

The sincerity in his eyes and the tremble in his voice made me tear up, made me feel like the most luckiest and the most loved woman in the world. And I believed I was. I really do.

"You're supposed to say 'Will you marry me?' and get on one knee," I joked, trying to control the urge to cry by teasing Eros, but it was becoming a lot harder every time he looked at me with such love-filled eyes and said such heart-warming words.

"Will you marry me?" Eros said, moving to get on a knee but I stopped him just in the nick of time.

"I'm kidding! And yes. A million, billion times yes!" I exclaimed.

I thought that I didn't really care for a wedding, but when it came down to it, I kind of… sort of… cared. And I didn't know why, but I was a little embarrassed that I wanted to be married.

When I was younger, I'd always thought that I didn't need marriage or love, that I was willing to live a lonely life with two pet goldfishes named Albert and Einstein. But now that I had Eros, I didn't want to be alone anymore. I wanted to marry him, too.

Maybe I was like every other woman out there, hoping for that perfect little wedding somewhere down the road in life, dreaming of getting married to the love of my life.

"I didn't know what kind of ring you wanted, so I went based off of one of your memories. If you don't like the ring, we can always trade it for another one," Eros said.

"No. No. I love it! I don't want another one." I exclaimed. "How much did it cost?"

"It's not important. What's important is that you like the ring," Eros said, avoiding another one of my questions.

Although I was really curious, I just shrugged it off and focused on the shimmering ring, watching it with utmost fascination and awe.

"Help me put it on?" I asked, looking up at Eros with shining eyes filled with tears of my fluctuating emotions.

If I still had my makeup on, I would look like a train wreck, again, like when Eros had first met me.

As Eros took the ring from the box and slid it on my ring finger, he said, "Once I get a little more free time, we can plan our wedding together."

I nodded, unable to say another word.

As I wiped at the tears on the corner of my eyes with one hand, I thought that Eros really deserved his second present.

"You look very beautiful today," Eros complimented suddenly, his long fingers slowly dancing across my uncovered arms, leaving a stream of tingles behind. "The red looks really good on you."

"You don't think I'm too pale for it?" I asked, surprised.

"Not at all. I like how the bow in the back makes you look like a present, like… my present," he answered, his fingers travelling from my arms up to my shoulders before dipping down my back to toy with the red bow dangling in the middle, absently stroking the sensitive skin with the tips of his fingers.

I glanced at him from the corner of my eye and felt as if this was going south quicker than I'd thought.

"Am I supposed to open this present, too?" he asked, his voice deep and husky, sexy and hypnotic as his lips skimmed across my burning red ears.

"Not yet," I said, pulling away from him before my legs could get too weak. "First, you need to go take a shower. Then, you can open it."

"Yes, ma'am." Eros chuckled but followed my orders.

After he went into the bathroom, I checked myself in the mirror before deciding to just stay in this outfit since I'd told Eros that he could take it off when he was done showering. But for now, I had to work up the courage and pray that I didn't make any mistakes or bite him, because I'd read that was a very common occurrence for beginners. And I didn't want to be *that* beginner.

How embarrassing would that be?

Other than that, I was glad that I'd made sure to thoroughly clean my mouth before Eros came into the room, or else it would have ruined this present when Eros guessed correctly again.

Nervously pinching the fabric of the red dress in between my forefinger and thumb, I pushed away the urge to grab my phone and do some last-minute studying. Because if I did, I would get even more nervous and have second thoughts.

After sitting for a little over ten minutes, Eros finally came out from the bathroom, his hair still dripping wet and his shirt now missing. The dark pants he wore hung low on his hips, and his abs glistened in the light because of the droplets of water dripping down from his hair.

I swallowed down the nervousness settling in my throat and found myself unable to tear my gaze away from his muscled chest and washboard abs.

*This sight never fails to capture my full attention. Never,* I thought, trying to think of what I was about to do next, before Eros distracted me with his yummy body.

"Can I open my present now?" he asked, smiling widely, probably because he'd seen the thirsty look on my face, as he wrapped his arms around my waist.

"You sure can," I said, almost slapping myself for the awkward reply.

*Why do I always have to be so awkward whenever we get down to business?!*

Eros chuckled as his cool fingers slowly brushed along my shoulders before untangling the bow and pushing the straps down my arms. Without the straps to hold the dress in place, the red fabric slid down my abdomen before collecting on the floor by my feet. I stepped out of the dress and kicked it aside.

The moment I turned around to face Eros in my lacy black bra and panties, I noticed that his eyes had darkened immensely, becoming almost predatorial as he ogled my entire body.

I held back a shiver and stood stock-still, feeling as if my heart were beating in my throat and throbbing like it wanted to come out of my body and fall at Eros' feet.

After a deep breath to calm myself, I took a hold of Eros' hands and led him over to the bed. When he sat down on the edge, I leaned over and draped my arms on his shoulders and around his neck, tangling my fingers into his damp hair.

"I want to give you a second present, Eros," I said, brushing my lips against his ear. I set my knee on his thigh and bit down on the rim of his ear, sucking lightly before caressing the reddening appendage with the tip of my tongue.

Eros' entire body tensed under my arms.

"What is it?" He breathed heavily, wrapping a strong arm around my waist to steady my body, in case I lost my balance and fell, further embarrassing myself.

"You'll see," I replied, trying to be as mysterious as possible.

"You're not teasing me again, are you?" he asked.

I laughed, remembering how I'd left him hanging the other night when I fell asleep while waiting for him to come out of the shower. I was so tired from running after the nine babies the whole day that, by the time Eros came back and we were about to get intimate, I fell asleep. Again.

*Why is this always happening to me now?! Why?!*

My body heated up and so did my face.

143

I coughed to dispel the guilt and said, "No. Not this time. I promise I won't fall asleep again."

After that affirmation, more to myself than to Eros, I went back to kissing and worshiping my way across his sharp, chiseled jawline with renewed vigor. My lips left moist kisses on the corner of his mouth and lips while my hands massaged his neck and shoulder.

When he'd relaxed enough, I parted my lips and deepened the kiss, mashing our lips and tongue together until there was no space left between us.

Since this was the first time that I was doing this, I wasn't really sure where to start. So I just decided to kiss my way down his body.

Eros' eyes were half lidded, watching as I licked his lips and kissed him tenderly before sucking his wet tongue into my mouth.

After a moment, I broke the kiss and trailed my lips to his neck. As I lightly bit down on his skin, I felt him shudder repeatedly beneath me. Then, I realized that this was the area where I would have marked him if I had been a she-wolf.

Without much thought, I bit down a little harder, close to the point of drawing blood, and heard Eros groan and pant my name.

From there, I kissed and licked a trail down his collarbone and straight to his abs, worshipping the steel-covered skin with my mouth, my tongue, and my teeth. When I reached his navel, I pushed his legs farther apart and kneeled in front of him, coming face to face with his tented pants.

"You don't have to, Emira," he said hurriedly, grabbing ahold of my forearms to stop me.

Though Eros said that, I had seen the way his breath held in his throat when he saw me drop down to my knees in front of him, the anticipation and surprise that had colored his face.

How could I stop?

"Why not? You've always done it for me. I want to do it for you this time. Please, Eros?" I said, looking up at him.

*I don't know if any woman has ever had to beg to give a man a blow job, but I feel as if I am the only one crazy enough.*

"Please?" I repeated.

After a minute of looking at me in the eye, Eros sighed and gave in. He brushed my hair back behind my shoulder and sat back to let me have more room.

"Let me know if I hurt you," he said.

"It should actually be the other way around," I replied, knowing that I might bite off his shaft because of my inexperience. Hopefully, that didn't happen.

With my index finger hooked on the waistband of his pants, I pulled the fabric down as Eros lifted himself so that it would be easier for me to remove. Then, I pulled off his boxers and stared at his magnificent length.

At this angle, his shaft looked extra-large, extra-long, and extra-thick. The veins were throbbing as blood collected while creamy liquid seeped out from the little slit on the top.

It was currently the only thing I saw.

Taking a deep breath to calm myself, I gripped his swollen girth and stroked up and down, experimenting with how much strength I should put into my hold.

"Do you want me to kiss it?" I breathed, looking at Eros' handsome face as I licked my lips.

Without waiting for an answer, I pressed a kiss on the tip of his shaft before opening my mouth to run my tongue along the little slit, licking off the precum that had collected and dribbled down the staff.

Once the bead of liquid was in my mouth, I was given the feeling of drinking milk. It was creamy and bland with a very faint sweet and salty aftertaste.

Eros didn't taste bad. At all. Instead, he tasted a lot more pleasant than I'd imagined. I had prepped myself for a really acrid, salty, and bitter taste and thought that I would give him blow jobs even if he tasted weird. But what I got was the opposite. And I was quite happy about that.

Tossing the thought aside, I licked my way down his cock and traced the veins with my tongue, watching his every reaction through the veil of my lashes. When I reached the top of the member, I sucked on the head and pressed the tip of my tongue into the slit, lapping at the tiny bit of liquid that trickled out.

"Fuck, Emira," he groaned, his head falling back for a split second.

At this exact moment, I felt empowered, like I could make Eros lose control because of me, for me. The elation of this knowledge filled my chest with heat.

"Does that feel good?" I asked, mimicking the words he'd used on me before.

"Yes," he panted as his fingers delved into my hair and tangled with the wavy locks.

After completely wetting his shaft with my saliva, I parted my lips and took him into my mouth as far as I could. My mouth felt strained because of how thick he was, and I almost gagged when the tip of his shaft hit the back of my throat. It brought tears to my eyes, but I held down the urge to pull back until the intense need died down.

In the end, I only managed to swallow half of his cock, so I had to stroke the other half with my hands and massage all the way down to his soft balls, squeezing the sacks in my palm with light pressure. As my hands kept busy, my head bobbed in a slow rhythm, trying to get myself used to the sensation of having something go down my throat, and my lips closed tightly around him, sucking until my cheeks started to hollow.

From above, Eros was panting heavily, petting my head or gripping my hair as he tried to hold his hips still.

*In and out and in and out,* I thought, breathing heavily through my nose and trying not to choke.

# CHAPTER 15

After about seven or so minutes, my jaw started to ache really bad, but I tried to hold on, that was until I accidentally scraped my teeth against Eros' skin.

"Sorry. Did that hurt?" I hurriedly took his length out of my mouth to inspect it.

"It didn't hurt. It just surprised me," he said, stroking my head encouragingly.

I smiled up at him before going back to sucking him off and basking in his heated gaze, occasionally looking up to see the rapturous expression on his face.

The way his eyes would flutter closed when I took him deep, the way he groaned when I sucked him hard, and the way he panted with his mouth partially open as sweat glistened on his temple made me wetter and wetter.

Gradually, I could tell that Eros was losing it as I bobbed up and down faster. After a couple of minutes, his hips pumped as he pistoned his thick shaft deep down my throat. The automatic urge to gag made my stomach turn but I forced it back along with the tears collecting in my eyes. My nose flared as I tried my best to keep breathing.

When he finally came, his length jerked in my mouth and sprayed stream after stream of hot semen into my throat. Since I was prepared for it, I swallowed as fast as I could to keep from choking and coughing. But Eros' load was way too much. It filled my mouth and dripped down the corner of my lips and chin, plopping on my chest and thighs.

"Spit it in my hand," he panted, holding his hand out for me.

Since I'd read that men really liked it when their come was swallowed, I swallowed everything in my mouth and went as far as to lick my lips clean of the slightly sweet and milky substance, staring at him the entire time.

Eros' eyes dilated at the sight and his shaft was quick to stand at attention again.

*I'm really going to great lengths for Eros today,* I thought to myself.

"God, Emira," he sighed, blue eyes turning so dark it bordered on black. "I want you right now."

My eyes widened at his words and I said, "Let's not do something that we're going to regret later, Eros."

He chuckled and stood, walking over to the nightstand to grab a box of something from the drawer.

"I was going to show you this later. But I don't think I can wait," he said, handing me the box once he'd opened it to take a small square item out.

As I held it in my hand, I realized that it was a box of condoms, said to be ultra-thin and ninety-nine-point-nine percent effective.

"Do these work for us?" I asked, turning the box around to read the description.

Eros nodded and tore the wrapper open.

"When did they start making these?" I looked at the package again to make sure this was really tough enough to handle whatever Eros was putting out.

"I had a friend look into making them for us. He just finished it the other day," he replied, pinching the tip of the condom before rolling it down his cock.

My eyes went wide, not too sure if I should be happy that there was a way for us to have sex without getting pregnant or embarrassed that one of his friends now knew of our bedroom struggles.

"Are they really safe?" I asked again, still hesitant.

"Yes. It's been lab tested and werewolf tested." Eros took the box from me and put me on the bed. He unhooked my bra and pulled off my wet panties before he spread my legs apart and lay himself in between them.

"Why are they packaged? Is he planning on selling them?" I was sure that werewolves weren't going to buy this since their conception rates were so low and most of them wanted to get pregnant.

"He's selling them to werewolves and humans alike."

"Wow," I said. "That'll surely bring in some business."

I was about to say something else but Eros blocked off my next words with his lips. He kissed me slowly, sensually and plundered my mouth with his tongue. Before long, I was lost in the haze of his touch and the sparks that it brought. All I could taste was Eros, all I could see was Eros, all I could hear was Eros, and all I could smell was Eros. Everything in my mind had taken the shape of Eros.

"Ah…" I moaned out loud and grabbed a fistful of the comforter in my hand, trying to keep myself anchored to the bed as Eros' mouth encircled a puckered nipple and bit down on the sensitive tip. Then, he ran his tongue over the pebbled flesh over and over again, leaving behind wet sounds every time his hot mouth made contact with my breast.

While his lips and teeth pleasured my right breast, his hand fondled the other one, squeezing the fleshy orb and playing with the nipples until they became hard and swollen. After one breast was wet and covered in his scent, Eros slowly kissed the skin in between the mounds before he played with the other nipple, sinking his teeth into the rounded globe.

I choked back a cry and clutched on to the covers, drowning in the pain and pleasure he brought.

As I squirmed beneath him, Eros pulled my legs wider apart and dipped a hand between them, teasingly tracing my extremely wet opening with his middle finger. After a few strokes, he inserted his digit and pushed it in as far as it would go, pumping his finger in and out at a slow pace while my juices gushed out to coat his hand.

Since we were such a tight fit, he'd always dragged out the foreplay because he didn't want to hurt me when we made love.

"Still so tight," he grunted, adding another finger as he tried to prepare me for his cock.

I arched my body and moaned under him, staring at the beads of sweat trickling down from his temple and glistening in the light, barely able to keep my eyes open because of the electric sparks. Though it felt good to have his fingers inside of me, the urgent need for something bigger, harder urged me to beg him.

"I want you, Eros," I murmured, my voice hoarse and raspy as I begged him with my eyes to put it in. But Eros refused to. He thrusted his fingers into my body faster and harder, almost relentlessly as he rubbed against my clit and forced me closer and closer to my climax, all the while massaging my nipples with his fingers and tongue.

My toes curled into the sheets and my entire body felt as if I were being electrified. Every single thing in the room dispersed into thin air.

After another minute or so, my stomach fluttered and my eyes rolled back when my orgasm finally hit, leaving me breathless and thoughtless at the same time.

It felt so good that I could barely open my eyes, and I knew that it was only going to get better from here.

Eros removed his fingers from my tight, sopping walls and put a pillow under my butt. He aligned his engorged member with my opening and rubbed the mushroom head against the juices trickling down from my entrance, breathing heavily the entire time as he held himself back to make sure that I was good and ready before he entered my body.

As soon as the bulbous head pushed forward and sunk into me, I could feel an uncomfortable, burning stretch of my inner muscles conforming to his shape and size. For some reason, this felt like my first time again.

Since I was too tight, Eros was forced to stop after a third of his cock had entered. He leaned down and kissed me languidly before pulling out and entering again, over and over, until my body started to open up for him.

"Just like that. Open for me, Emira," he said, burying his face into my neck, breathing heavily as sweat dripped off his chin and plopped on my belly.

My breath held in my throat as I counted every slow and torturous thrust, waiting until he buried himself deep inside of me. In over fifteen slow strokes, my body gradually gave way and swallowed inch after inch of Eros' throbbing cock, sucking him into my depths until he was balls deep.

When we finally became one, I gave a strangled cry and wrapped my legs around his waist, biting down on my lip as he kissed me again and tangled our tongues together.

After I'd adjusted to the feeling of having him inside of me, of being completely filled by him, the raging desire came back and I craved for more.

"Faster," I murmured against his lips, biting down and arching my hips to meet his delightful thrusts.

Eros kissed me frantically as he picked up the pace. Before I knew it, he was slamming roughly into me, pounding into my body with each thrust of his powerful hips. And with each thrust, his shaft would bite into my cervix and send a burning pain through me that eventually ebbed and turned into mind-blowing pleasure.

"It feels so good," I gasped as Eros lifted my legs up against his shoulders and groaned a reply.

Other than the sounds of my uncontrollable moaning and cries of Eros' name, I could hear the sticky sound of Eros' every entry and exit and the panting groans that left his mouth as he fucked me hard, rough, and fast. And I loved every minute of it.

My stomach clenched, my toes curled, and tears fell from my eyes as the pleasure and pain mixed together to give me one of the most intense orgasms I'd ever had. Though my mouth fell open, nothing came out, not even a squeak, as I reached a new ecstatic high. White fireworks burst before my vision and my abdomen clenched in timing with my fluttering inner walls. But Eros didn't give me a break. He continued to thrust into me, slamming against my swollen G-spot as he pushed my thighs flat against my breasts and had me hold them in place.

Before I had even come down from the orgasm, my loins burned intensely, like I was going to pee, like I had held it in for too long that it was going to come out at any second. And this made me panic. I made a move to tell Eros but the buildup was fast and intense, erupting within seconds. I barely had the time to open my mouth when he rammed hard and fast against my G-spot, and I felt myself let go.

Eros slowed his thrusts before pulling out completely to watch as a stream of clear liquid came up and out of me, almost like a water fountain.

The feeling was intense like an orgasm had overtaken me. My whole body was trembling and my stomach was heaving as wave after wave of uncontrollable ecstasy coursed through my veins and burned every fiber of my being. This orgasmic feeling continued for almost fifteen seconds while the stream of liquid continued to come out for the next ten, wetting Eros abs and thighs in the process.

When I was able to think again, I covered my face with my hands and felt like crying, too embarrassed with myself that I didn't know what to do. If only I could just disappear on the spot.

"I think I peed, Eros," I wailed, embarrassed beyond my imagination.

*This has never happened before,* I thought, disgusted with myself for the first time since a long time.

"You didn't pee," he said, chuckling at my misery. "You squirted. Some women squirt when they're feeling really good."

*Squirt?*

I opened my mouth to ask him what he meant but Eros was quick to kiss my lips and insert his cock back in, thrusting with renewed vigor like he'd taken a huge dose of Viagra when I wasn't looking, not that he needed it.

I had to grab a hold of his forearms as he pushed my thighs flat against my breasts and pounded into me again, going out of his way to rub against my G-spot every chance he got. The orgasmic feeling had me quaking in place while every part of my body throbbed with intense pleasure, causing me to feel lightheaded as my vision became foggy.

I had a feeling that Eros was really aroused by the fact that I had squirted, and he was probably very proud of himself, too.

Another twenty or so minutes of rough and intense love making passed before he panted and came into the condom. At first, I'd thought that he was done because he pulled off the condom, tied it, and tossed it into the trash by our nightstand. But I was wrong, because he grabbed another one from the box and put it on. Then, he shifted me to my sides and entered again, starting a new rhythm of hard thrusts that sent bolts of pleasure through my core.

At this point, I had become a pile of sweaty, wet mush and I couldn't do anything other than hold on to Eros for dear life. My limbs felt heavy and moving required too much effort.

"One more time," he said against my ear, kissing the appendage endearingly. "Just one more time."

After he'd made me squirt for the first time ever, Eros made it a mission to make me do it again by stimulating my G-spot and my clitoris repeatedly. The whole entire night. And his "one more time" ended up being more than I could count.

*This will probably be the last time I am this brave,* I thought to myself as another intense orgasm washed through me.

. . .

After Eros' birthday, I had a couple of weeks of peace with the babies and Granny Ada, until the Werewolf Council came knocking on my door and demanded to be seen.

It was the same group of old men who had delivered the verdict at the trial against Eros and the late Alpha Jared. The ones who wanted me to get "marked, mated, and pupped."

They'd shown up on pack lands after giving a warning in advance by thirty minutes and expected to see the "Sentinels" immediately. So, Eros had to call off training to entertain them while I dressed the babies and made sure they were presentable, which was total bull crap.

Why did I have to show those old men my babies when I didn't even want to?

They were my babies, and I knew I had a right to keep anyone I didn't like from seeing them. Because, who knew what these old men had in mind? What if they declared that I wasn't fit to be the mother and wanted to take the babies away from me? That wasn't possible. But still.

*I don't know.*

My mind was blowing up with so many questions, and I couldn't do anything about it because they were the Werewolf Council. Even though Eros had reassured me multiple times that they couldn't take the babies away, I was still in the defensive, uncaring if I was going to offend them because of it. I had the right to be worried for my babies' safety.

"Alpha Eros, congratulations on the nine pups!" they greeted and congratulated, grinning widely at Eros, who was opening the door of our room so they could enter.

When they saw me, they greeted me as well. "Alpha Female Emira. We hope you are doing well."

"I am," I said, nodding my head at them with a fake smile on my lips.

The only thing they'd called me in the past was Breeder, so I wasn't too sure how they knew my name when I'd never introduced myself to them. But I wasn't going to ask.

"They must be the pups," Samson, one of the Council members, said, leaning over to smile at Kyra, who looked like she was going to bite him if he took a step closer. In fact, all the pups had taken the defensive now that there were unfamiliar people in the room. "They look very strong already."

Strong? What on earth did he mean?

They were only a couple of months old. How strong could they look?

"What are their names?" another one asked, turning to me.

Unwillingly, I heaved a sigh and introduced them to all of the pups, starting with Silas and ending with Kyra.

After they'd all had a good look at the babies and chatted amongst themselves, Samson said, "It is a good time to start training the Sentinels, Alpha Eros. With the war coming, they will be utmost needed and will contribute to our win over the humans."

At his words, I bristled and turned my head to give Eros a wide-eyed, not-too-happy look.

What made them think that my babies should be training already? That they should become a part of the war when they weren't even grown up yet?

*Are they insane?*

I didn't know why, but I was getting very, very angry. And it was just building and building until I felt like I was going to cry if I didn't do something about it, like I'd turn into the hulk and just smash everything and anything to bits and pieces.

After I'd given birth, those turbulent and uncontrollable emotions seemed to stay with me.

I always got angry very easily and very fast. It didn't take but a few seconds for the anger to build up just because someone had said something that I didn't like or looked at me in a certain way, which was not like me at all to act like this.

*This isn't postpartum, is it?*

Even though I'd heard of postpartum depression, I'd never heard of postpartum anger.

"And if you need help with the training, we have a few candidates to suggest," Samson said.

Eros declined their offer and led them out of the room before I could blow up in their faces and ask them to leave. It was either that or punch them all in the face, over and over and over and over again.

When Eros came back, I was quick to ask him about what those old men meant by the training.

"Why do they want us to train the babies?" I asked, feeling betrayed by Eros' sudden silence.

Eros sighed after a moment and tried to explain, "At this age, they're supposed to start training already."

"This age? They're only five months old!" I exclaimed in disbelief. "How do you expect them to train?"

"Our pups are Sentinels, Emira. They were born to be different from others. If they don't find a way to expel all their energy, they will only become more and more violent—"

Why was it that the more Eros tried to explain, the more confused and the more angry I became?

"But they're my babies, too! I don't want them to train and I don't want them to become a part of this war, at least not until they could make their own decisions when they're grown adults!" I cried, trembling so much that I couldn't even concentrate on what I was saying. "They're babies for crying out loud! And I don't care if anyone says otherwise!"

Eros reached out to touch me, to comfort me, but I pushed his hand away, turned my back to him, and tried to walk to the babies. But before I could get very far, Eros' arm wrapped around my waist and anchored me against his body.

The moment I was enveloped in his calming scent and aura, my shoulders slumped and a part of my anger gradually scattered like scared pigeons. I deflated like a hot air balloon.

"Just let me explain, Emira," he said softly, calmly.

"Fine," I harumphed.

"I know that they might be babies to you, but they are Sentinels, warrior werewolves." Eros sighed again. "They're not like regular babies or regular werewolf pups. They were born to fight, defend, and protect. If they don't have a purpose, they will not survive. So they have to channel their power into something or else they will go into bloodlust and become crazed. Then, they'll hurt anyone and everyone around them, including you. It's the same concept as when humans get a sugar rush, except more deadly."

My brows knitted together into a line as I gnawed on my bottom lip and picked at the cuticle on my fingers, an action that I hadn't done in quite a while.

After a long moment to digest what he'd said, I asked, "Are other Sentinels like this, too? Do they become more violent unless they train?"

"Yes. Most of them start training when they are two to three months old," he said. "We're actually a little later than them."

I didn't know what to say after that.

"Can I think on this? Before you start training the babies?" I asked, trying to hold back the uncontrollable tears as I untangled Eros' fingers and pulled myself out of his warm embrace.

"I can't concentrate right now because I'm too angry, and I don't even know why I'm so angry," I sobbed, wiping at my cheeks to erase the evidence of my weakness.

Eros tried to reach for me again, but I was too mad at myself, too mad at the world to let him.

"You're channeling their anger and frustration, Emira," he said, pulling my hands away from my face to wipe at my tears with his fingers.

"The babies aren't angry... or frustrated," I sniffed, trying to deny his words about the babies' anger issues.

"Look at them, Emira. Tell me they don't look angry."

Eros' hands settled on my shoulders as he turned me around and made me look at the pile of babies on the floor, clawing and biting at each other.

The babies had been this way for over two days now, starting with Kyra who was always very volatile to her other siblings.

At first, I'd thought they were just playing around, like how puppies play fight with each other, except the babies were a little rougher due to them being wolves. But now that Eros was explaining everything, I realized that what I'd thought wasn't the case. At all. At this point, I couldn't deny his words or ignore the problem any longer.

# CHAPTER 16

Since our very first fight, Eros and I had been getting into more and more arguments lately, especially when it came to the babies and their training. Well, it was just mainly me fighting with him while he'd calmly tell me his thoughts on the matter.

I was as hard headed as a mule because I didn't like the idea of the babies training or going to war, but what was I to do when this was what they were born for? When they could possibly die if I stopped them from doing it?

All these questions made my head hurt, and I hadn't come up with an answer yet. But if I had to choose between my babies dying now or training and going to war, I would choose the latter, even though they had a chance of dying if they went to war.

As the days passed, I came to realize that maybe letting the babies train was a good idea. Because Eros had been right about the pups getting more and more aggressive if they weren't given something to release the pent-up energy in their little bodies. They fought with each other almost every minute of the day, and there was nothing I could do to make them calm down.

Each day had become torturous and stress filled. And today was no different, except things went downhill really fast when I tried to stop Kyra from taking a chunk out of Silas' face. Her little claws had come out and dug themselves into Silas' arm while Silas' had his claws digging into her belly.

When I tried to untangle Kyra from Silas, I noticed that Kyra's eyes seemed to be turning from pink to red at a really fast pace. Just the sight of it was enough to make me feel like I was having a heart attack.

"Kyra!" I screeched, panic coloring my voice.

Kyra suddenly turned her head away from Silas and opened her canine-filled mouth to take a bite at my arm.

Since I was unprepared for the attack, her sharp teeth bit deeply into my forearm and sank in to the gums.

Blood gushed down my arm and dripped on the floor as I screamed and tried to get her to let go, but she wouldn't. It was like she was rabid or crazed or something. She dug her claws into my wrist and hung onto me for dear life. I wanted to just drag her off but I was scared that I would hurt her or she would end up with a chunk of my arm in her mouth.

With how she was drinking my blood like she was a starving vampire, I was fearful that she would eat the chunk of my flesh. And that would be really, really creepy.

As of this moment, I didn't know what to do. I was scared out of my wits and in tremendous agony. The pain was nothing that I could comprehend, it hurt and ached and felt as if my arm had been lit on fire and left to burn at one thousand degrees inside of an incinerator.

Within a matter of seconds, the area she had bitten started to turn purplish-blue as it traveled up my arm, all the while my spilt blood became as black as coal.

Since the room was soundproof, I doubted anyone in the packhouse had heard me scream, so there was no way anyone could come to my rescue right now, except for Eros.

*'Eros, Kyra bit me and now my arm's turning blue and she won't let go,'* I said anxiously, urgently through the mind-link, extremely worried for myself at this point.

'Stay right there, Emira. I'm coming right now,' he replied.

159

Within the next two minutes, Eros was already in the room and growling at Kyra in werewolf tongue, sounding authoritative and extremely scary.

Just the sound of his anger was enough to make the hairs on my entire body raise and my heart skip a beat. But whatever he was saying didn't seem to work.

Kyra didn't let go of my arm, instead, she seemed to cling even tighter as she ground her jaw, as if she were going to rip my flesh out.

I gave a startled, pained squeal in protest.

"Command her. Tell her to stop," he said quickly.

"How? I've told her to let go already, but she won't," I replied, scared to tears.

"Try to be as authoritative as possible. Think of her as your subordinate, as your follower and make her obey your command."

I breathed out sharply and willed all the fear off my face to replace it with a stern, angry look.

*I'm her mother. I'm her leader. She needs to listen to me,* I kept chanting to myself.

"Let go, Kyra!" I exclaimed, pushing all my pent-up anger to the forefront as I bellowed in Kyra's face.

She startled and looked up at me, seeming to shrink into herself as her claws detached from my wrist and her teeth ripped out of my arm. Then, she whimpered in the back of her throat and tried to nestle her face into me, as if to seek comfort, but Eros grabbed ahold of her and set her on the ground.

By this time, Granny Ada was in our room, gasping at the sight of my blood everywhere on the ground and my extremely blue arm.

"Get her to Khanh. Quick! I'll watch the rest of the pups. Hurry and go," she urged.

Eros then picked me up off my feet and whisked me off, like a whirlwind, before I could lose consciousness.

When we got to Khanh's office, she was already standing by the door with a syringe and vial of something in her hand, probably because Eros had mind-linked her to let her know we were coming. I barely had the time to sit down on a chair when she jabbed the middle of the bite mark with the needle and injected me with the clear liquid.

"Hurry and drink this, Emi," she said, holding out the vial.

I tried to grab it from her but my hands were shaking too much, so Eros took it instead and poured it into my mouth. Since I was so out of it, I didn't really remember what it tasted like.

"That was a really close one, Emi. You need to be careful in the future," Khanh said, sighing out in extreme relief, just like I did when Eros showed up.

"I will. I definitely will," I breathed out, trying to catch my breath and calm my chaotic thoughts.

"Just avoid this area and don't let water touch it until it heals completely." Khanh helped me clean all the blood on my arm and patched up my bite before she applied gauze and tape.

I nodded my head.

After that traumatic visit to see Khanh, I learned that the babies had venom in their teeth and their claws, a type of dastardly and deadly toxin that could kill upon contact. But since I was the Mother, I had a type of antibody inside of me capable of combatting against the poison and saving my life.

Although I wasn't immune to the venom, I was able to endure it for a longer period of time, which was about ten minutes, before I passed out and died.

If it had been anyone else, that person would have died within the span of a minute and turned into a rotting corpse within ten minutes. I was lucky that it didn't take but five minutes for Eros to come and escort me to the doctor. Because if he hadn't, I would have been that rotting corpse lying in our room next to the pile of fighting babies.

I was just that close to courting death, and in the hands of my own baby to make matters worse. Although Eros had warned me not to let the babies scratch or bite me, I didn't think too much of it because the babies were always biting and scratching each other over the last few days, and nothing happened.

So, due to my stupidity, I'd just caused myself to suffer, even though I had been warned in advance. And now that that had happened, I was extremely wary of the future and what it would mean for Eros and me and the babies.

. . .

Ever since that chaotic experience with Kyra, I realized that I knew nothing about Sentinels. Although I had learned a little about Sentinels from when I still worked at the lab, my tiny bit of knowledge was nothing as in depth as it needed to be. If I hadn't been jolted by that venomous bite, I would have continued to stubbornly believe that I should raise my children like human babies instead of the warrior werewolf babies that they were.

How stupid was that?

I shook my head and folded a pair of little pants to add to the pile of folded laundry to my left.

"You're right, Eros. I think we should train them," I said.

He had just finished his long training with the pack members and had come back earlier than usual, so I was able to converse with him before I prepared for bed.

The babies were already asleep now, but that was only because I had to "command" them to do so. Everything they did now had to be "commanded" by me, and it was breaking my heart and making me cry myself to sleep too many times to count.

I didn't want to tell them to eat, sit, lie down, or go to sleep like I was their owner and they were my pet. But it had become the norm because they were just so aggravated that they couldn't function on their own.

Without me ordering them to do certain things, all they'd do was fight with each other or cry and scream. And they didn't even speak to me anymore. Before all this, I'd hear them call me "mama" several times. But now, all I heard was angry growling full of suffering and pain.

Eros had respected me and let me have enough space to think things over. And now, I had come up with my answer.

I wanted to have them trained. I wanted them to go back to normal, to the way they had been before whatever this was took over them. I wanted my babies back.

"Are they going to stay like this?" I asked worriedly, trying to stop the tears from welling in my eyes.

"No. They'll go back to normal again. Don't worry," he said, kissing my brow delicately as his thumb stroke away the tear that had fallen from my left eye. "Once we get them to moving around and expelling some of that energy, they'll be fine."

"Are you going to train them?" I asked tearfully.

Since Eros was so busy with training the pack members, I didn't really know if he had any time to train the babies. And I didn't want him to spread himself too thin, either. His training was probably stressful enough.

"I'll take some days off and train the pups," he said.

"But what about the pack members? They have to train, too," I said, worried that this would disrupt their plans and ruin our chances when it was time to fight with the Hunters.

"It'll be fine. I'll have the Gammas take over in the meantime," he replied, tucking a stray piece of hair behind my ear. "We'll probably start training tomorrow and see how it goes."

"Can I watch? I promise I won't disturb you," I pleaded.

I really wanted to know how he was going to train them when they were this little. Were they going to learn hand-to-hand combat or start working on their baby abs?

Somehow, just imagining the babies doing pushups or trying to lift dumbbells made training seem a lot more cuter and funnier than it should be.

"Of course. You'll need to be there anyway," he said.

"Why?" I picked up the pile of baby clothes and put them in the drawers before turning to face Eros again.

"They most likely won't listen to anything I say, so you'll need to tell them what to do until they can function by themselves." he explained, encircling me in his arms and comfortingly rubbing my back.

"I'm sorry, Eros," I muttered, leaning my face on his chest and inhaling his fresh scent. "I should have just listened to what you said. I'm an idiot."

"You're not. You're one of the smartest people I know," he complimented, though I didn't really believe what he was saying.

"Don't lie, Eros. You probably think I'm stupider than a jar of rocks," I joked, trying to take the seriousness out of the situation.

After a little pause, Eros said, "Sometimes."

"Eros!" I exclaimed, my eyes widening as they filled with disbelief.

Eros chuckled and said, "I'm kidding. I think you're smarter than a jar of rocks."

"That doesn't make it any better!"

. . .

As soon as the sun came up, I'd noticed that Eros was already awake. He was holding up a pair of pants and was trying his hardest to put them on Noah, who was squirming and kicking and trying to get away. By the time he'd managed to get it on, the other babies were awake and trying to run away, while I lay on my side with my head propped on my hand, watching Eros struggle to get all of the babies dressed and ready for their training session early this morning. He was smart to change their diapers when they were sleeping or else that would have been terribly time consuming.

With a yawn, I dragged myself out of bed and walked into the bathroom to brush my teeth and wash my face. I knew that we were going to be outside for a couple of hours today so I made sure to apply sunscreen on myself first before applying baby sunscreen on the babies. I wasn't too sure if they'd burn or not, but I didn't want to risk it.

Once I was done getting dressed and the babies were also done, we all sat down at the table to eat our breakfast. I was having a more human meal consisting of a big bacon, egg, and cheese breakfast burrito and some precut fruit, while Eros had eggs over easy with pan seared steak strips, four slices of toasted bread and roasted baby potatoes.

As for the babies, they had raw chunks of beef because they no longer drank my milk. Ever since they'd started walking, they got hungry a lot easier and required a more nourishing meal, so Granny Ada started feeding them chunks of slightly seasoned meat instead. Sometimes she would just brown the outside and leave the inside raw or she'd just season it a bit and not cook it at all. The babies seemed to like it raw more than lightly cooked.

"Sit and eat," I ordered as the babies started to get antsy and angry again, almost getting into a fight with each other. But after my command, they all sat down and started to eat their meals.

When we were done eating, I grabbed all of our lunchboxes and drinks out of the fridge and packed them in a cooler I'd borrowed from the kitchen.

"Ready?" Eros asked, picking up Wren, who was getting really sleepy after breakfast.

She'd literally had her whole face in the plate because she couldn't decide between eating or sleeping, so she just did both at the same time. I was really worried that she'd asphyxiate herself when I'd first seen her do that, but after I tried to stop her, to no avail, I just gave up and kept my eyes on her until she finished her meal.

Eros also assured me that she wouldn't asphyxiate so I wasn't too worried after that. But how she was able to eat and sleep at the same time still amazed me.

"Yes," I said, taking a hold of Kyra's hand. Since she was one of the most easiest to anger and aggravate, I wanted to make sure she didn't get too far from me or get in a fight with one of the others.

As my eyes trailed over Kyra's angelic face, I couldn't help but be reminded of the feeling of her canines latching deeply into my forearm and tearing my skin open. My skin crawled at the thought.

Was it weird that I was kind of scared of my babies now? Of the things they were capable of that regular babies weren't?

"Are we going to take the car or walk over there?" I asked, taking a hold of Nicholas while commanding for the others to follow along.

"It'll be a lot faster if we take the car." Eros grabbed the cooler I had packed and we all went down the stairs. As we walked through the house, I hadn't seen a single pack member and knew that they were probably busy training with the Gammas.

When we got to the front of the pack house, there was a white van already parked at the front. I opened the back doors and helped Eros load the babies into their car seats before taking a seat in the passenger side. Eros got into the driver seat and we were quick to drive to the training destination.

At the sight of the familiar road and scenery, I realized that Eros was taking us to that smaller arena Lia and Rora had taken me to before. But this time, the inside had been completely renovated. Gone was the barren and desolate center. In its place were obstacle courses stretched from one side of the field to the other.

It reminded me of the ninja courses I'd seen on TV.

"Wow. When did you set this up?" I asked in complete awe.

"A couple of days ago after training with the pack," he said, leading us through the obstacle.

There were monkey bars, climbing nets, slacklines, and so much more, some of which I didn't even know how to describe. But I was assured that the babies would be able to release all of their energy going through these courses.

"We'll start training them in their human forms first before training them in their wolf forms."

"Follow your dad," I said to the babies, urging them on to try the first obstacle course.

The babies all followed my command and ran after their father to start stretching their tiny little bodies. Although they were closing in on six months, they looked older than that. I would say they looked almost as if they were two years old.

As I watched them crawl through the tunnels and run around on the track, I tried to think of this as them playing and having fun on a large playground instead of training for a war.

Because only then did I feel a lot better about commanding them to do things.

"Crawl your way through, Cillian. Don't be scared," Eros said, kneeling to Cillian's level to help the little fella start on the next course.

The way Eros directed them through each course made me realize how cut out he was for this job, how perfect he was as a leader. But as I looked at the picture as a whole, it was mighty funny how a grown man standing over six feet tall was pep talking a six-month-old who was a little over thirty-six inches in height. What was even funnier was him shuffling all nine of them through a tunnel and telling them what to do.

While they were busy doing all of this, I whipped out my phone and started taking pictures and videos of this event for future reference or for when I needed a good laugh.

"Do you want to try, Emira?" Eros called, turning to face me for a second while the babies were taking a little break.

"I don't know if I'll be able to do it," I replied truthfully. "My arms are like soggy spaghetti sprinkled with a layer of salt."

Ever since I "trained" with Lia and Rora the other day, I hadn't gotten the chance to do it again because of the lack of time and energy. Just dealing with the babies and the bite had taken at least a dozen years out of my life, so I didn't want to put any more stress on myself. At least that was what I was going to say if anyone asked.

"You can train with the pups to make them hard, dried spaghetti," he chuckled, waving me over with his right hand.

I sighed under my breath and got up out of my seat, abandoning the last bit of relaxation I had.

"Try stretching first," he said, turning back to the babies to make sure they were doing what they were supposed to.

After I'd stretched for over ten minutes, Eros made me try climbing on the folded spider web ropes that came to a point at the very top. I'd thought that climbing this web would be very easy until I got on the thing and felt it wobble and move in all directions around me.

The web itself was very loose so I had to keep a steady hold and not let it control me into moving where it wanted me to move. As I climbed, my entire body was tensed to keep myself from being thrown off, because I'd almost slipped and twisted my ankle through the hole.

When I finally got to the top of the web, I was already sweating and I considered just rolling down the rest of the way. But what was the fun in that? Right? I was being sarcastic.

*I hate exercising.*

At first, I'd thought that climbing would be the hardest part, but it wasn't. Climbing down was.

Since the web kept swinging around whenever I moved, I kept missing the next step down and had almost slipped off again and again. And knowing me, if I had fallen off, I would have probably landed on my face or broken something.

# CHAPTER 17

"You're doing great, Emira," Eros said from over my shoulder as he led the babies through the monkey bars.

He held them up by their waist and made each one use their own strength to climb instead of helping them out.

Compared to me, a thirty-seven-year-old woman, who was struggling on the web, they did way better for being only six months old.

Just looking at how easy it was for them to go through every course made me feel very embarrassed and sparked the need for me to try harder.

The next hour went by in a breeze when Eros called me over to the babies and him.

"Tell them to shift with your mind, Emira."

I panted for breath and wiped at my sweat with the sleeve of my shirt before saying, "Will they know what that means?"

"Their instincts will automatically submit to your command, even if they don't understand what you are saying," Eros explained.

"But how do I tell them with my mind?" I scratched the back of my head in confusion.

"Like when you are mind-linking me, try calling to them that way," Eros said, leading me to the front of the babies before he removed Darius from his spot and set him very far away.

I took a deep breath and looked down at their flushed cherubic faces, trying to calm my mind enough to open a mind-link like I usually did.

*'Darius, shift into your wolf,'* I ordered, holding my gaze constant on his face.

Darius seemed almost hypnotized when he tilted his head at me and completely zoned out. In the span of five seconds, I heard the sound of his bones snapping and then clicking back into place. As this happened, his body started to glow so brightly that I was eventually forced to close my eyes.

Although Darius didn't look like he was in pain, I couldn't help but feel like he was. And it made me feel really bad.

When I opened my eyes again, a black wolf the size of two stories stood before me, drooling and wagging his tail excitedly back and forth in the air.

*Oh my goodness.*

My mouth dropped open.

"H-how is he so big? Is he going to grow anymore?" I gasped, gawking at the massive size of my son, who had been only thirty-four inches several seconds ago.

At this point, if Darius grew any taller, I would look like an ant to him. And he could probably blow me over by breathing in my direction.

"His wolf has already grown to full potential and probably won't grow any more than a few inches in the future," Eros said, not too surprised at the sight before him.

"But how is that possible?" I murmured.

"That's just how Sentinel wolves are. They usually grow to their full height within the first few months they are born. This is the reason why they are trained at such a young age and are able to guard and fight for their pack."

Once I was over the shock of Darius in his wolf form, I used the mind-link to make the rest of the babies shift.

"What are they going to do in their wolf forms?" I asked Eros, who was leading the whole group outside to an area that was fenced. I didn't really see the purpose of the fence because the babies were almost three times its height. If they wanted to get out, they could just step over the fence and run.

"It'd be good to let them wrestle and fight each other in this form, that way they could get used to being one with their wolf."

I nodded my head and watched as the babies all started to wrestle and spar with one another. Though I tried to keep track of which baby was which, I soon lost count when they all became balls of black, running and chasing each other.

Every time one of them fell over or jumped, I felt the earth shift beneath my feet, as if there were an earthquake.

So, to keep myself from falling over, I took a seat on the grass and watched them wrestle each other, letting the breeze brush through my hair and chill my flushed cheeks.

"Come have a seat, Eros," I called, patting the grass next to me with a smile on my face.

Eros walked over to me and sat down before wrapping his arm around my shoulder and pulling my weary body against his heated one.

I sighed under my breath and leaned my weight into him, thinking of what our future might look like.

. . .

It was almost five in the morning when my phone suddenly vibrated on the nightstand. I could barely open my eyes. My body felt like lead, and I didn't want to move a single inch.

*Who in the world is messed up enough to call someone at this time?!*

Grumbling to myself, I blinked away the fog in my vision and looked over at the nine cribs to see that the babies were still asleep and Eros was already out of bed. Though I wanted to ignore the call, I didn't.

I grabbed the phone off the nightstand and swiped to answer before I could even take a look at the caller ID.

This happened to be mistake number one, because when I put the phone against the side of my face, a very, very familiar voice seeped from the speaker and into my ear.

171

"Hello? Annie? It's me," she said, as if she were expecting me to just recognize her voice after so many years of separation. But sadly, I recognized her just from the first intake of air, from the rasp that bordered a cough when she spoke the letter H.

It was my birth mother, the woman who I'd been trying to ignore for over twenty-five years, the only woman who continued to call me Annie, regardless of the fact that I had changed my name a long time ago. Her voice was the same as what I'd remembered. Low and gravelly from the long years of smoking cheap cigarettes and drinking grocery store beer.

"Hello?" she said.

"What do you want, Janet? You haven't contacted me since I was adopted. Why are you looking for me now?" I asked, failing to cover up the bitterness that tainted my voice and layered it thickly with hate and anger.

I started calling her Janet after the first year of adoption and didn't want to call her "mom" anymore because she'd left that title behind her years ago when she abandoned me for her abusive ex-boyfriend.

"I…" she trailed off, probably taken aback by my hostility. "I just want to know how you're doing, and let you know that I'm getting married next month."

"So what?" I replied, not really in the mood to play catch up with her.

"I want to invite you to my wedding," she continued, biting back a cough.

"I'm not going. And tell me the real reason why you're calling me, because I know that's not all."

"Annie!" she exclaimed before breaking into a coughing fit.

I didn't say another word. Instead, I waited for the moment when she would crack and get down to the real reason why she'd called me at five in the morning and disrupted my sleep. As the first minute ticked by with just the sound of her coughing, I tried to go through the list of people who had my number and knew her. But I could only think of two names.

Bennet and Abeline.

They knew that I didn't want anything to do with my mother, so I was sure that they probably didn't give her my number. But then, who did it? Who went against my wishes and did this?

"Who gave you my number?" I asked, too impatient to wait any second longer.

"I saw Katelyn the other day, and she gave me your number. She'd told me you were married and doing really well."

*Katelyn, that bitch,* I thought, grounding my teeth together.

"Alright, if this is all you want to say then I am going to hang up. Oh, and by the way, congratulations on your third marriage."

"Wait! I… Let's meet up and talk, Emira," she said quickly.

"No. I don't have the time or the energy," I declined without a second thought.

"I know you're mad at me. But please. Just once. I promise I won't bother you ever again," she begged, making me wonder why she was so desperate.

Why would she bother contacting a daughter she'd abandoned for over two decades? What could her ulterior motive be?

I closed my eyes and breathed deeply, trying to calm my billowing anger. "At least tell me what you want from me."

"It's a long story. I'll tell you when we meet up," she said mysteriously.

Janet sounded suspicious, and I didn't trust her. Not now, not ever. She'd lost any trust I had in her when she broke her promise. But if I didn't meet with her, she was going to keep bothering me until I did, just like all those relatives she'd stalked and harassed to lend her money for her addictions. Since I knew of her psycho capabilities, I'd rather just meet with her and get it over with than let her find the pack house and stalk me here.

*I don't want her anywhere near my babies.*

After a very long pause to think, I said, "I'll decide on the meet up spot."

"That's fine with me, Annie," she sighed, as if relieved.

"Stop calling me Annie. I know that you know about my name change," I said, grinding the words out through the cracks of my teeth.

"No matter what you change your name to, you'll always be Annie to me," she said, obviously refusing to refer to me by my new name.

"Whatever. I'll text you the address. You come here, and we'll talk like you want." I quickly ended the call before she could get another word in.

"What's wrong?" Eros asked, coming into the room all dressed and ready to go.

"Janet just called," I grumbled, extremely grouchy now that I was awake.

Since Eros knew every single thing about me, I didn't really have to explain anything to him, which was kind of nice.

"What did she want?" he asked, grabbing some diapers to start the tedious task of changing the babies.

"She wants to meet up and 'talk.' But I have a feeling that she wants something more than just that," I said, telling him what I really thought. "And I agreed to meet up with her because I didn't want her to keep bothering us. You know how crazy she is."

Eros nodded his head.

"And she's being so suspicious that I keep thinking something's up! Do you think I should just tell her that I'm not going? That I changed my mind?" I asked, getting out of bed to help Eros change the babies' diapers.

"Even if something is up, the Gammas will be able to take care of it. You have to trust them, Emira." Eros pressed a kiss on Silas' sleeping face.

"I guess I'll just go and see what she wants."

Though I kept saying that I didn't want to go, I kind of did. I just wanted to ask her the questions that had bothered me all these years, ask her why she never came for me like she'd promised.

As of this moment, I wanted closure, even if it meant that I would have to permanently cut her out of my life from now on.

. . .

I'd texted Janet the address of a local café in town and said that if she didn't make it, I wasn't going to bother going out of my way to clear my schedule again. She'd texted back that she would make it and that she was driving all the way from my hometown to here, so she'd be here by Thursday afternoon. Though I had the babies training and my own exercise routine keeping me busy, I was still really anxious and stressed out about seeing her again.

In the past, I'd only caught glimpses of her running through the grocery store or filling her car with gas at the gas station. Seeing her face to face was a completely different matter.

Just the thought of sitting in her presence made me feel like I was being reverted back into that twelve-year-old who was being sent away to live with a new family, who had been forsaken because I was a nuisance and the cause of all of my mother's failed relationships.

Although I knew that it wasn't my fault, I couldn't stop myself from believing I was the problem. And it was very hard to change this belief because it'd been with me since I was little.

I breathed out a deep sigh and gripped my handbag, feeling reassured when the cold gun laying inside bit against my fingertips. Since this was a pretty risky situation I was in, Eros decided to give me one of the guns filled with Ziron-e, just in case things get out of hand and the Hunters showed up. Though we both trusted that the Gammas would keep me safe, the gun was there to give me comfort and peace of mind.

I just hoped that nothing happened, because I knew my aim was still not very good. If I were lucky, I'd hit a Hunter, but if I were not lucky, I'd hit a Gamma.

As the car turned into the parking lot of the little café and stopped, I thanked the Gammas, opened the door, and got out, feeling the extremely cold breeze chill my entire body. Today happened to be a lot colder than yesterday. The clouds were covering the gray skies and there was no sun present.

This weather completely mimicked how I felt about meeting with my birth mother for the first time in twenty-six years.

I took a deep breath and stepped into the café, looking around the small shop until I found Janet sitting by one of the booths by the window.

"Annie! You look so good... and young!" Janet praised as soon as I walked over.

She was early today, for once. In the past, she had always been late to everything by over thirty minutes to an hour. Even a rare visit to the doctors had to be rescheduled several times because she was always late to the appointment.

Before I came, I was really considering showing up a little later because of her habits. But I was glad I didn't, because she'd managed to surprise me this time.

"Thank you," I replied curtly, letting my vision sweep over her sitting form as I took a seat across from her.

Although all her features were the same as it had been years ago, indicating that she hadn't gotten the rhinoplasty she always wanted, she had aged a lot.

Her wrinkles were a lot more prominent and her skin seemed quite sallow, even though she'd applied makeup to cover up her imperfections. The grey roots of her blonde hair were showing by over two inches and her cheeks were completely hollow, showing the state of health she was really in.

By looking at her like this, I estimated that she was probably less than ninety pounds.

"I didn't know what you'd like so I got you a green tea. It's healthy for you and helps you lo—" she said, pushing the white cup in my direction.

"Let's make this quick, Janet," I said, before my patience could run out.

She made a face when I called her "Janet," but didn't object.

"I… I need some help," she said, pausing for some time to come up with the right words.

"With what? Cigarettes, alcohol, or… drugs?" I asked, staring her dead in the eye.

Embarrassment colored her face.

"No. I… I need some money," she said. "Ben, my fiancé, got in a fight last week and busted someone's head open with a crowbar. They filed a criminal charge and had him put in jail. I used all our retirement money to get him out, but now he has to pay for their hospital charges and lawyer fees."

I pinched my brow, wondering why I was still sitting here in the seat letting her talk.

"How much?" I asked.

"A little over fifty-nine grand. The man had to get brain surgery because of the injury." She shakily grabbed her cup of coffee and took a slow sip.

"Fifty-nine grand?!" I exclaimed, outraged that she would even ask this of me. "Do I look like a money tree to you? Where do you think I'm going to get that kind of money?"

"I heard that your husband is a CEO—" she said, probably not even feeling an ounce of shame or remorse for her words.

"Katelyn told you that?" I said calmly.

She nodded her head.

"What makes you think that I would take my husband's money to help your fiancé? No. I'm not going to. You're better off selling yourself on the streets," I bit out, swallowing the curse words that wanted to come up.

Even if I were to give all of Eros' money to charity, I would never give her a single dollar. *I won't. I refuse to.*

"Is that how you talk to your mother?" she scolded, frowning deeply at me, as if she were still a mother figure to me.

"What kind of mother do you consider yourself, Janet? You abandoned me when I was twelve and never came back for me like you said you would. It's been twenty-six years. Twenty-six years since you've said a single word to me! And now you're asking me to hand over fifty-nine thousand dollars! You're insane if you think I will."

"I'm sorry, Annie, but I've been very busy," she said, trying to come up with an excuse that didn't really cut it.

"For twenty-six years?" I mocked, looking up at the ceiling to stop the tears from falling and trying to cover up the fact that she still affected me. "Don't you know how ridiculous you sound saying that?"

"I'm sorry. I-I just… I forgot. I was having a hard time when I went through that first divorce and lost everything," she babbled, wracking her brain for a good excuse.

I chuckled bitterly under my breath.

"I knew you wouldn't change. What made me think that you would?" I said angrily to myself.

It went quiet between us as I wiped at my tears with a napkin on the table, trying to calm myself before I said something else to her.

"Just help me out, Annie. I really need the money. If we don't have it, Ben will have to go to jail again and our wedding will have to be called off.

Don't you want me to be happy?" She looked at me with a pitiful expression on her face. But I laughed at her words.

"No. I don't. I want you to live as miserable as I had," I said.

"Please, An—Emira. Please. You're my last chance. The bank won't loan me anymore money and I've already borrowed from all of my relatives and friends. Please," she begged pathetically, reaching out to grab my hand, but I pulled away from her as if she were a poisonous disease. "I'll never bother you again. I promise. After this, I will disappear from your world. Permanently."

My mouth clicked shut.

I didn't know what I was even looking for when I came to meet her, but it sure wasn't this.

"You're lying, Janet. I've heard you use this line so many times on your friends and family that I'm just tired of hearing it. My answer is no, and it will remain that way. Go find someone else to exploit." I picked up my bag and stood, turning away from her before the tears could fall from my eyes.

"And don't bother calling me again. Because you'll really regret it," I said, opening my bag just enough for her to see the gun laying inside.

She gasped and started to cough uncontrollably.

As I walked out of the door, I thought that maybe this was the conclusion I needed, even though she didn't answer very much about why she'd never came for me. But I didn't really need to know anymore.

When I successfully left the shop and got back into the car, I realized that I was just being extra paranoid. Nothing had happened like I'd thought, and the gun I had in my purse laid in there unused.

Well, it was always better to be safe than sorry.

# CHAPTER 18

Patting around on Eros' side of the bed, my brows wrinkled. I opened my eyes to stare at the cold and empty spot. Checking to see if Eros was back in bed was something that I'd been doing this whole entire month. But no matter how many times I woke myself in the middle of the night to check on him and the babies, it was only me sleeping in the bed.

Ever since I had that talk with my mother, I didn't have the chance to see or converse with Eros. He'd completely disappeared for days on end, and he didn't show up to train with the babies, either. Instead, Lia and one of the Gammas were there in his place. Though there were times that I could feel him nearby, I never caught a glimpse of him. It was like he was avoiding me, and that stressed me out because my mind kept supplying me with images of him going somewhere nice with a pretty young woman, having dinner and chatting it up. Even though I knew this wasn't true, the thoughts could not be quelled. Instead, it escalated. And I became scared of the implications, but I was too afraid to ask him about it.

*Eros is probably busy with something important. Stop scaring yourself,* I tried to convince myself.

I rolled over and glanced at the clock to notice that it was already seven. Though I tried to go back to sleep, my mind was already whirling with unnecessary thoughts, so I ended up getting out of bed to check on the babies, who were still sleeping soundly.

Ever since their training started, they'd gone back to normal and slept a lot more than they used to. All of them were a lot happier and didn't fight aggressively with each other anymore. And life had become a lot easier than it was before, making me so relieved because of those changes.

Other than that, they've also started talking a lot more now, more so in real life than in my mind. Though most of it were just simple words like "mama," "dada," "baba," and so on, it was a very beautiful process I enjoyed seeing on a daily basis.

When I finished brushing my teeth and came out of the bathroom, I gave all of the babies a morning kiss and got them changed to go eat in the dining hall today.

As the ten of us entered, I spotted a free table and ushered the babies to their seat. I commanded them to stay put before I headed into the kitchen to get their big platters of meat from the enormous cold vault stationed on the far end.

I quickly opened the door to the cold vault and grabbed the big platters of meat and vegetables I'd prepared yesterday night. When the babies were sleeping, I'd cut all the meat into tinier chunks to eliminate their chances of choking and added the seasoning. Now that everything was left to sit the entire night, it was ready to be cooked.

I grabbed a pan from the cabinet and put some oil in before dumping the mixture in to slightly sear the surface but not cook it completely. Then, I quickly dumped the meat out on a giant platter filled with green lettuce, tomatoes, and cucumber. I repeated this process multiple times for each child before scooping a giant heaping of rice on to the side of the plate. It didn't take me any more than fifteen minutes to get everything together.

After that, I put all the platters on the food cart, grabbed my leftovers from yesterday, and pushed the cart out to the babies.

"How are you doing, Emi?" Rora asked excitedly, helping me place the plates down in front of each baby.

As soon as the plate was placed in front of them, they all started to dig in to their food with extreme enthusiasm.

"Not very good," I answered, rubbing my eyes as I thought about the loneliness I'd been feeling due to a whole month of not seeing Eros. And really, it had been a whole month since that last time he'd come back into the room to shower and get some clothes.

I didn't know what he was busy with but it was really giving me anxiety just thinking of the things he could be doing.

"Why? What's wrong?" Rora asked as Lia brought her tray of food over to the table and took a seat across from us.

"It's nothing big, but Eros has been gone the whole night for the last month or so, and it's really bothering me," I admitted.

A couple of days ago, I'd asked some of the pack members, who usually trained with Eros, what time they got home, and all of them answered that they were home by ten. Everyday.

This only meant that Eros wasn't training with the pack throughout the night. But if that was the case, then what had he been doing this whole month?

"Maybe Alpha Eros' was busy doing something…" Rora comforted.

"Or someone," Lia added before quickly covering her mouth and giving me a wide-eyed look that seemed kind of apologetic.

"What?!" I screeched, clenching my legs to keep myself from jumping out of my seat.

"I'm joking, Emi!" Lia exclaimed.

"That's a bad joke, Lia!" Rora cried, staring at Lia with a disapproving look.

"Sorry! I didn't mean to say that. It just came out all of a sudden," Lia said, digging into her rice and beans. "But really, Alpha Eros would never do anything like that. Everyone here knows he only has eyes for you."

"I know he won't. I just want to know what he's been doing and when he's done doing it. That way he can come back to me and the babies," I murmured, picking at my chicken and cheese enchilada leftovers.

"I think he will talk to you about it soon." Rora bit into her club sandwich full of bacon and partially cooked meat.

"If you're so worried about it, why don't you go ask him?" Lia suggested.

"I can't. I don't even see him anymore," I replied, popping a bit of chicken into my mouth.

After chewing a bite of her steak and egg omelet and swallowing, Lia said, "Emi! If he doesn't come to you, then you go find him and ask him. It's as easy as that."

"Right! Why didn't I think of that?" I exclaimed.

Lia shook her head at me, causing her long blonde hair to flutter around her head and reveal the red love bites all across her neck.

My mouth fell open into an O.

"What's with that face?" she asked, raising a brow.

"Your neck," Rora said, pointing her index finger at Lia, who was quick to cover the hickeys back up with her hair.

"Is it that noticeable?" Lia nervously smoothed her hair down.

"Yes," I said.

"Lia! You know you shouldn't be doing that with anybody except for your mate!" Rora whispered lowly, even though there was literally no one in the pack house except for us.

"How do you know it's not her mate who did that?" I raised a brow.

"Is he your mate, Lia?" Rora asked, though her expression and tone didn't quite sound like she was asking a question.

Lia shook her head.

As I thought of who could have possibly been getting down with Lia, an image of her and Gamma Qian came into my mind.

The other day when the babies were training with Gamma Qian, Lia had tagged along with me to keep me busy. While I was exercising on the course, I thought I'd seen Gamma Qian hold Lia's hand. But since it such a fast glimpse, I thought that I'd imagine it, because after I asked Lia, she denied it.

"Is it Gamma Qian?" I whispered.

Rora nodded her head for Lia, who remained quiet.

"It's not something serious. We're just fooling around," Lia said nonchalantly, keeping her eyes on her food.

"You know things like this don't end well, Lia. Don't let it get too out of hand. Because one of these days, Gamma Qian's mate is going to show up and you'll be left behind," Rora warned, her words full of wisdom.

I grimaced, feeling really bad for Lia all of a sudden.

Even if she loved Gamma Qian, it might not work out in the long run, because they were not soulmates. And it was believed that they would not be blessed by the Moon Gods if they were to mate. But I was sure that there were people who had gone against this rule and mated with someone who wasn't their true mate. It just made it really bad for their true mates, who had probably been waiting for them for hundreds of years, like Eros had waited for me.

If I had married some other guy, he would have been forced to remain single forever. And though Eros could find someone else, I didn't think he would.

. . .

When the babies and I were done eating, I sent them off to Granny Ada and went back to the room to quickly change and go find Eros. But as I opened the door and looked in, Eros was standing in the bathroom washing his hands and looking extremely weary. His clothes were dirty. There were stains all over his jeans and his shoes, while his hair and hands were covered in dust and dirt.

If he had been going out and having a good time, he wouldn't be looking like this... like he'd been rolling around on the ground for over two hours after falling into the river and drying out in the sun.

"Hi," he greeted, picking up a pair of stained gloves from the sink to stuff into his pockets.

Before he could leave the bathroom, I said, "Eros, is there something I should know?"

"Hm?" He turned his head to me with a questioning look on his tired face.

"Where have you been this whole month?" I asked, putting my hand on my hips to try to intimidate him while interrogating him at the same time.

I was on the verge of exploding on him like an erupting volcano, but after seeing the condition he was in, I changed my mind.

"It's a surprise. Just a little longer and you'll see what I've been working on," he said, grinning impishly at me with twinkling blue eyes.

Eros was obviously trying to use his good looks to seduce me into dropping the subject. And it was working.

*Damn it. I can never hold myself together whenever he looks at me like that.*

"I hope it's a good surprise," I said, glancing at him from the corner of my eye.

"It is. I think you will love it," he said, still smiling at me.

"I'll take your word for it, Eros." I sighed, deciding to drop the topic and move on.

"I haven't had the chance to ask you this, but how did that talk go with your mother?" Eros asked, grabbing some clean clothes from his closet.

"Not very good. She wanted me to give her fifty-nine thousand dollars to help pay for her fiancé's problems. I don't have that much money so I told her no and left," I admitted, frowning in remembrance of the conversation.

"If you want to help her, you can," he said, reaching out to comfort me before pulling back because of how dirty he was.

I shook my head. "I'm not going to use your hard-earned money on someone like her. If we give her money once, she'll just keep coming back for more. She's the type of person to never know when it's enough."

I knew this from experience, prior to my adoption.

Everyone she befriended always started out feeling sorry for her, so they always fell for her pitiful stories and let her borrow their money. From one hundred to several thousands, they never realized that she wasn't going to return their money, that she'd avoid them once she had the dollar bills in her hands.

Janet had scammed so many people in the course of the twelve years I'd lived with her that I knew exactly what her lines would be when she found herself a prey. First she'd make light conversation and slowly build a relationship with that person, preying off of their emotions until they were unable to refuse anything she wanted.

She manipulated them and she was smart about it, too. Every time she borrowed money, she made sure never to leave any evidence behind that could incriminate her when they tried to sue her to get their money back.

Throughout my childhood, I could only remember her going to jail briefly for a couple of months because she'd borrowed money from a relative and refused to pay it back. From then on, she'd devised a strategy to keep herself from going back in there. And it has worked to this day.

Janet was probably "busy" building relationships with all these people that she'd never had the time to come back for me.

I was glad that I hadn't heard from her ever since I changed my number.

*Thank goodness.*

. . .

The weather was starting to become a lot warmer now that spring was here. The grass had become greener, the flowers had budded, and the birds were chirping away in a merry tune. Though the weather was beautiful and the breeze was nice, I could feel the tension in the air and the anxiety in the pack.

War was coming. Very, very soon.

Ever since the government had declared war over a week ago, Eros and the pack members were all training from day to night, hoping to be ready enough before the first battle broke out and hoping to have an advantage over the Hunters and the human army.

Though the supernaturals were a lot stronger, there were a whole lot more humans. If one human were to die, many more would take his or her place.

I heard from Eros that the Hunters and the human army had gathered together in a big camp in the west side of the states, while the vampires, animal shifters, and other supernaturals collected in our area and towards the east of our pack.

Now that everyone had gathered into one area, Eros was appointed with training and preparing more people for this war. I could tell that he was becoming more and more stressed as the days passed. But he'd never taken any of it out on me. He was still calm and full of love for me and the babies, and I didn't think that would ever change.

"Mama. I want to go see papa," Ace said, grabbing a hold of my hand and yanking me to follow him. If I hadn't clenched all the muscles in my body, I would have fallen on my face because of the strength and force coming from Ace's little hands.

"Don't pull me, Ace," I said. "You know I'm not as strong as you."

"Okay, mama. Can we go now?" Ace asked, looking at me with puppy dog eyes and his bottom lip sticking out. I honestly didn't know where he learned that from but I found it very hard to say no to him.

*He's just too darn cute to deny.*

"We'll go after everyone has had the chance to use the toilet," I said, kissing his chubby cheeks and pointing him to the bathroom.

As they all took turns to go get their business done, I took a seat on the bed and thought about how fast the last four months had passed. The babies went from talking gibberish to speaking in full sentences now, from wearing diapers to going to the bathroom by themselves, from looking like little babies to looking like four-year-old toddlers. It was crazy how fast they were growing. Although I wished they could stay small forever, that was just wishful thinking.

"We're done, mama," Silas said.

"Did you wash your hands?" I asked them all.

"Noah didn't want to wash his hands so I made him do it," Kyra said, grinning with a really proud expression on her face.

When I saw the water spots all over Noah's shirt. I sighed under my breath. "You didn't bully him did you?"

"No. I was very nice when I put him on the sink," she responded quickly, glancing anywhere but at me.

"He only needed his hands washed, not his entire body," I said, taking a new shirt from the drawer for Noah to change into.

"I'm sorry," she replied, like she always did when she got in trouble.

"Are you going to do it again?" I asked, even though I knew that she would.

She shook her little head of black hair vigorously and said, "No, mama. I won't do it again."

"Alright. I'll believe you this time," I said, pulling off Noah's wet shirt to put on a short sleeve shirt.

Once everyone was done putting on their shoes, we walked our way to the training grounds. Since I hadn't ever been out there before, I had to enlist Rora's help because I didn't want us to get lost while we were on our way.

"We're ready to go," I said, meeting up with Rora by the front door before getting all the kids into the van.

Since the training grounds had been remodeled to accommodate more people, it was now a little farther from the pack house. So we had to take a van and drive almost fifteen minutes to the east before we got there.

As we parked the car, I saw a line of warriors marching around the area and monitoring everything to make sure there were no intruders.

The only reason I felt so safe now was because of the warriors. They literally walked all the way around the border between the defense line and the attack line almost twenty minutes in front of the packhouse all day, every day. If there were anyone trying to cross the boundaries with bad intentions, the warriors would have taken care of them in less than a second. I was extremely confident in that, because I'd seen it with my own two eyes.

"Have you talked to Lia recently?" Rora asked, opening the back door to let the kids out.

"No, I haven't seen her in a while now. Have you?" I got out of the passenger side and grabbed the small sack of snacks out from the back of the van.

Rora shook her head. "I think she's having a falling out with Gamma Qian."

"Really? What happened?" I asked, surprised that they were having problems already.

"He met his true mate a week ago when Alpha Ara's old pack joined ours. I heard him say that she's from Hunan just like him," Rora said.

"Holy crap. That was so quick!" I exclaimed, feeling even worse for Lia.

Though she'd said that what was going on between them wasn't serious, I had a feeling it *was* serious, because the way she looked at him mirrored the way I looked at Eros. Lia loved Gamma Qian. There was no way that she didn't.

"Did they break up?" I asked, not really sure if they were even dating to begin with.

"I don't know. But Lia has been acting strange lately. Really sad and depressed."

I grimaced.

After greeting the warriors at the front of the guarded gates, I led the babies through with Rora in tow. As my eyes swept over the entire training ground, I was in awe. What was in front of me was magnificent. Something I had never seen before in my life.

There were people sparring so fast that they became blurs to me, while others were going through scary training courses adapted for more advanced warriors.

The one course that caught my attention the most was the shooting course surrounded by giant walls of glass. It was nothing like the shooting range I'd been to with Rora and Lia. Instead of shooting at targets, whoever entered the course became the target and had to dodge the bullets at various speeds and various forms.

Just looking at the entire area made me realize that I could never be of any help in the war. I was better off staying in the back and making sure I stayed safe with the babies. Because, with my amateur skills, I'd get killed off faster than I could blink once.

"Do you see Eros?" I asked Rora.

I wasn't able to spot him because of the big crowds of people training everywhere. If I were to go looking around, it'd probably take me more than thirty minutes. And I didn't want to mind-link Eros so that he could come get me because I wanted to surprise him.

Rora raised her head into the air and breathed in deeply before she pointed me towards the makeshift dining area, which was just basically a giant gray canopy tied to metal bars with several tables and chairs lined underneath it.

I squinted and finally saw Eros several yards away. He was standing next to two very tall males. One male had dark blonde hair with golden eyes while the other looked very serious and had pale blue eyes and sunny blonde hair. Though both were extremely good looking in a god-like way, I had to say that Eros was the handsomest to me.

Eros glanced at me from the corner of his eye, and I immediately realized that I forgot to put the mental barrier up around my thoughts again.

*Damn it.*

The babies and I quickly made our way over to him, dodging the courses and sparring pairs.

# CHAPTER 19

"This is Alpha Xavier Thaeos, the Southern Cardinal Alpha, and Alpha Deimos Ventrie, the Northern Cardinal Alpha," Eros introduced, gesturing towards the citrine-eyed Alpha first before gesturing at the blue-eyed male. "And this is my mate, Emira and our pups, Silas, Noah, Nicholas, Darius, Cillian, Kyra, Wren, Erik, and Ace."

"It's a pleasure to meet you," I said politely, adding to my words with a picture-perfect smile.

"The pleasure is all ours," Alpha Xavier said, grinning down at me before turning to look at the trail of nine kids behind me.

"That's quite a few you have there," Alpha Deimos said, his face cold like a shield of thick ice.

After hearing his words, I was given the feeling of déjà vu because Gemini, his mate, had said the exact same thing when she counted my babies while they were still in my belly.

"Gemini said the same thing," I pointed out, wondering if they were on better terms now.

"Did she?" Alpha Deimos stated more than asked.

From his facial expression, I didn't know if he was happy or not.

Although I found myself kind of scared by both Alpha Xavier and Alpha Deimos because of the power and authority that leeched off them in waves, I was more scared of Alpha Deimos.

His facial expression remained rather bland but that hint of seriousness at the tip of his brows made him look very scary, kind of like a stern father figure every child was afraid to cross.

"Don't mind this block of ice. He's always like that," Alpha Xavier joked, grabbing a bottle of water for both him and Alpha Deimos. "We'll leave you two to talk."

Once the two were out of sight, I turned to Eros and asked, "Aren't you going to ask me why we're here?"

"Did you come to see me?" he asked, handing me a water bottle from the cooler on his left as all the kids surrounded him in a circle.

"Yes. We all wanted to surprise you," I said as Kyra latched herself onto Eros' leg.

"I wanted to come and see you, papa!" Kyra cried. "Did you miss me and mama?"

Eros patted her head lovingly and picked her up into his arms, kissing the top of her brow with a warm smile on his lips.

"Yes, I did," he said. "I missed you all very much."

"We miss you, too," the babies replied in unison, acting like they were all twins, for once.

"Alright, get off of your papa and sit down. He's tired enough as it is," I said, ushering them into their chairs and handing them their beef jerky snacks to get them to sit still for a bit.

Eros took a seat in one of the chairs next to me and chugged down a whole bottle of water before inhaling and exhaling deeply.

Since the day was rather warm, he was sweating quite a bit, probably because of the strenuous training he'd been doing since three in the morning.

If it were me in his position, I'd probably be buried six feet deep already, so I wasn't going to try.

"Beef jerky?" I asked, holding out a stick of jerky for him.

Eros shook his head.

I shrugged my shoulders and took a bite out of the stick before thinking to myself that it was a little too spicy for my tastes, probably because I wasn't too good at eating spicy foods so I felt like it was more spicier than it actually was.

"Do you want to see the surprise?" Eros asked suddenly.

"You're ready to show me it?" I cocked my head to the side and looked at Eros.

It had been months now since Eros started on his little surprise, and now that he was willing to show me it, I was a little nervous and excited at the same time.

Eros nodded and said, "Come on. I'll take you to see it."

"You want to show me it… now? What about the training?" I grabbed his forearm and tried to stop him.

"I'll ask Xavier to take over for me. Give me a second." Eros pressed a kiss on my temple before he turned to go find Alpha Xavier.

"I'll load the kids into the van then," I called after him.

Almost immediately after he disappeared, I had all the babies pick up their jerky and head back out to the van.

"Where are we going, mama?" Erik asked, licking his mouth to get rid of the little flakes of pepper sticking on his lips. Then, he shoved the whole stick in his mouth and started chewing really fast.

"Don't do that, Erik. You're going to choke," I said, handing him a water bottle. "Your papa's going to take us somewhere. Let's go back to the van and wait for him."

"Can I have another beef jerky stick?" he asked, licking his lips again, as if he were reminiscing the taste.

I sighed and handed him another stick, looking over his rounded body and wondering if I should change his meals to make it a little more healthier. But then again, how do I make meat more healthy? Erik just liked to eat too much, and I couldn't really blame him for that.

"Really?! Hurray!" Kyra shouted, bumping into Wren when she hurriedly jumped out of her seat. "Sorry, Wren."

Wren glanced at Kyra from the corner of her eyes but didn't say anything, opting to take another bite of her jerky as she walked over to me.

Out of all the babies, I'd have to say that Wren was the most mellow and chill. Albeit Silas was also pretty calm and quiet, he didn't give me that Wednesday vibe like Wren did. She was just in a class of her own.

As for Kyra, she was very spunky and outgoing. She was also very "handsy" and loved to talk. A lot. If she wasn't talking about her toys or making up stories about them, she was talking about what she saw on TV or in the pack house.

Cillian was pretty much a crybaby. He cried about everything and was not very good at sharing toys compared to Erik, who was fine with letting everyone have his toys, as long as they shared their food with him. Erik liked to eat way too much and was always picking food off the other siblings' plates.

As for Noah, he was really energetic. He could run around the whole pack house and still be up for more running. He lasted the longest during training with the Gammas. Yet whenever he fought with Kyra, he was always the one to lose. Sadly.

When it came to Ace, he was the one who liked to joke and play tricks on the others. He was always finding ways to make Cillian cry and he could never stay in one spot for very long.

Though all the babies looked like copies of their father, Nicholas was the only one to look the most and act the most like Eros. He was pretty calm and caring. Even though Ace played tricks on him, he was always one step ahead and was always able to keep himself from becoming the victim. He was very smart.

And last but not least, there was Darius. He was the most stubborn and opinionated compared to the rest of his siblings. Though he could be as hardheaded as a bull, he was also very righteous and stood up for those being picked on, like Cillian for instance. He was also the one to tattle tale the most on Ace.

Now that I thought about each of their traits, I couldn't help but wonder if they would remain this way or change in the future.

"Get in the van, guys," I said, fastening Cillian in his car seat before helping the rest of them into their spots.

As I got in the passenger side and closed the door, Eros opened the driver side door and got in. He closed the door and fastened his seat belt before turning to me with a wide smile on his face. He said, "Ready to see the surprise?"

"I am." I nodded and smiled back at him.

Eros ended up driving us back to the pack house before turning north and keeping on the road for another five minutes. When we got to the destination, he made me close my eyes and cover them with my hands, which only added to the mysteriousness of the situation. Though I was tempted to peek, I decided not to ruin the surprise.

Eros led me out of the van while I had both of my hands on my face, staring at the inside of my eyelids.

"Open your eyes, Emira," he said against my ear.

As soon as I opened my eyes and looked at the scenery before me, I was almost brought to tears. I couldn't process what this meant, couldn't process that this was the surprise Eros had been working on for so long.

"What is this, Eros?" I said shakily, holding my hand over my mouth in complete shock.

I couldn't believe what I was seeing.

"It's our house," he said.

"This isn't a house, Eros! It's a freaking mansion!" I exclaimed, unable to stop the waterworks from wetting my entire face in a matter of seconds. "Did you do this all by yourself?"

Standing before us in its mighty glory was a beautiful home that was a mixture of modern and traditional, along with a giant pool in the front, filled with beautiful clear and blue water. It stood two stories tall, had a set of red cedar doors, and was layered with white brick all the way around. The windows were Palladian style and there were balconies on the top floor.

"It took me a while but it's finally done now. Do you like it?" he asked, searching my eyes for the answer.

I nodded repeatedly before croaking, "I love it!"

Out of all the things that Eros could have gotten me, I never could have imagined that it would be this. Not in a million years.

"Was this what you'd been working on every night?" I asked, letting Eros wipe all the tears off my face with the pads of his fingers.

Eros hummed a response, and I was crying even harder.

While the kids were running gleefully around on the lawn and staring at the pool in complete awe and happiness, I was sobbing my heart out on Eros' shoulder, unable to do anything other than hold on to him and cry.

"Why didn't you say anything? I could have helped you," I said, finally calming myself enough to talk.

I couldn't believe that he had forgone sleep and rest to build our family a house.

"I wanted to surprise you and the pups," he said, making a move to kiss me but I quickly retreated out of his arms and stood a foot away from him.

I said, "Don't kiss me, Eros! I have snot all over my face. I'm disgusting right now."

"You're not disgusting," he reassured, pulling me back into his arms to press a firm kiss on the corner of my mouth.

"Let's go inside. I want to see what it looks like," I said, grabbing a hold of his warm hand.

"Mama! Is this our new house?" Kyra asked, skipping up to us with sparkling blue eyes.

I smiled down at her and said, "Yes, it is. Your papa built us this house."

"Yay! We have a new house!" Noah screamed, running around the tree at the front of the house while all the other kids laughed.

"Here," Eros said, handing me the key to our new home.

After telling the kids to follow us, I took the key from him and led them up the steps and to the door. With a shaking hand, I stuck the key in the lock and opened the door to peer inside of the marvelous home.

My breath stuck in my throat.

The interior was even more beautiful than the exterior. Everything looked so clean and fancy. The walls were a beautiful creamy light gray color with white intricate wall trims on the bottom, the dark wood flooring was shining in the light, and there was no carpet at all, which I loved. Because I was not a fan of carpet since it was so hard to clean and dry, unlike wood. Having wood or marble flooring also helped lessen the dirt and pollen inside the house.

"You furnished everything?" I gasped, trailing my fingers on the nice gray sofa before touching the glass table in the center of the living room.

"If you don't like it, we can always change it," he said nonchalantly.

"No. I love it! But there's something really familiar about it. It's giving me déjà vu," I said, unable to put my finger on it.

Eros smiled.

"I based it off of your dream home when you were in high school," he explained, stepping over the beige rug to show me the shelf on the wall where he'd assembled pictures of me, him, and the babies.

"You did!" I exclaimed.

Back when I was still in high school, I'd created a collage of my dream house during my home economics class. As I looked at everything in the house, there were definitely some items I'd put into the collage that were now a part of our home.

"You're making me cry too much today," I murmured, falling into his embrace as tears formed again.

"Thank you, Eros." I sniffled.

"Papa can I pick a room? I want the room upstairs!" Noah called from the stairs.

"I want a room upstairs, too!" Cillian said.

"Me too!" Ace screamed from the other side of the room.

"Me too! Me too!" Kyra said repeatedly.

I turned to little Wren who was sitting on the couch with her head on her hand, looking like she was asleep, and asked, "What about you, Wren? What room do you want?"

"I don't care—no, I do care. I want a room far away from Kyra," she said.

Kyra harrumphed and screamed, "I don't want a room next to Wren, either!"

"Girls, stop fighting," I said, shaking my head at them.

At this moment, I could already imagine what they would be like in their teenage years.

*Havoc will be wreaked and chaos will ensue.*

This was my imminent future with teens in the house.

I could just see it now.

. . .

It took Lia, Rora, and me two days to move everything into the new house. From all the beds to the cabinets and toiletries. Once our bedroom had been completely cleaned out, I felt kind of sad but relieved at the same time.

Ever since the kids grew in size, they didn't fit in the crib anymore so we had to jam nine little beds into our room.

There was literally no walking space because the beds were all in the way.

Now that the room had been cleared, it looked way more spacious than it had been for the last couple of months.

Since this was the biggest room in the pack house, I wondered who was going to move into it now.

"Do you know if someone is moving into this room?" I asked Rora, who was helping me clean the bathroom and walls.

Rora glanced at me and parted her lips to say something before deciding not to. After a long moment of her replicating a fish, I asked, "It's not Zanthos, is it?"

She made a gasping noise and snuck a glance at me, probably to see if I was mad about Zanthos moving in.

"So it's really Zanthos?" I tossed the sponge back into the soapy tub and stood.

"Zanthos will be moving into the pack house with his mate while he joins in this battle to destroy the Hunters," Rora stated.

"He's helping in this war?" I gawked at Rora, who simply nodded her pretty little head.

"Wow. I guess if he's joining the fight, then he can have the room," I said.

"Are you guys done yet?" Lia called from the door, glancing in to see me spraying down the tub after bleaching and soaping it.

"Just about," Rora said, washing her hands and wiping them off.

"I think that is good. If Zanthos wants anything else clean, he can do it himself." I quickly washed my hands and wiped with a paper towel before following Lia and Rora out of the bathroom.

"So…" I trailed off, looking at Lia, who was abnormally quiet today. She hadn't teased me or made a bad joke the whole day. And that was just weird to me. "Are you okay, Lia? Do you want to talk about it?"

"I'm fine," Lia said, leaning against the wall.

"Did you and Gamma Qian break up?" Rora asked bluntly, ignoring the look I gave her.

"We did for a bit. But after talking it out, we've decided to continue seeing each other," Lia admitted.

*Holy cow.*

That wasn't the response I was expecting.

"What do you mean?!" Rora seemed incensed by Lia's words. "You're just going to continue dating him? Knowing that he's met his true mate? That he might leave you later on?"

"Qian's not going to leave me. We love each other," she said adamantly, not backing down.

My eyes widened at the word "love."

I knew it!

"Yes, but have you thought of how his true mate will feel? You're stealing her mate!" Rora argued.

"It's not technically stealing. We were together before he met her. And she's already pregnant with someone else's child anyway," Lia said, dropping the second bomb of the day.

I wasn't one to judge but—damn—this was some messed up stuff.

"She's pregnant?" Rora asked, as shocked as I was.

"Two months pregnant with her best friend's baby," Lia continued, tucking her blonde hair behind her ear and revealing the bite marks all over her neck. "So do I get your approvals or what?"

"But what about your true mate? What if he's a wonderful guy who's been waiting for you his whole life?" I asked, thinking of what would have happened if I had missed out on being with Eros. I couldn't even imagine how miserable I would be without him.

"I'm not the type of person who thinks about the future, Emi. I live in the present and I love in the present. I don't want to miss out on Qian. I really love him," she said, gazing at me with eyes full of anguish.

I pursed my lips and really contemplated her situation before saying, "Well, if that's your choice, then I will respect it."

"What about you, Rora?" Lia asked, turning her face towards Rora, who was chewing on her bottom lip.

"I will respect it, too," Rora said, sighing deeply, probably at the thought of what Lia's future might be when her true mate and Gamma Qian fight for her.

"Thank you," Lia said, grinning brightly like she always did.

"I just hope you're happy, Lia," Rora sighed.

"Me too," I agreed.

# CHAPTER 20

"You have to stay safe, Eros. For me and the babies. Please," I said, holding back the urge to tell him not to go, to tell him to stay here and forget everything about the war and the Hunters and the government. But I couldn't. He had to protect his people, fight for their rights to live, and fight for our family. It was something he had to do, no matter how much I wished otherwise.

With the long months of preparation and training, the first battle was finally here, and I was not ready for it. I'd cried every single night for the last three nights after I found out about the upcoming fight.

My eyes were extremely red and hideously swollen, even though I had iced them for fifteen minutes before coming out here to send Eros off. I'd thought that I was done crying, but I wasn't. Tears were still building in my eyes and blinding my vision of Eros' face.

I'd never known how the wives of soldiers felt when they sent their loved ones to war, but as of now, I did. And it was a very terribly painful and hard thing to do. It felt like my heart was being ripped apart, because I couldn't stop thinking about the things that could happen to him.

Though I had seen Eros fight before and knew how strong he was, I was still very worried and I didn't think that I would ever stop worrying about him.

"Don't worry, Emira. I'll be back before you know it," he said, cupping my face and stroking my pale cheeks with his thumbs.

His warm breath fluttered across my face as he pressed a soft kiss on my dry, cracked lips.

I wished that this moment would last forever and I didn't want Eros to leave me.

*I guess I'm really selfish, after all,* I thought sadly, trying to push down the emotions that cut across my heart and burned my eyes.

"I love you," he murmured, smiling warmly at me like he wasn't heading face first into a risky battle filled with Hunters and silver bullets.

Just the thought of silver bullets made me think of how he'd almost had his heart cut out of him, how he'd almost died in the hands of the Hunters.

"I love you, Eros," I whispered, my throat tight as I choked on a sob and tried to swallow it down with the rest of my uncontrollable desperation for him to stay.

"Remember to stay with the pups in the house at all times, Emira. Don't let anyone in, even if you know them," he reminded.

"I know," I said, sniffling.

"Don't cry," he said, trying to wipe the never-ending tears off my face, but to no avail.

"I can't help it," I said, grabbing a hold of his hands and pressing it to the side of my face.

"Eros?" I murmured.

"Hm?"

"You better come back. Or I'm going to find myself a handsome man and remarry with the kids," I threatened.

"You won't have the chance, so don't even think about it, Emira," he replied, putting on his hard helmet while looking at me with narrowed blue eyes.

I laughed, the sound rather hollow and bitter.

"You better go before I change my mind and make you stay," I said, trying to give him a smile, but I was sure that the expression on my face was probably very ugly and forced.

"I'll see you soon, Emira," he said, pressing another lingering kiss on my lips before marching off to the front where all of the pack members were lined up in rows. I watched Eros command them to go, watched until Eros and the pack all disappeared from my sight. And still, I stood there like a statue for almost an hour.

"We should go back, Alpha Female," Gamma Chandni said, breaking me out of my stupor.

I nodded my head and got back in the car with her to go back to the house where Gamma Sebastian was watching the kids.

Now that the whole pack was gone, Gamma Chandni and Gamma Sebastian were the only ones still left to guard me and the babies. They were at the house every hour of the day and they never left their post, usually eating with me and the babies every day.

As soon as I opened the front door and walked into the house, Kyra was right in front of me. She hugged my leg and looked up at me with sparkling eyes full of tears.

"Mama! Wren's being mean to me!" she cried, showing me a doll whose head had been completely burned off. The scent of burned plastic was enough to make my nose wrinkle.

"I was not." Wren had her arms crossed over her chest as she stood by the sofa.

Even if I didn't know what had happened, I knew that Kyra probably instigated something, again.

"What happened?" I asked Wren, who glanced at Kyra once before looking away.

"Kyra kept hitting me in the head with her doll so I thought I should take care of one of the problems," she said nonchalantly, shrugging her little shoulders like it was no big deal that she had burned the doll's head off.

"So you burned the doll's head?" I asked, wrinkling my brows.

"Wren was going to burn Angela to death if I hadn't saved her from the fire. She's a ps-pi-psycho, mama," Kyra said, tugging on my shirt.

"Don't call her that. It's not nice," I said to Kyra, before turning to Wren. "And Wren, you shouldn't be touching the lighters. It might burn you if you're not careful."

"It wasn't a lighter. I put the doll on the stove," she corrected. "And I cleaned the mess, too."

I took a deep breath in and closed my eyes for a second before taking the doll out of Kyra's hand.

"Don't burn Kyra's dolls," I said, breathing out.

"So I can burn other things?" Wren asked, looking at me with eyes full of hope.

"No. No more burning things. It's dangerous," I said in finality, ignoring the crestfallen look on her cute little face. "What would you do if you accidentally burned the house down?"

"I would put the fire out with a fire extinguisher," she said calmly, as if that was the reaction I wanted from her.

I pinched the bridge of my nose and said, "Just don't burn anything anymore, Wren."

"Fine. I won't," she said, pouting as she climbed back up the stairs and disappeared from my sight.

"Mama, Wren just said that she'd smash all my dolls if she couldn't burn them," Kyra said.

"Just leave her alone if you don't want her to destroy your dolls," I stated.

"But I haven't done anything to her," Kyra argued, frowning as if she were wrongly accused.

I heaved a sigh as another headache rapidly formed on the right side of my head.

"Mama," Cillian sobbed, running up to me with tears covering his entire face. Even the front of his shirt was wet because of how much he'd cried.

"What's wrong now?" I asked, kneeling to his level to wipe his tears.

"Ace put cat hair all over my bed!" he exclaimed, rubbing at his eyes.

"Cat hair? Where'd he get the cat?" I asked.

We didn't have any pets in the house because of Silas.

He was extremely allergic to animal dander.

"Noah found it in our back yard near the trash and brought it inside. And now Silas is itching all over and sneezing a lot," he said, still crying and breathing hard.

This entire situation made me want to tear out all of my hair. But I couldn't, so I had to put my big-girl panties on and fix all the problems, like a mom should.

"I'll clean up the cat hair so don't cry anymore," I said, retrieving the bottle of Benadryl from the medicine cabinet and the vacuum from the closet before following him up the stairs.

As soon as we reached the top of the stairs, I could hear Silas sneezing repeatedly.

"How are you doing, Silas?" I asked, opening the door to his room to see him and Darius sitting on the rug, watching TV.

"Good," he wheezed before sneezing.

"Silas, did you touch the cat?" I asked, noticing the hives covering his entire arm.

He shook his head.

"Ace threw the cat at him," Darius answered for Silas.

I opened the bottle of Benadryl and poured a cup of the antihistamine out for Silas.

He drank the full cup without blanching, thanked me, and went back to watching cartoons with Darius. It didn't look like he was even mad at Ace for throwing the cat at him. Sometimes, he was too calm and peaceful for his own good.

*But I guess that's better than fighting all the time.*

Once I was done with Silas, I went into Cillian's room and was extremely appalled by the amount of cat hair all over the fleece cover. There were balls of orange and white sprinkled everywhere. Everywhere!

*Good gods!*

I hoped the cat didn't have any fleas because the babies might all get it.

"Did Ace shave the cat or what?" I asked Cillian. He shrugged his shoulders and was still hiccupping from his crying.

"Go drink some water, Cillian. I'll vacuum this and get you a new cover and sheets."

After I'd finished vacuuming all the fur, I replaced the dirty cover, sheets, and pillowcase with new ones. And when I was done with that, I went to find Noah and Ace.

"Ace! Noah!" I called, opening Ace's door to see that it was empty and the lights were off. I knew that he must have hidden himself because of what he'd done.

"Erik, put that snack down and help me find Ace and Noah," I said, waving Erik over to me.

"But I'm hungry," he protested, looking at me with knitted brows, as if he were contemplating if he should help me or not.

"You can eat it after you help me find them," I said, sighing under my breath.

"I don't have to come with you, do I?"

"No. Just tell me where they are," I answered, helping him open the bag of fruity snacks.

"They're in the study room," he said, popping a green gummy bear into his mouth.

"Don't eat too many of them. You'll ruin your lunch," I told him, heading off to the study room.

As I stepped up to the room and opened the door, I said, "If you two come out now, I promise I won't yell at you too much."

Silence was all I heard in return.

"Hello? Noah? Ace?" I called, turning on the light.

"They already ran when they heard you talking to Erik," Nicholas said from behind me. "Do you need me to go get them, mama?"

"You don't need to. I'll just mind-link them." With that last word, I opened the mind-link and commanded, *'Ace and Noah. Come here. Now.'*

Within seconds of saying that, Ace and Noah came to a standstill in front of me, both avoiding my gaze because they knew they were in big trouble. I crossed my arms over my chest as I tried to play the role of a strict mom and said, "Why did you bring the cat in the house, Noah? You know that Silas is very allergic to them."

"Because… because… because I thought the cat was really cute. So I wanted to show him to everyone," Noah said.

I knew he was just trying to come up with an excuse because his eyelids were twitching. Every time he lied or was nervous, his eyelids would twitch nonstop.

"Uh-huh." I obviously didn't believe him. "What about you, Ace? Why'd you put all that cat fur on Cillian's bed?"

"Because it was funny," he answered, a lot quicker than Noah did.

"How is that funny? You made him cry," I said. "And what did I tell you about bullying him?"

"I'm not bullying him. It was just a joke," he said, looking at me with big blue eyes and a pouting lip.

"That's not a joke, Ace. He's still crying because of you," I stated, setting my hands on my hips and looking down at him with a serious look on my face.

"I'm sorry," he said, kind of curling in on himself.

"You don't need to apologize to me. You need to apologize to Cillian. Now go," I ordered.

After Ace went into Cillian's room, I asked, "Where's the cat?"

"It's in Ace's room," Noah said.

I immediately went into Ace's room and waited for Noah to take the cat out from the bathtub.

"What did you guys do to him?" I exclaimed, putting a hand over my mouth in extreme shock.

It was obvious that Ace had shaved the cat.

Because it was completely naked and wrinkly and just really hard to look at.

The poor thing look traumatized as it shivered in place and looked back and forth between me and Noah.

"Ace shaved the cat," Noah said, throwing Ace under the bus.

From across the hall, I heard Ace yell something.

"What did he use to shave the cat?!" I asked, beyond incensed at this point.

"He used papa's razor and papa's shaving cream."

"Ace, you're not allowed to watch TV for the next two weeks. And you, Noah, you're not allowed to either," I said just as Ace came back into the room, still pouting.

"Can we keep him?" he asked, full of hope.

"No," I said, watching as all of his hope was dashed.

"Why not? He doesn't have any fur now. So Silas will be fine if we keep him," he said, whining.

"No. We don't know whose cat this is. They might come looking for him," I replied, picking up the cat to inspect the collar on its wrinkly neck.

There was no tag so I wasn't too sure who to contact, but I knew that it belonged to someone since it had a collar.

"Please, mama? Can we keep him if no one comes for him? Please," he pleaded, looking at me with puppy dog eyes because he knew I was weak to that look.

"No," I said sternly.

As I looked down at the naked cat still shaking like a tree during a tornado, I sighed.

Now how was I going to tell the cat's owner what happened to all of its fur?

. . .

I didn't think that I was going to be such an emotional wreck once Eros was gone, but I was. And I couldn't help it.

The kids still didn't know about the severity of the situation we were in, and I wasn't going to tell them anything about it. I just wanted them to grow up carefree.

Maybe later on when they were old enough I would tell them about how heroic their father was and the war that he'd help fight. But for now, I was content with running after them and fixing the problems they caused. Like that bald cat, for instance.

Speaking of that cat, it was now a part of our family because no one had shown up for it. I'd tried putting a post online at the town page about finding the cat, but no one had claimed it. Instead, they commented under my post about how ugly it was and asking what had happened to its fur. Since I didn't want to say that my son had shaved the thing, I didn't answer them.

Now that it had been with us for a little while, the hair was growing back and I didn't know what to do with it. I had Ace put the cat in a cage and keep it in his room at all times. But that didn't make Silas' allergies go away because the dander got everywhere, even though I made Ace and Noah wash their hands and change their clothes after they were done touching the cat. There was just something about the cat that had caused Silas' allergy to act up all the time, and I was getting frustrated that he had to keep taking Benadryl because of it.

*I don't know why Ace and Noah liked the cat so much. Since they're canines like dogs, shouldn't they hate them?*

Out of everyone in the house, Ace and Noah were the only ones interested in the cat. Cillian hated the poor thing with a fierce passion ever since Ace put all that fur on his bed. Kyra and Wren didn't care for it. Darius wanted to get rid of it because of what had happened to Cillian. Erik and Nicholas didn't really care. And Silas was extremely allergic.

I just hoped that someone was going to come for the cat soon because I was going to go crazy if they didn't.

"Are you going to train with us, mama?" Kyra asked as I tied her black hair back into a small ponytail at the top of her head and wiped off the sweat on her forehead.

"Not today," I said, watching as she jumped out of the chair to run back to the group.

Every morning, the kids and I would go train with Gamma Chandni and Gamma Sebastian. It had become our routine ever since Eros left. But since I was so stressed and tired today, I decided to be lazy and take a little break.

Instead of working out, I did a little stretching and watched the kids spar with the Gammas.

In the beginning, they worked with the training courses and did a lot of repetitive exercise in order to become more stronger and faster. When the training courses became too easy for them, they'd switched to sparring and learning defensive fighting. Now that they had learned everything they could, they were sparring with the Gammas. It was pretty incredible how receptive and smart the kids were. Though they were only half the size of the Gammas, they fought pretty viciously and gave Sebastian and Chandni a hard time defending against them.

As for their poisonous claws, I always commanded them to keep them retracted in case things go wrong. And since that could happen, I made sure to grab some antidotes from Khanh when I last saw her some weeks ago.

*'Are you busy right now, Eros?'* I asked through the mind-link, hoping to chat with him throughout the time the kids were training.

*'Not too busy,'* he replied, his voice sounding extremely exhausted in my mind.

*'Are you resting?'* My brows wrinkled.

*'No. Just going through some maps and attack plans for tomorrow,'* he stated. *'What are you doing?'*

*'I'm watching the babies spar with Gamma Chandni and Gamma Sebastian. They've all been doing really well with their training, especially Wren and Noah. They fight like nothing I have ever seen before. If I weren't their mom, I would have probably been buried six feet deep somewhere in the desert,'* I said exaggeratedly, my eyes following Wren's little body as she ducked out of Gamma Sebastian's grasp and swept his legs out from under him.

Eros chuckled.

*'How did your last battle go?'* I asked.

*'Not so well. I think the scientists have created an upgrade for the Hunters because they've gotten a lot stronger since we last fought them.'*

My face fell.

*'But I know we can win this next one,'* he continued.

*'I hope so,'* I replied solemnly.

*'Take care of yourself and the pups, Emira. I have to go to a meeting with the other Alphas and leaders now,'* Eros said hurriedly.

*'Take care of yourself too, Eros. I'll talk to you later.'* I turned off the mind-link and stared blankly ahead.

Ever since Eros left, I tried to talk to him every day through our mind-link to check on how he was doing and see if everything was okay.

As of now, he was still safe and alive, much to my relief.

Since that first battle I'd sent him off to, things had become a lot more serious. Although we were able to make the other side retreat because of the Ziron-e bullets, the government had changed up their game plan by enlisting all the human soldiers into the war. This made the Ziron-e become useless.

While our side no longer had an upper hand, the enemy side still had silver bullets and all types of poisons and chemicals to combat the supernaturals on our team. I knew that they had the upper hand now because of all the research they had gathered on the supernaturals throughout the years, some of which I had contributed to during my short time working there. And even though I had racked my brain for some ideas on how to help, I kept drawing a blank.

As a human, I knew that we were very tenacious creatures. We never gave up and we'd rather die than fail, especially when we were defending our country. Though we weren't as strong as the supernaturals, we were united and there were many of us. It didn't matter how strong the opponent was, we would win because of our numbers.

I sighed dejectedly.

If only I could help Eros in some way, instead of just sitting uselessly at home with the babies while everyone was out there fighting for their lives. Even Granny Ada had gone to help and she was over a thousand years old!

"Mama, I'm hungry," Erik said, pulling me from my thoughts.

"Are you guys done training?" I asked, realizing that I was losing track of time because of my thoughts.

Erik nodded his head repeatedly as I picked up all our stuff and got into the car with everyone.

# CHAPTER 21

The seasons were passing by in a blur. From summer to winter and back again as the leaves grew and fell from the trees surrounding the house. It was close to the third year of the war and—still—there was no end in sight. Eros was still gone from our home, just like the pack members were missing from the pack house, while I was surrounded by our lively children, who had gone from looking like toddlers to looking like preteens. And this was all in the span of three years after they were born, meaning that they were only three years old.

Both the girls were about five inches shorter than me while the boys were seven to eight inches shorter. In just a little more time and they'd be taller than me. And I kind of hated how fast they grew.

*It's really unfair,* I thought.

"Mom, there's people outside the house," Darius stated, his squeaky, pre-pubescent voice grating on my ears as he pulled the curtain up so I could see outside the window.

As I peered out, I saw a white SUV parked at the front of our house that I didn't recognize. Since the kids and I had been locked inside the perimeters of our house and the yard, we hadn't had any visitors for over two years now, other than Sergio, Chandni, Qian, Sebastian, and Beta Toren, who had traded with each other to train the kids whenever they could.

Just at the sight, my heart dropped and I stopped in my tracks, fearing the worst because of my previous experiences.

"It's the Werewolf Council members," Chandni said, sending me a reassuring look, probably because she'd noticed how my entire body had tensed in response to seeing the SUV.

But after hearing her say it was the Council members that had shown up at my door, my body remained tense. Because, whenever they showed up, nothing good ever happened.

The last time I saw them, Eros and I had gotten into a fight and continued to fight for days. And now that they were here again, I couldn't help but get defensive.

When the Council knocked on the door, Chandni opened it and let them in.

"Hello, Emira," Samson said, greeting me with a smile compared to the other three men, who stood staring at my kids like they were looking at pieces of priceless artifacts.

"Hello, Samson," I greeted in return, gesturing for them to take a seat on the couches.

"It's been a long time since we've seen your pups now, hasn't it?" he said, trying to start small chitchat. But I wasn't having it.

"Is there a reason for your visit today?" I asked, going straight to the question.

He sighed and folded his hands in his lap. "We need the Sentinels to join the war."

At his words, my jaw clenched as anger billowed inside of me.

"No. A million times no!" I stated. "I can't believe that you're suggesting such a thing!"

"Our casualties have risen, Emira. We cannot continue to let our kind die. If the Sentinels do not join, we will lose the war and the lives of everyone in it." His face became stern as his white brows furrowed into a line.

"So you want to sacrifice my children for your own benefit? You have no right!" I bellowed, squaring my shoulders defensively.

"It is their duty. They were born to protect our people," he said calmly.

"No. They were not. They were born to be whoever they want to be, to do whatever they want to do," I argued, sending a message to the kids to make them all go upstairs.

"As the Mother, you need to encourage your pups to fight. That is their sole purpose in life. Yet you coddle them when they are to be treated as warriors," another Council member interrupted.

"Stop. You're not going to come into my house and tell me how to raise my children," I stated, frowning deeply as Chandni set a pot of hot tea down on the table and poured everyone a cup.

"We are not telling you how to raise your pups. We only want what's best," Samson said.

"I don't care. My babies are not going to go to war for you." I crossed my arms over my chest and glared the old men down.

"It is not for us. It is for the good of everyone. Do you know how many of us will die without the Sentinels protection? They are our only hope."

"But how do you expect babies to fight your battle? They're only three years old! What fighting skills do they have?" I asked. "They're not seasoned warriors built to fight and destroy, Samson. They're my children, and I will not send them to die."

. . .

By twelve in the afternoon the next day, Eros came back to the house, dressed in normal clothes instead of his bulletproof uniform. And I had a feeling that he was sent back by the Werewolf Council.

This was the first time I'd seen him in months, and he hadn't changed much except for that black stubble on his chin and the dark bags underneath his eyes. My heart ached just looking at him like this.

He looked so tired.

"You're not here to persuade me into letting the children join the war, are you?" I asked as we sat down at the dinner table together, staring at our food instead of eating it.

Eros shook his head. "I will respect whatever you choose, Emira. If you don't want our pups to fight, then they won't."

His words hit me right in the heart and I broke down in front of him, sobbing like a baby.

"I don't want to be selfish, Eros. I just want to protect them," I wailed. "Is that wrong?"

Eros got out of his chair and came over to me before kneeling by my feet. He grabbed a hold of my cold hands and held them in his, kissing the knuckles delicately. He said, "Following your heart is never wrong."

"But it's not about what I want. It's about people dying. If the children don't join the war, then more people will die," I said, choking back a sob when I saw the children all peeking in from the doorway.

"Mom, there's something we want to tell you," Silas stated.

"What is it?" I asked, quickly pulling my hands out of Eros' hands to wipe the tears off my face.

"We know about the war and we want to fight in it. We want to help dad," Silas spoke up, standing by his eight other siblings who nodded their heads in agreement.

The pleading looks on their faces made me cry, and the words to refuse them were stuck in my throat like a mixture of molasses and peanut butter.

"All of you want to?" I asked through a bone-dry throat.

They all nodded and said, "Yes."

I looked at each child's face, trying to determine if they really meant it or not. But after staring at their unfaltering faces for ten minutes straight, I knew that they weren't kidding.

"Please, mom. We're tired of always staying at the house. We've trained hard enough for this. We're ready," Kyra whined and pleaded.

"Let me think about it," I breathed out, feeling the stress collect on my temple.

"Please, mom. Please!" Noah begged, dropping down to his knees right next to Eros.

After he'd done that, Kyra, Nicholas, Silas, Erik, Cillian, Wren, Darius, and Ace all got on their knees.

My mouth fell open, and I became speechless when all of my babies kneeled at my feet, along with the man I loved.

"Eros?" I called, hoping he could help me make the decision.

"It's your call, Emira," he said, being no help at all.

After a really long pause, possibly longer than ten minutes, I gave in to them.

"If that's really what you all want… then yes. You can go," I told them, glancing at Eros from the corner of my eye. "But you have to listen to your dad. If any one of you don't, you'll be going back home."

"Yay!" Kyra squealed, jumping up and down as if it were a party that she was going to and not a dangerous battle.

I sighed and shook my head before grabbing Eros' arm to pull him up.

"Thank you, Emira," he said, pulling me into his arms where I belonged.

"I knew you were here to convince me to let them join," I muttered against his shoulder. "I just knew it!"

Eros chuckled, rubbing my back in circles, and didn't say anything more.

. . .

The whole family had arrived at the base by one in the afternoon the next day. I'd packed up everything we needed the day previous for Eros to deliver to our temporary apartment on base. So we didn't have to carry anything in as we toured the site.

Everywhere we walked, people stared. They looked at Eros first and greeted him before they said their greetings to me and the children. By the looks of it, they all knew me and the babies, even though I had no clue who they were.

After taking all the kids to their shared rooms, Eros led me up the apartment building to where we were going to be situated.

"This will be our temporary room," Eros said, leading me into a small apartment with only one bed and a small kitchen in the same room.

At the left side of the bed was a door, which I assumed was the bathroom, a rack that had Eros' clothes hanging on it, and the luggage I had packed yesterday for myself. There was nothing else to address in the room other than the old ceiling fan that was collecting dust and the yellowing paint on the walls that had different-colored crayon scribbles all over it.

Someone with kids must have lived here previously, because the walls at our house looked exactly like these walls when the kids were a little younger.

"Is that the bathroom?" I asked, hoping it was because I didn't want to share bathrooms with everyone. That would be torturous on my bladder if someone was in there and there was a long line of people.

"Yes," he said, looking at the door with peeling paint and scratch marks all over it.

The room smelled kind of weird, like a mixture of dust and mold, but it was livable, and I couldn't ask for better conditions because of the situation we were in.

We were going to war, not going on vacation.

*I guess this room is a lot better than the tents being used by some of the people outside,* I thought as Eros left the room.

Since there was no air conditioning system, Eros had to set up a fan on the nightstand by the bed.

Just as he was done turning the fan on to help with the stuffy feeling inside the room, some kind of siren blared long and loud and scared the complete crap out of me.

"What is that?" I asked, fearing there was some sort of attack on the base.

"We're being attacked," Eros confirmed, grabbing his dirty bulletproof jacket off the floor.

"I have to go, Emira. You stay here and wait for me to come back," he said, opening the door and running out before I could say anything back to him.

With one hand pressed against my throbbing chest, I opened the door and followed him out, ignoring his order for me to stay inside so that I could go check on the children. By the time I'd managed to climb down the stairs to the lower floor, I saw all the kids come out of their rooms.

"Where are you all going?" I asked, although I kind of knew the answer.

"We have to go protect the base, mom," Darius said, avoiding my gaze because of the tears in my eyes.

I was crying already, and I didn't even know it.

"We'll be okay, mom. We've trained a long time for this. Believe in us," Nicholas said, pulling me in for a hug.

I wiped at my face with my sleeve and looked at the cracked ceiling, trying to stay strong, even though my heart was breaking into millions of pieces.

"Stay safe, please. All of you. I-if you can't handle it, then leave and come back to me. I'll take care of it," I said, my voice cracking mid-sentence as they all circled around me in a giant group hug.

"Mom, you're not as strong as us," Kyra said, laughing at me.

"I might not be strong like you but I've gotten away from death several times, Kyra. Don't judge a book by its covers," I said, knocking her softly on the head with my knuckle.

She pouted.

"Aren't you guys going to change into some type of uniform or something?" I asked, noticing that they were still in their regular clothes.

"They'll be shifting into their wolves, so it won't be necessary," Beta Toren answered as he came up to us, nodding at me in greeting.

"Will you be taking them out there?" I would be a lot more relieved if he were able to take them out there himself.

"Yes. Alpha Eros, the Gammas, and I will be bringing the Sentinels out there together. We will put their lives above ours, Alpha Female," he promised.

I covered my mouth for a second and said, "Thank you."

"You're welcome, Alpha Female. It is the least we can do," Beta Toren said.

"Is there any way I can supervise them?" I asked, hoping that I could watch them fight and check on their safety from time to time.

"You can't come with us, mom," Silas interrupted, his brows furrowing together, probably because he was worried for my safety.

Though I was extremely scared of going on the battlefield, I would do anything for my children. As a mother, I wanted nothing more than for them to be safe, even if I had to risk my life to make sure they survived.

"Alpha Eros said to take you to the watch tower if you want to supervise," he said, probably mind-linked by Eros before he came here. "It is safer there."

I nodded my head and followed Beta Toren and the children out of the apartment. All around us, people were running to their vehicles, dressed from head to toe in protective clothing.

I watched as all the children were loaded into three different jeeps and whisked off, while Beta Toren stayed behind to take me to the watch tower.

As I got into the car and started praying for everyone, I didn't notice that the person who had gotten into the driver's seat was not Beta Toren.

By the time I'd noticed, the car had already started rolling.

"Hi, Emi," Zanthos said, giving me a creepy smile from the rearview mirror as I looked up and saw him in the driver seat.

My heart literally stopped in my chest, and I froze in my seat like an ice statue.

"W-what are you doing here, Zanthos? W-where's Beta Toren?" I stuttered, feeling myself become more aware of my surroundings as my skin crawled at the idea of what was going to happen to me next.

*Why didn't I pay more attention?! Why did I let him drive me off?* I berated myself over and over again in my head, starting to panic because Zanthos didn't say anything in reply. He only smiled at me and continued to maneuver the vehicle on the road.

"Stop the car, Zanthos! Let me off!" I cried frantically, glancing at the lock to see that all the doors had been locked by him.

At this point, the hairs on the back of my neck stood on end and I was seriously contemplating if I should jump out of the car or try to take the steering wheel from Zanthos, like I'd seen in the action movies. But if I did something as stupid as to fight for the steering wheel, the car might crash and I might die while Zanthos might come out of it alive, having achieved his mission.

*What do I do? What do I do?*

I gnawed on my bottom lip as I panicked full force.

I couldn't call for Eros to come save me because he was busy with the battle. If he were to come for me, I was sure that a lot of people would die because of his absence.

*What can I do?*

My heart felt like it was going to jump out of my chest, my hands were sweaty and shaking, and I felt tears of frustration form in my eyes.

"Don't jump out of the car. It's dangerous and you might lose a limb," he cautioned.

After Zanthos had apologized to me, I was rather neutral with him and I was starting to let my guards down.

First, because he apologized.

Second, because he sounded sincere.

And third, because of Anira.

But now... now I just wanted to rip his throat out and stomp on it.

"Where are you taking me?" I asked, depleting in energy as hopelessness set in. I was regretting every single life decision I'd made regarding Zanthos.

"To the watch tower," he said, grinning like a maniac.

"To the watch tower?" I repeated, extremely confused by his words.

"I'm taking you to the watch tower. It's only two minutes away," he explained, shaking his head at the stupefied expression on my face.

"But why are you taking me to the watch tower? Aren't you trying to kill me? Where are the Hunters?" I asked, looking around to see if we were getting surrounded or not.

Zanthos couldn't contain it anymore, so he burst out into loud and obnoxious peals of laughter.

"There's no Hunters," he said in between chuckles.

"No Hunters?" I asked, trying to clarify the situation.

"No hunters," he confirmed.

"You're not trying to kill me?" I cocked my head to the side and looked at him.

"No. Beta Toren asked me to take you to the watch tower and I agreed," he answered calmly.

"Why didn't you say anything when I asked you?" I was almost hysterical because of how bad he'd scared me.

"It was too funny how scared you were. So I didn't want to interrupt you," he said, still chuckling.

"You are sick, Zanthos! I can't even believe you would do that! Do you know how terrified I was? You bastard!" As I spoke, I felt my blood pressure skyrocket the more I thought about it.

*At this rate, I will never forgive Zanthos. Not even when I am ninety.*

When Zanthos stopped the car in front of the watch tower and we both got out, the first thing I did was slap him in the face.

My hand bounced off his cheek and the sound of the slap rang loud in my ears.

"I deserved that." He shrugged it off and continued to give me that shit-eating grin.

"And this," I said, slapping him again and again and again, even going as far as to stomp on his toes and kick him in the knee.

The man stood like a tall oak tree and didn't move in the least, letting me continue my assault of him. For some reason, I felt as if all the anger I had towards Zanthos finally had an outlet, and I was using this outlet well, although there was really no visible damage done to him.

"What's wrong with you?" I cried, rubbing my right hand that had now gone red because of how hard I'd slapped him.

"Now, if you feel better then let's get going." He brushed the dirt off his pants and gestured for me to go first.

I didn't say anything as I walked towards the tall watch tower several yards away from us.

"Eros said there's a surprise up there for you," he said, pulling a cigarette out from a box in his pocket and lighting it.

"You have a bad sense of humor, Zanthos," I said.

He shrugged his shoulders and replied, "To each their own."

I huffed and started my climb up the watch tower.

# CHAPTER 22

When I finally got to the top of the tall tower built by cinderblocks and thick, fortified glass walls, I saw a short-haired female sitting in a chair by the clear glass windows, staring outside with a machine gun within hand's reach. Though the image of her back was familiar to me, I drew a blank as to who she was.

"Hi," I said as she turned around to look at me.

"Hi, Emi," she said, smiling until I could see the cute dimples on both sides of her plump cheeks.

My mouth dropped open.

She smiled even wider because of the shocked expression on my face.

"Asuka?" I breathed in disbelief, letting my eyes trail from her short black hair to her bulletproof uniform. I couldn't believe that my co-worker from the lab was still alive. The last time I'd seen her, she was crying pitifully as we separated and ran for our lives from Kent and the members of his pack.

"How are you still…" I trailed off.

"Alive? It's a long story," she said, waving me over to take a seat on the chair next to hers.

I quickly walked over to her, gave her a big, firm hug and took a seat in the cushioned chair.

"What happened? I remember hearing you scream when Kent came after us. So I thought something bad had happened to you," I said, reminiscing the moment like it was yesterday.

"I thought I had died too, but I didn't," she started. "When Kent ran after you, one of the other werewolves in his pack had me cornered by the river. I was stuck between jumping into the river and drowning or letting him kill me."

"Oh, right! I almost forgot that you couldn't swim," I exclaimed. "So what did you do?"

"I decided to take a chance in the river and let myself fall back. But I never fell in. Someone caught my arm and pulled me up before my feet could even touch the water." She smiled with a faraway look in her eyes, probably remembering the magical moment in her mind.

"Then, what happened? Were you saved?" I set my elbow on the table and propped my chin on my palm.

"Yes. My mates saved me." She grinned and glanced at me.

Hearing her words, my mouth fell open, once again.

"Wait a second, did you just say 'mates'?" I asked.

"Yes." She was still grinning.

"Mates?! You have more than one?" I almost jumped out of my chair at the ecstatic news.

"Yes. I have two mates, Weston and Rowan. If it weren't for them, I would have been dead by now," she explained.

I was really surprised, completely mind blown. Though I'd never seen this coming for her, I was glad that she got over Daryl's death and found love again. Twice.

"I'm happy for you, Asuka. I really am. Congratulations," I said sincerely, reaching out to give her another hug.

"What about you? Are you married yet?" She pointed towards the ring on my finger.

"Engaged," I corrected, grinning as I showed her my ring and she showed me hers. "Your ring's really pretty."

"Yours is, too," she replied, smiling widely.

"I also mated a werewolf, and we have nine children together," I said, dropping the bomb to see what her reaction would be.

"Nine?" she croaked, her eyes bulging out of their sockets.

I nodded my head and crossed my legs.

"But it's only been like three or four years," she protested, probably wondering if I'd adopted them.

"I had them all at the same time. Have you heard about the Sentinels?" I asked.

"You're the Breeder?" She gawked.

I nodded again.

"Wow. It's probably a good thing that the lab had been ransacked when it had. Or else you would have become our next specimen."

I grinned from the truth in her words. "I guess some things happen for a reason."

"Yes, it does." She nodded her head in agreement, too.

"Are your mates treating you good?" I asked out of the blue, wondering how she was able to keep up with two virile werewolf males while I had trouble with just one.

"Better than I could ever hope for," Asuka said, blushing.

I gave her a sly look and said, "Good to know. By the way, how'd you get this job?"

"I can shoot pretty well so they decided to let me keep watch," she stated, shrugging her shoulders as if it were something very small and simple.

If it were me, I doubted I would even be considered for this position.

"Cool. Is there any way for me to see farther out?" I asked her. "I'm supposed to supervise my children but I can't see anything from here."

I grinned sheepishly as I thought of how I'd forgotten about the children once I saw Asuka again.

"There's binoculars in the drawer or you can look through the scope on the machine gun," she said, pointing to the drawer underneath the table.

"Awesome."

I grinned and pulled my chair closer to the machine gun, rubbing my hands together like I was doing something diabolical.

I'd only seen one of these in the movies so I was super excited to put my hands on it, even though I wasn't going to use it because of my bad aim.

As I touched the top of the gun and the sides, I stayed away from the trigger and looked through the telescopic sight.

Since the gun was aimed at a closer distance, I had to move it around a bit to use it as a binocular.

"Is it dangerous to be up here?" I closed one eye and looked through the scope.

"Usually it's not," she said. " My mates made sure that the glass walls are all bulletproof. So not much can hurt us when we're in here. There's like five sheets of bulletproof glass."

*Five sheets? Talk about protective mates.*

I raised a brow but didn't question it. Instead, I moved the gun from area to area in search of the battle and saw a couple of men dressed in the puke-green uniforms commonly seen on the members of the human army.

"Asuka, I think the enemy is on our base," I said, pulling my face away from the gun to see that Asuka already had her finger on the trigger.

It was funny, in a sad kind of way, how I considered the human side to be the enemy now.

"I see them," she said, squinting into the telescopic sight while sliding the window open a little to clear room for her gun. "You might want to sit a little farther away from me. The shells might burn if it hits you."

I quickly pulled my chair and the machine gun all the way to the corner of the table.

Next thing I knew, rounds started flying as the shells bounced all over the place. And I was glad I was wearing a long sleeve shirt.

When I peered into the scope and looked in the direction I'd seen the men, their bodies littered the ground. Every shot from Asuka's gun hit them straight in the head, ensuring that they died instantly and there was no need for a second shot on the same man. In a matter of minutes, the ten men were all lying dead on the dirt.

"Holy crap! You don't just shoot 'pretty well,' Asuka. You're like a sniper," I praised in awe of her amazing skills. "Can you teach me to shoot one of these days? I've been told that I suck balls at shooting a gun."

"Sure," Asuka replied, giggling at my word choice... well, Lia's word choice.

"Really?" I glanced at her.

"Yes. I didn't do very well when I started out, either. But with more practice, I got a lot better," she admitted.

After a moment of comfortable silence between us, I asked, "Asuka? How'd you know it was me?"

Since she'd never seen my face without makeup caked on it, I was wondering how she was so sure that I was "Emi." Because I knew that the current me looked nothing like the me before. At least I hoped I didn't.

"I guessed. Because your eyes looked really familiar along with your hairstyle," she said, pointing at my bangs, the ones I'd styled the same for over ten years.

"You're always so good at figuring out the details," I muttered, grabbing a pair of binoculars from the drawer because I was getting tired of moving the gun around.

"Not always," she said, shrugging her dainty shoulders.

As I adjusted the eye-cups, I was finally able to see the battle happening at a farther distance away from us.

There were supernaturals of all shapes and sizes and human soldiers inside of armored vehicles everywhere on the battlefield, probably because of the close range by which our side fought. If the humans didn't have the armored tanks and metal suits to protect themselves, they would have died a lot faster within the jaws of the shape-shifters.

As I looked around, I finally spotted my children fighting with the armored vehicles. They were in their shifted forms, towering over the tanks as they tore those things apart and crushed the humans inside with their mighty bodies, leaving no survivors in the aftermath. From what I could see, every move they made was precise and deft. When they were shot at, they would dodge the rain of bullets with quick maneuvers of their powerful hind legs, regardless of the fact that they were gigantic in size, which made them a better target to shoot at.

How they were able to remain one step ahead of the bullets was a mystery to me.

While I had been extremely worried about their safety, a part of me knew that they were way too strong to be hurt. I'd seen how viciously they trained, how tenacious they were when they fought with the Gammas and the Beta one-on-one and won. Now that they were using those skills in battle, I realized that they weren't giving it their all during training. Just the amount of gruesome blue and black bodies on the ground were proof of that. I watched in mild horror as my babies ripped off their enemies' head and severed human limbs from bleeding bodies, toying with their preys as their eyes gleamed gleefully, delightedly. I could tell that they enjoyed every second of this fight, enjoyed watching the light die from their opponents' eyes.

But I didn't want to admit this. I didn't want to admit that my children were born to fight, that they were born to be killing machines used on the battlefield. It didn't sit well with me. At all.

At the sight of people dying and the bodies that littered the ground in massive amounts, I couldn't help but feel melancholic. Although I didn't know any of these people, it hurt to see them dying. Even though I knew that the human side was the enemy, I still felt really bad seeing them die, fighting for what they believed in, defending our country and our people. Because, beneath this title of Breeder, I was also human. And I didn't want any more people dying, be it humans or supernaturals.

*What is wrong and what is right? Where does the line between good and evil blend? Am I making the right decisions?*

Those were the questions that I'd repeatedly asked myself ever since the war started, and it ate at me every time I turned on the TV to see the news reporter talk about the war and the casualties.

Shaking the saddening thoughts off, I went back to focusing on the battle before me.

Other than my nine babies playing with their opponents like little ragdolls, I saw Eros in wolf form killing everyone within his reach, all the while making sure to stay in the same area as the babies to try and protect them as he fought. His every move was impeccable and deadly, and the broken bodies around him were starting to pile up. Though he was doing a great job, his fur was matted in some areas and my heart cinched at the thought of what that could mean. I knew he'd been injured but I didn't know to what extent because his black fur made it very difficult to tell if it was his blood or his enemies' blood.

As my eyes strayed from him to the dark blonde wolf next to him, I noticed that this wolf could take a lot of silver bullets without showing any signs of agony or anger. He didn't dodge the bullets like Eros did, instead, he let them shoot him. When they did, he killed the enemy with a swipe of his claws or bit off their heads. After having been shot over and over again, the bullets that had entered his body were spit back out, falling to the ground aimlessly and surrounding him in a mass of silver.

At the sight, my memory was jogged.

This powerful wolf was Alpha Xavier.

I remembered that he had become immune to silver after mating with Maya, who was also fighting in the battle. The red-haired sorceress was deflecting everything sent at her and sending toxic potions at the enemy in massive amounts. What surprised me the most were the little yellow triangles she threw that transformed into giant gray-skinned men, who were over two heads taller than the human soldiers and seemed to be very strong, too.

Now that I was seeing Alpha Xavier and Maya fight with my own eyes, I was really amazed by this power couple. And I wished that I could be helpful to Eros the way Maya was helpful to the war and to Alpha Xavier.

"What's wrong?" Asuka turned away from her gun for a second.

"I feel really useless," I said, frowning.

"What do you mean useless?" Asuka's brows wrinkled.

"Everyone is out there fighting and I'm just sitting here watching them like a creep," I said, pursing my lips.

"You're not useless, Emi. Look at your children fighting—" she tried to say.

"But that's my children. I just wished that there was something I could do to help out," I interrupted, dropping the binoculars on the table before folding my hands in my lap.

I couldn't bear to look anymore. The chaos and destruction, death and decay were making me physically sick.

"Well… maybe you can go over to the field hospital and help with the wounded," she suggested.

I perked up at her words.

"Where's that at?"

"It's about five minutes from here. You see that white tent right there? That's it," she said, pointing at the tent really far away.

"Thanks, Asuka. I'm going to go over there and see if there's anything I can do to help. I'll see you later," I told her, quickly hopping off the chair to go down the stairs.

"Do you need me to call someone to take you there? Because I can if you need me to," she said, pointing at the phone hanging on the wall.

I took a look outside the glass and saw that the vehicle I'd come in was still there, so I said, "No, thank you. I think my ride is still down there."

"Bye, Emi. Come visit me when you have time," she said, waving as I quickly descended the stairs.

"I will!" I called.

When I got to the car, Zanthos was sitting inside with his elbow sticking out of the window as he smoked his cigarette.

"Done talking?" he asked, snuffing his cigarette as soon as I opened the door and got into the back seat.

"Yes. Can you take me to the field hospital?" I pulled on my seatbelt and turned my head to look at him, still a little bothered by his joke from earlier.

"You sure you can handle going there? It's a lot of blood and dead people," he said, starting the car before stepping on the brake to shift gears.

"Of course," I replied, turning my gaze to the window as the conversation between us died down.

After a moment of awkward silence and me clearing my throat for the second time, I asked, "How's Anira?"

I hadn't talked to Anira for a couple of months now. Ever since she'd quit her job at the research facility and joined our pack, she was always busy working with the secret lab to create more Ziron-e and experiment on ways to bring down the Hunters, a job completely opposite of what she had been doing for years.

"She's fine," he sighed. "She's still working with the pack members at the lab."

From his sigh, I knew that he hadn't been able to see her because of her work. Anira was the type to cut herself away from the real world to focus on her experiments. She immersed herself in her own little reality and kept everything else out until she was good and ready. This meant that anyone trying to contact her would be ignored until she was done doing whatever it was she was doing, including me. I'd tried calling her a couple of times in the past six months, only to go straight to her voicemail and receive a message saying that she was fine and busy with her work. From then on, I opted to periodically send her texts asking if everything was okay.

"Thanks, Zanthos," I said, getting out of the car when he reached the field hospital.

Zanthos grunted a reply and waved at me before speeding away in the direction of the battle.

*I never thought I'd thank Zanthos in this lifetime, but I had to give credit where it was due.*

"Emi! What are you doing here?" Rora called, coming out of the giant white tent to wave at me.

"Hey, Rora! I just wanted to see if there was anything I could help with," I said, walking with her into the tent and noticing the amount of filled beds lined up horizontally against the wall. From the looks of it, there had to be at least one hundred of them.

"Oh! There's plenty of things needing done here," she said, pulling me along.

As soon as we got inside, two armed males carried in a wounded female whose arm had been cut off by something and was lying right next to her on the thick green fabric used as a makeshift stretcher.

"We have someone whose arm has been blown off, Gemini," Granny Ada said, helping the men move the blonde-haired female onto the clean bed.

The Moon Healer was quick to move over to the bed and take a look at the arm. She picked it up and rearranged it back on the stump that was left. Once that was done, she lifted her hands and set it about five inches away from the wound. Then, her hands glowed with soft white light, just like when she had touched my belly at the gathering three years ago.

What I saw next made my eyes widen in astonishment.

Within seconds of the white light touching the blonde female's skin, her hand started knitting back together. Broken bone reconnected, tendons reattached, and skin healed over like the arm had never been removed from its owner before.

"You're all good to go," Gemini said, pulling back as the glowing on her hands disappeared.

The female thanked Gemini several times before she ran back to join her team.

"You're amazing, Gemini," I complimented, unable to believe what I'd just seen.

"Hi, Emi," she said, smiling at me with extremely tired eyes.

I didn't know how long she had been doing this, but I could tell that it was definitely taking a toll on her. There were bags under her eyes and her chubby cheeks were starting to disappear. From the way she carried herself, I could tell that she was at her limit.

Other than Gemini having to put body parts together, Khanh and a lot of Pack Healers were also there to help. It was just too bad that we didn't have any more Moon Healers like Gemini.

"Is there anything I can help with?" I asked, watching Granny Ada remove a bullet from someone's bruised leg.

"You can help me wrap this young man up, Emi," Granny Ada said, cleaning the wound off and applying a clear layer of ointment before going to the next bed.

"Leave it to me," I stated, grabbing some gauze off the tray Granny Ada had left on the side of the bed.

After I greeted the patient, I used gauze and tape to patch him back up before sending him off to do whatever else he needed to do. This job was a lot easier than any of the other jobs that the pack healers were doing. Less gruesome, too. And I was beyond happy to do it.

For the next few hours, I spent my time wrapping people up and removing bullets from their wounds, trying not to cringe or throw up because of the state some of them were left in.

By working like this, I was given the opportunity to keep myself and my mind busy, while being helpful at the same time. That way, I wouldn't have to keep thinking about unnecessary things or making myself feel guilty for the decisions I'd made.

"Emi," Rora called. "They're bringing Wren in."

I immediately dropped the gauze back on the tray and ran over to the front of the tent. My heart was beating a thousand miles a minute, and I couldn't stop my hands from trembling.

"What's wrong?" I asked, my eyes darting to the two men carrying Wren in. At the sight of Wren lying on the makeshift stretcher, I was already in tears.

"Wren, baby," I whispered hoarsely, walking alongside her.

My baby had blood all over her body. It stained her dress and covered her features completely from view.

Some of the blood had dried over several times while others were still glistening and sticky. And because of all the red coating her, I couldn't tell where her injury started and where it ended.

"Please call Gem, Rora," I said, my hands shaking uncontrollably as I dug my nails into the skin of my palms to keep myself from breaking down and crying.

*This is not the time for tears,* I told myself.

As soon as the men put Wren down on the bed, I grabbed her little hand and held it in mine, praying to every god I knew.

"Mom?" she whispered, her eyelids quickly coming down on each other.

"It's me, baby. I'm right here," I cried, choking on my tears. "Keep your eyes open for me. Don't close them."

"I can't, mom. I'm so sleepy…" she trailed off, taking a slow and deep breath.

"Don't, baby. Don't!" I screamed, voice becoming hoarse because of my emotions. "Don't close your eyes. Please!"

As I was sobbing my heart out, watching as Wren's eyes closed while feeling helpless, Gemini tapped me on the shoulder and said, "I don't know how to break this to you but… Wren is okay. She's just sleeping."

Gemini's words made me feel like I had been punched in the throat.

"What?" I choked on my sob and started coughing like mad.

"She fell asleep. The only wound on her is her broken fingernail," Gemini said, trying to keep a calm, professional expression on her face, but the quivering on the corner of her lip betrayed her.

My face deadpanned.

"What about the blood?" I asked, still in disbelief.

"It's not hers. I think it's from either the Hunters or the soldiers," Gemini explained, pinching her lips together to keep herself from laughing in my face.

*Well, this is embarrassing,* I thought, feeling my cheeks burn.

"Why am I not surprised?" I breathed out, trying to hold down the urge to pick Wren up and shake her awake. "You can laugh if you want."

Right after I said that, everyone laughed. From Granny Ada to Rora to Gemini to—basically everyone in the tent.

*I don't think I've ever been this embarrassed in my life.*

Releasing a deep, shaky sigh, I rubbed my aching temple with my hand and knew that my face and my ears were probably the color of a tomato.

"Gemini, please come take a look at Kent," the red-haired female, who was the late Alpha Jared's mate, called, stopping everyone's laughter.

*Thank goodness.*

I turned my head to look at the bed on the far corner and gasped at the sight of the black hole in between Kent's brows, thinking that there wasn't much help for him now. And my words became reality when Gemini shook her head and said, "He's been dead for too long."

After the red-haired female heard Gemini's words, she stood stock-still and didn't say anything.

To me, she didn't look very mournful or even a tiny bit sad that Kent had died.

Her face was neutral and emotionless. But maybe she was numb to everything and was mourning in a different way.

I wasn't too sure.

"You killed him, Bailey," a male with brown hair said to her, pointing a finger at her face in a rather rude manner.

"What are you talking about? I didn't kill Kent. I love him," she denied, avoiding the male's gaze.

"Love him? Ha! What a bunch of bullshit!" the man said. "I saw you shove him into the bullet with my own two eyes. Is that what you call love? Because if that's love, then you must have 'loved' Alpha Jared a lot, too."

Anger filled Bailey's face for a split second before she smoothed out her dirty shirt and calmed herself. "I know you are very upset with Kent's passing. But I will not stand by and let you accuse me on baseless claims."

I shook my head and turned away from the arguing pair because of the disrespect they were showing to the dead. By the time they were done arguing, Kent had been taken away and neither of them had noticed. Though he'd been a source of my fear and worries for a long time, he didn't deserve to be disrespected like that. No one did. Not when they were already dead.

# CHAPTER 23

"Emi, can you help me wrap him up?" Granny Ada asked, handing me a roll of gauze and moving over so I could take her place. I nodded my head and took the gauze from her as she went off to help another person.

When I turned to the patient, I noticed that he was just staring at me the whole time.

"Hi," he greeted, smiling roguishly at me.

*I don't know why but his smile makes the hairs on my arm stand on end, and not in a good way.*

"Hi," I replied politely, taking a look at his arm and trying to finish up as quickly as possible. Something about him gave me the creeps.

"You're Emi, right? I heard the little old lady call you that," he said, extending his arm for me.

I paused for a second before saying, "Yes."

I quickly applied a thin layer of medicine on the black hole in the center of his forearm to help combat the silver still running through his system. Then, I cut some gauze and applied it over the wound before taping it down.

"I'm Liam, Alpha of the Forusk Pack," he introduced. "It's really nice to see a beautiful woman like you here."

I tried not to blanch at his flirting, but it was really hard to maintain a professional facial expression.

"Nice to meet you," I replied robotically, packing all the items back on the tray to move the stand to the next bed in need of help.

"You have a bit of the stuff on your arm," he said, suddenly reaching out and swiping the clear liquid off my wrist with lingering fingertips, all the while smiling at me in a flirting and inappropriate way.

I froze for a millisecond, stunned that he'd touched me, stunned that he was acting this way while everyone was fighting for their lives.

"Please don't touch me. I'm mated," I said, extremely irritated as I sent him a look to back off, but he didn't seem to be bothered by it.

"I know that you're mated. It's just some friendly flirting. Nothing serious, Emi," he said calmly, not even bothered by the fact that I was a mated woman, whose mate could kick his ass to Neptune and back.

I gave him the what-the-hell look and said, "Then you shouldn't be doing it at all. Alpha Eros, my mate, won't like it."

I tried to bring Eros out to scare him into backing off but the guy just wouldn't take a hint.

"He's not here. He won't know." He tried to touch me again but I took a big step back, almost running into the metal stand in my haste.

"I don't care if my mate knows or not. I know. And it's disgusting what you're doing. I don't appreciate it and I hope that you stop. Now." I tried to put my foot down, but after he continued being a creep, I decided to push my stand away from him.

"I don't mean any harm," he called from over my shoulder as I walked away as quick as I could.

I closed my eyes for a split second to calm my anger but it could not be quelled.

"Do I look like someone who will cheat on their mate?" I asked Gemini.

She shook her head and said, "Next time when he's bleeding out from silver, I'll leave him there for a little longer."

"Aw, thank you, Gemini!" I gushed.

"You're welcome," she said, patting my shoulder.

As I helped out the entire afternoon in the white tent, I was finally given the chance to go eat dinner and head home. So Rora and I decided to go back together. We made it to the car parked on the gravel at the other side of the building when I spotted that Liam guy again. He was standing by a jeep talking to a bunch of men, but when he saw me, he immediately stopped what he was saying to come towards me. Even though I was tempted to ignore him, I knew that he wasn't going to give up just like that. I could tell.

"I'll be in the car," Rora said before she quickly climbed into the driver seat and rolled up the windows, leaving me stunned at how quick she'd left me behind.

I didn't get why Rora always cowered when she was in the presence of an Alpha, but it was not something that she could change. I'd tried many a times, with no result. Perhaps, it was something in her DNA that made her instinctively scared of them.

*Who knows?*

"What do you want, Alpha Liam?" I asked bluntly, not one to beat around the bush like a lot of people.

"I just want to talk to you, Emi," he said. "I've been thinking about you all day."

His words almost made me puke, but I held it back with a stiff frown on my face.

"Day? You've only met me this afternoon," I retorted.

*What can I do to make this guy go away?!*

He chuckled and rubbed his neck sheepishly, tossing some of his blonde hair around. "It's enough to make me feel like it's been a day."

"Look, Alpha Liam. I don't know what your problem is but I have a mate and I'm not interested in your 'friendly flirting,' so please, just leave me alone."

"Emi—" he tried to say, before I cut him off with a raised hand.

This guy just pushed my last button.

"Have you seen my children, the Sentinels? Because I'm sure they are interested in seeing the man who's stupid enough to flirt with their Mother,"

I said, threatening him with my children now that nothing else had worked. Once the words left my mouth, I realized how ridiculous I sounded trying to use my children to scare off a full-grown werewolf.

Alpha Liam paled.

*That's the reaction I am looking for,* I thought, grinning evilly to myself.

As I opened my mouth to say something insulting, I noticed that Alpha Liam was no longer looking at me. Instead, he was looking at something behind me, something that scared him enough for him to sweat bullets down the sides of his face.

My face immediately fell because I had a feeling that a certain black-haired, blue-eyed male was behind me.

"Alpha Eros," Alpha Liam choked out, his body becoming tense like someone had grabbed him by the tail.

*I don't know why, but I feel as though I have just been caught in the act by Eros, even though I haven't done anything wrong.*

"Don't flirt with my mate, Alpha Liam. Or I will make sure that your pack will have a new leader by tomorrow morning," Eros warned, stepping in front of me and covering my view of Alpha Liam.

I didn't have to see Eros' face to know that he was pissed. Really, really pissed. Because I could feel the anger seeping off from his body in roaring waves.

"I wasn't flirti—" Alpha Liam never had the time to finish that sentence because Eros' fist was already in his face. He flew back from where he stood and slammed into a dead tree several yards away, bringing the tree down with him.

*Oh, shit!*

"Get in the car, Emira," Eros said, making his way across the gravel to where Alpha Liam was lying. "I'll take care of him."

"Okay," I squeaked, quickly making my retreat into the car where Rora was cowering in her seat.

"Rora! I can't believe you abandoned me like that!" I whispered.

"I can't help it," she said, her teeth chattering as she peered out the window. "It's just in my DNA to submit to an Alpha."

"But Alpha Liam isn't even your Alpha!" I exclaimed.

"I know," she replied, seemingly frustrated with herself.

From the corner of my eye, I saw Alpha Liam go flying again, so I went back to watching Eros beat the living daylights out of the guy.

Alpha Liam kind of deserved the beating, if you asked me. Not only did he try to flirt with me, he had touched me. And this did not go well in Eros' book.

For being a werewolf himself, I didn't know why he would even try to go after a happily mated female. That was a completely prohibited law for werewolves.

If Eros and I took it a step further, instead of just beating him up, he could have been forced to face a court trial for his actions with the Werewolf Council and he could have lost his position in his pack because he was in the wrong.

If it weren't for his Alpha title, he would have been shunned from his pack and left to die.

This was a serious offence in the world of werewolf.

*Shame on him,* I thought, chewing on my fingernail as I waited for Eros to finish up.

By the time Eros was done with him, Alpha Liam was kneeling on the ground like he was groveling for forgiveness, saying something that I couldn't hear. His entire face was black and blue and blood was everywhere. Even that arm I had helped wrap up was bent in another direction and a chunk of meat had been gouged out.

*Now he's going to have to go back and see Gemini. But too bad that she's going to torture him when he does.*

I cackled evilly to myself.

"Why are you laughing like that?" Rora asked, sending me a weird look before putting the key in the ignition.

"Nothing. I'm just happy Eros took care of the problem," I said to her, coughing a little awkwardly to hide the smirk on my face.

Eros opened my car door and said, "You can come out now, Emira."

"Are you okay?" I got out of the car and closed the door before waving Rora off.

He nodded and wiped his bloody hands on his pants.

"Alpha Liam won't bother you again, Emira," he said, shooting a sharp glance at the group of men Alpha Liam had been talking to previously. They all cowered and didn't dare to come help Alpha Liam.

Truthfully, I didn't really think Alpha Liam was that interested in me. He was more interested in the power that he thought I had because I was the Sentinels' Mother. But now that Eros had made an example out of him, no other supernatural would be stupid enough to test their luck. Hopefully.

"I saw all the blood on you when you were on the battlefield, Eros. Let's go and have Gemini take a look," I said, grabbing a hold of his right hand.

"I'm fine, Emira. I've already taken the bullets out myself," he said, squeezing my hand reassuringly.

"What? Why didn't you go to the field hospital? They have an ointment and some medicine that can help take out the silver," I explained, my brows furrowing.

"I'd already used some before coming here," he answered.

"Are you sure?" I looked up at him.

"Yes. The wounds are already closing up," he said, stroking the back of my hand as we walked to the front of the tent. "If you're still worried about it, I can show you later tonight."

"…" I glanced at Eros from the corner of my eye before getting into the jeep parked in front of us with Gamma Sergio and Beta Toren already in it.

"Wait, where are the children?" I asked, suddenly remembering about our babies.

"I took them all back to the apartment a little earlier," he said, taking a seat next to me in the back.

"Are all of them okay?"

"They're fine. No serious wounds." Eros closed the car door before Gamma Sergio started driving.

"Did you get Wren, too? She was in the field hospital," I said, turning my head to look back at the white tent.

"Yes. I had Darius carry her back," he confirmed.

"Carry her back?" I repeated, knitting my brows. "She's *still* sleeping?"

"She probably wore herself out from the fight," he said, chuckling all of a sudden.

Hearing him laugh made me realize that he must have seen that embarrassing scene earlier between me and Wren.

*Ugh. I don't think I'm ever going to live this down.*

· · ·

Later that night when Eros and I were lying in bed, playing twenty questions, I noticed that he seemed a lot more happier now, probably because we were together again and the babies were safe.

"What are you thinking about?" I asked, turning to rest my head against his chest while trying to ignore the damn creaking from the bed.

Every time we moved, the cheap bed frame would creak like we were doing something, but we weren't. It was truly annoying. I considered removing the frame and leaving the bed on the floor, but I was afraid that spiders, cockroaches, or rats would crawl on us in the middle of the night. Since this apartment building was so old and decrepit, I was sure that this would happen.

Eros chuckled and said, "You. I'm thinking about you right now."

"About me what?" I looked up into Eros' blue eyes and smiled at him.

"About how wonderful you are," he said. "About how lucky I am to have you as my mate. About how excited I am to spend the rest of our lives together. About how—"

"Okay! Okay. I get the picture. If you praise me anymore, my head is going to get too big and I won't be able to walk without having to hold it up," I stated. "And I'm happy to spend the rest of my life with you too, Eros."

Eros hugged me closer and tucked me against his chest.

"But really, I am pretty wonderful, aren't I?" I grinned.

Eros smiled and said, "Yes, Emira. You are."

"When do you think this war will be over?" I asked, changing the subject.

"Maybe in another two or three years," he paused, "That's two questions, Emira."

Compared to Eros, I thought it might take a little longer than that. Like five times longer.

*You know how stubborn us humans can be.*

"I'll skip a turn next time," I muttered, holding back a yawn until the corners of my eyes became wet. "What do you want to ask me?"

"Do you still have feelings for Bennet Mathias Miller?" he asked nonchalantly, as if he were unbothered, but I knew that he probably was.

"You know I don't. It was just a stupid crush, Eros. It can never compare to anything you and I have. If you hadn't brought him up, I would have forgotten all about him." I leaned up and kissed his chin endearingly.

All of my words were true, because when I thought about Bennet, nothing really came up other than old memories and empty feelings.

"Can I ask another question?" A sudden thought suddenly popped into my head and I wanted to ask Eros before I forgot.

"Go ahead," he said, quite pleased with my previous answer.

"Did you like me better when I was pregnant?" I asked, seeing Eros' expression change for a split second. "It's true... isn't it? Because you were always aroused every time you looked at me and my pregnant belly. But now that I'm not pregnant anymore, I barely feel anything from you."

"..." Crickets chirped for almost five minutes while the wheels in Eros' head spun nonstop.

"Aren't you going to say something?" I asked, looking at him with a mischievous smirk on my lips.

Eros choked on his spit and started coughing for a minute or two.

"Something about you carrying my pups made me a lot more... excited than normal. Perhaps, it was your sweet, ripening scent accompanied by the scent of your arousal or the way you looked so beautiful when your belly swelled with our pups," he explained, threading a hand through my hair to massage my scalp. "But I don't love you any more or any less just because of it, Emira."

"You make it seem like it's my fault," I accused, a little embarrassed because of his words.

"It's both our faults. How about that?" Eros patted the back of my neck gently and went back to massaging me.

I grinned, happy with the answer.

"It's my turn to ask a question, isn't it?"

"Uh-huh," I murmured against his shirt, feeling sleepy again.

"When do you want more pups, Emira?" he asked suddenly.

At his shocking question, I propped my head on my hand and looked at him as if he were crazy.

"More pups? Are you out of your mind, Eros? Nine is already more than enough for me." My eyes were wide open now because Eros had managed to shock the sleep out of me.

How was he suggesting more pups when the children were still babies?

"It's always been my dream to have a big family," he said, rubbing my neck to calm me down.

"And you think our family isn't big enough?" I asked incredulously.

He nodded his head and said, "I would like to have more pups one day. Not now. But someday in the future."

Eros was looking at me with this expectant glint in his eyes as he tried to use his good looks to make my resistance falter. Though I tried to withstand the pleading gaze within the depths of his eyes and the handsome smile on his lips, I couldn't do it and gave in after a while.

"Fine. But like in twenty years or something," I muttered. "Now can I go to sleep?"

"Twenty years?" He raised his brow.

"Twenty years," I repeated, yawning.

"I'll mark this in my calendar to remind you in twenty years," he joked. At least I hoped he was joking, because I just said a random number to get him to go to sleep and stop asking me.

If I had known that twenty years from now I would be pregnant again with more babies than my first pregnancy, I would have slapped myself in the face. Several times.

But it was kind of late to cry over spilled milk because the words had already left my mouth and Eros seemed to have taken it seriously.

As my eyelids came together, I prayed one last time to the universe. I prayed that the war would end soon and everyone would live peacefully with each other. I prayed that all the soldiers and warriors would be able to return to their families safely. And I prayed that my family would be healthy and happy for as long as we lived.

# EPILOGUE

My everyday life for the last three years had consisted of waking up to an empty bed, eating a simple breakfast, and running off to visit Asuka in the watch tower or heading straight to the field hospital.

Sometimes I would get the chance to see the children before they geared up and headed out to have some "fun," while other times I would end up wrapping their wounds and sending them back out to fight.

Before I knew it, my children had all grown even bigger and stronger. They stood taller than me and looked to be in their early twenties when they were just six years old.

*I still haven't gotten over the shock of their rapid growth.*

As for Eros and me, we barely had the time to see each other. Though we slept in the same room, we were dead tired by the time we were back in bed that we did nothing except for saying a couple of words before falling asleep half way through.

Though I didn't like the war, I knew it was necessary to attain peace. This world needed to change. It needed to acknowledge and accept that there were supernaturals living amongst us, needed to stop killing them and experimenting on them. Once this change happened, we would finally be able to live normally again, perhaps, even better than before. Because no one would be forced to hide and run or fear for their lives.

By the third year of me joining the war, the enemy side finally called for a peace treaty, unable to take the strain of economic losses and the numbers of casualties. Though both sides had a lot of losses, more humans had died than supernaturals.

The door suddenly opened and pulled me out of my thoughts. As I looked up, I saw Eros come into the room.

He was dressed in a black tuxedo and white dress shirt, looking cleaned up and fine as ever, and his hair had been combed back to give him this really sleek and sexy look. I would have been drooling over how good he looked, but I didn't want to ruin my makeup since it had taken an hour and a half just to put it on and do my hair for the wedding.

Speaking of that, we'd finally had the time to sit down and plan our wedding these last few months after the war had ended.

Eros and I had decided on having an outdoor wedding in front of the pack house, where the grass was green and really pretty. It would be a lot more convenient for all the guests to see the ceremony and enjoy the party afterwards.

Early this morning, we'd set up all the chairs and decorations, along with the canopy in case it got too hot outside. Then, I went to get my hair and makeup done by Jemma, a talented witch who had a salon in the town next to our pack.

"Are you ready, Emira?" Eros asked, holding his hand out for me to take.

"Just about ready," I said, slipping on my pair of white and gold heels.

I was dressed in an elegant white dress with no train because I didn't want anyone to accidentally step on it.

It was one of those wedding dresses with off-shoulder sleeves and lacey floral details all over the chest and the long, puffy skirt. I really loved how it hugged my chest and flared out at the waist.

As for my hair, Jemma had put it up into an updo and left little curls out at the front to frame my face.

She'd attached a beautiful floral hairpiece to the back of my head and pinned the veil to the top.

With my makeup, she had helped me create a simple and natural look that was flawless and elegant.

I didn't really want anything too jazzy.

After smoothing the dress down, I took a hold of Eros' hand and let him lead me out of the room.

Since I didn't really have a father figure in my life, other than Anira's father, who refused to come to my wedding, I was forced to walk down the aisle by myself, which was fine by me.

But Eros didn't want me to walk by myself so he thought he'd walk with me.

I told him that I'd never seen anyone do that and it might be weird, but he said that we could always start a new trend. So I just shrugged my shoulders and let him have his way.

Eros weaved our fingers together and led me to the front of the packhouse, where everyone was already seated and waiting for our arrival.

In the center of the columns of chairs was a white aisle runner that led straight to our pastoress, who was dressed in an all-black gown and standing with a book in her hands.

To both sides of the aisle runner were pink and white rose petals scattered all over the green grass, and there were pink and white flowers everywhere to decorate the center aisle.

Just seeing all the pretty decorations made me really happy, although I was also very nervous at the same time.

When everyone noticed us coming, they all turned their heads in our direction and smiled.

I could see Granny Ada and the kids sitting in the front row with the rest of the pack members in the other rows.

Standing in the front on the left side of Adeola, the pastoress, were Rora, Asuka, Anira, Gemini, and Lia, dressed in long, blush pink bridesmaids' gowns.

On the right side stood Alpha Xavier, Alpha Deimos, Beta Toren, Gamma Qian, and Zanthos, dressed in snazzy black suits.

Through the buzz of everyone whispering and the pastoress starting the ceremony, I couldn't hear a single thing.

My mind was just somewhere else as I started to become nervous in the presence of the entire pack and my family.

"We are gathered here today to join our bride and groom in the sacred ceremony of Holy Matrimony…." Adeola started as I completely zoned out. "As friends, family, and comrades, do you support the union of this couple today?"

*If anyone dares to object, I will send my children after them,* I thought, praying that no one was stupid enough to ruin our wedding by objecting, even if it was a joke.

My hands started sweating and my mouth became extremely dry, and I was unable to stop myself from biting on my bottom lip.

Since I really didn't want her to say "speak now or forever hold your peace" at our wedding, like I'd seen in a lot of movies where some random person comes in and objects, she'd changed the line to something else.

"We do," the entire crowd said, to my immense relief.

"Let this ceremony now commence." Adeola opened her book and started on the usual ceremonial information and thanks to all who had come to our wedding before she went to the vows.

"Eros Hall, do you take Emira Snow to be your lawfully wedded wife, to have and to hold from this day forward, for better or for worse, for richer or for poorer, through sickness and health, to love and to cherish, till death do you part? If so, say 'I do,'" Adeola said.

Without any hesitation, Eros said, "I do."

At this time, tears were streaming down my face, even though I was trying so hard not to ruin my makeup.

"Emira Snow, will you take Eros Hall to be your lawfully wedded husband, to have and to hold from this day forward, for better or for worse, for richer or for poorer, through sickness and health, to love and to cherish, till death do you part? If so, say 'I do.'" Adeola turned to me.

"I do," I said, smiling happily through my tears.

After we'd completed our vows and exchanged our rings in complete silence, Adeola said, "You may now kiss the bride."

I quickly wiped my face with the back of my hand and leaned in to meet Eros' kiss.

The moment our lips met, the crowd of people erupted into thundering applause, making this moment feel even more magical than ever before.

. . .

"I hope you're not mad about mom and dad not coming to the wedding," Anira said, handing me a glass of wine.

I shook my head and didn't take it in fear of spilling it all over my white dress.

"I'm not mad," I said.

When I'd called and invited Logan and Jennifer, my adopted parents and Anira's birth parents, to our wedding a month and a half ago, they'd blatantly said that they weren't coming and Logan would not walk me down the aisle because they did not approve of my marriage to a werewolf. They'd lectured me on my choice in partner and said that Eros was going to kill me and eat me one day because werewolves were vicious, crazed creatures not capable of love.

I believed that their anger had a lot to do with Anira breaking off her engagement to Wyatt and mating with Zanthos. Since Eros was Zanthos' brother, they wanted nothing to do with him, too.

Other than the Zanthos thing, their anger and bitterness might also come from the fact that humans had lost the war between the two kinds, but there was nothing I could do to make them change their mind. So I didn't say anything when they gave me a thirty minute lecture about how I should live my life.

If they were to ever found out that the Sentinels they hated so much were my children, they'd probably cut ties with me.

"Well, if it makes you feel any better, they're not coming to mine, either," she said, taking a small sip of the red wine. "This is good wine."

"Eros had it shipped all the way from some famous winery in Italy. So it better be good," I said.

Though Eros didn't tell me how much the red wine was, I had a feeling that it must have been very, very expensive.

*I'll probably enjoy the wine later when Eros and I are alone tonight,* I thought, hoping there'd be some left when the party was done.

"They still nag me about the whole breaking-up-with-Wyatt thing. Apparently, they think the only man I should ever be with is Wyatt because us breaking up is ruining their business relationship with his parents," she ranted, sniffing indignantly.

"They'll eventually come around," I comforted.

"I don't care if they do or not. If they don't want to be a part of my life and my baby's life then it's on them," she said, shrugging it off like it didn't matter, though I knew that it probably did to her. Her parents had always loved her to death, so it was probably hurting her a lot for them to shun her because of this breakup.

"Wait, what do you mean by 'baby's life'?" I questioned, suddenly catching those words after a little while.

She made a regretful expression and said, "Damn it. You weren't supposed to know about that until next week."

"You're pregnant?" I gasped in disbelief.

"Yes. I've been pregnant for over a month now. I didn't want to take the spotlight off of you today so I wanted to wait and tell you later." She frowned.

"That doesn't matter, Ani," I paused, "Congratulations! I'm so excited for you! I bet the baby is going to be so adorable!'

As my eyes went from her face to the wine cup in her hand, I gasped.

"Why are you drinking wine? You're pregnant! Stop!" I exclaimed, knowing that any type of alcohol was very dangerous for the baby. Her child could have fetal alcohol syndrome even if she'd only drank one cup!

"I only took a sip to taste it," she said stubbornly.

"Even a sip can endanger your baby! Maybe we should consider getting your stomach pumped to get it out." I swiped the wine cup from her and the thing I hoped wouldn't happen, happened. Because I took the cup too fast from Anira, the contents splashed out of the cup and dripped down the side to make a landing on my dress. And I had no one to blame but myself.

Anira and I both looked down at the splotchy red on my dress and looked back up at each other.

"Oops," she said as I stood completely still in disbelief.

"Damn it!" I exclaimed, tempted to stomp my feet.

Anira grabbed the wine cup back and put it on the table, before she took a hold of my hand and pulled me into the pack house.

"If we hurry and get it off, it won't stain too bad," she said, pulling out her cellphone—from who knew where—and started searching for ways to remove wine stains.

We ended up spending over thirty minutes in the kitchen with a bottle of dish soap, hydrogen peroxide, vinegar, salt, and water, trying many methods until the stain wasn't as noticeable anymore. At first, I didn't think that anything was going to work because of the white, but Anira made it happen, somehow.

"Mom!" Kyra called, waving me over to her the moment she saw me come out of the pack house.

"You look so pretty today!" she complimented.

"Thank you," I said, smiling as I watched her stuff a whole chunk of the wedding cake into her mouth.

After she'd swallowed, she said, "I want to get married, too!"

"No, Kyra. You're only ten," I stated, shaking my head at her.

"But why?" Her pretty face fell.

"Because I said so." I ended up using the line that all parents used on their children at least once in their lives.

"But why?" she asked again.

"Stop annoying your mother, Kyra," Eros said, coming over to my side.

Kyra pouted and went back to eating her cake.

This was what I meant by all my children being immature, even though they looked like they were twenty-four.

*But I guess a twenty-four-year-old can still be immature too… right?*

Because of this, I couldn't send them to school. If I send them to college, they would struggle because their mentality was not at the same level as the other college students. If I were to send them to elementary school, no school would take them because of how old they looked. There was no way that I could explain why our six-year-olds looked like they were twenty-four.

It was too confusing for me, so Eros decided that we would have the kids homeschooled to lessen the confusion. Though I was told that a school for supernaturals was available, I didn't want to send my children there because it was a six-hour drive from our home. So we were stuck with letting Granny Ada, who volunteered herself, and Eros teach them, because I didn't have the patience to deal with their shenanigans. I felt like I was too old and too impatient for the job.

I sighed and looked up to see Lia pulling on Gamma Qian's arm before she leaned up to kiss him. Lia and Gamma Qian had waited until Lia met her mate before they decided to complete their bond last year. She'd told her true mate that she was in love with someone else and that she could not be with him. Surprisingly, her true mate took it pretty well. He'd actually wished her the best and left without causing any problems, which was so not normal to me. But at least there was no fight.

"Cake?" Eros asked, holding a plate out for me to take.

"Yes, please," I said, quick to grab myself a fork.

By the time the party ended, everyone had helped clean up before they left.

I was dead tired when we got back to our house, empty of screaming kids because Granny Ada had taken them over to the pack house for the night.

The first thing I did was take a hot shower to get rid of all the aches and pains in my entire body. Then, I opened that wine Eros imported from Italy and poured myself a cup before taking a swig.

"What are you doing?" Eros asked, coming out of nowhere in his bathrobe.

I almost choked on the wine if I hadn't stopped drinking it at the right time.

"Eros! I thought you were taking a shower," I said, holding my glass out for him.

"I was done," he replied, taking the glass and putting it back on the counter.

"Oh… I guess I'll go get ready for bed," I said, pausing awkwardly before quickly heading back to our room to brush my teeth.

By the time I got out, Eros was lying completely naked in the bed, looking at me with shimmering blue eyes and a wide, sensual smile on his lips. His thick shaft was already facing the sky.

"It's our wedding night, Emira," Eros said suddenly.

"It sure is," I replied, wanting to facepalm.

And there it was… me… being awkward. Again.

"Do you still have those condoms from the other night?" I asked bluntly, tired of the dirty talk that I never seemed to be very good at.

Eros tossed two packs on the bed, and I felt my face sting with the realization of how long this night was going to be.

"Can we use just one of those boxes?" I asked, regretting my life decisions for the Nth time today.

"You promised that I could do whatever I wanted on our wedding night," he said, smirking at me because he knew that I never went back on my promises.

"…"

*Damn it.*

# READ THE FIRST BOOK IN THE CARDINAL ALPHA SERIES NEXT

Want more of Alpha Xavier Thaeos, the Southern Cardinal Alpha? Read about him in Blood Bound.

Find Blood Bound at: **http://www.authortayt.com**

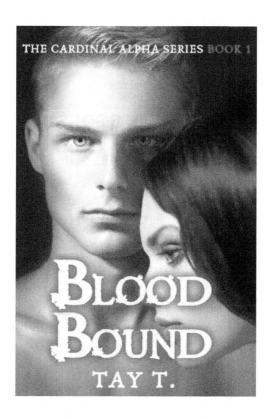

## CONNECT WITH THE AUTHOR
Follow on Facebook: http://facebook.com/authortayt
Follow on Twitter: http://twitter.com/authortayt
Website: http://authortayt.com
Mailing List: http://eepurl.com/gWglqf

**Join Tay's mailing list for information about new releases, teasers, sales, and giveaways. No spam, guaranteed.**

http://eepurl.com/gWglqf

## DON'T MISS THESE BOOKS BY TAY T.

**The Cardinal Alpha Series:**

Book 1: Blood Bound
Book 2: Heart Bound

**The Breeder Series:**

Book 1: The Alpha's Breeder
Book 2: Eros: A Short Character's Point Of View
Book 3: The Sentinels' Mother